ELDRITCH

NECROMANCER!

By Rex Talionis
Illustrated by Henry Hubert

Black Circle Collective

Copyright 2024 © Black Circle Collective
First Published 2024 on Paperback
Cover, Design by Black Circle Collective
Illustrations by Henry Hubert
ISBN: 9798329587562

All rights reserved. No part of this publication may be reproduced, distributed, or transmitted in any form or by any means, including photocopying, recording, or other electronic or mechanical methods, without the prior written permission of the publisher.

Introduction

Welcome to **NECROMANCER!** A Grim Dungeon-crawling Gamebook.

According to the ancient lore of *Thorns*, it is said that immortality and omnipotence could be attained by tapping into *Æther*, a rare essence. This elusive substance is primarily found in the ethereal planes, but some of it has leaked into the *Realms of Thorns*, causing the dead to walk and spirits to haunt the land. *Æther* holds the promise of immeasurable power, and with enough of it, even an undead being could be restored to a state of normalcy and vitality.

Long ago, in the now desolate kingdoms of *Krator*, there existed mighty rulers known as the *Regii*. These ancient kings harnessed the power of *Æther*, storing vast quantities of it in the catacombs known as the *Necropolis*, their burial site, to prepare themselves for *The Reckoning*; to ready themselves for the *Final Battles* in the *End of Times*. Deep within these crypts, a repository guarded by a device crafted by the *Great Wizard* held the *Æther*, intended to be released during the prophesied times of *The Reckoning* to awaken the deceased *Regii*. However, when *Krator* fell into ruin, the *Great Wizard* perished and the last of the *Regii* was dead. *Krator* and the *Necropolis* was soon forgotten until the Great Lich *Mortis* ventured into the depths of the catacombs and claimed the *Æther* for himself. With this power, *Mortis* transformed himself into flesh and blood, and turned the *Necropolis* into his fortress, and it is said that he is now building an army of undead to serve his dark ambitions, which will be unleashed upon the realms of *Thorns*.

You are a NECROMANCER, trained in the *Dark Arts*, and couldn't care less about helping the people of *Thorns* against the undead army. But you have set your sights on the *Necropolis*, to attain the *Æther* for your personal use, to gain immortality and its omnipotent power, and maybe to build your own army for world domination at some point?

Prepare yourself NECROMANCER, for you are to venture into the perilous depths of the *Necropolis*, where you must navigate the treacherous catacombs, confront the accursed creatures within, and ultimately challenge the Great Lich himself. The fate of your soul and the promise of immortality lies just beyond your grasp. **Before you start your adventure, you have to first build up your character and get familiarised with the rules.**

Building your Character

You are about to embark on a dangerous descent into the eldritch depths of the *Necropolis*. Before embarking on this, your first adventure, you must first build up your Character, a NECROMANCER. Pages 20-22 is the *Character Sheet*, which you may use to record the details of your adventure. You are advised to either record on it with a pencil or make photocopies of the sheet for future uses. **You also need a dice for the game.**

1. Core Attributes

As a NECROMANCER, you will start your quest with default attributes. These attributes will evolve over time based on your decisions and the outcomes of your encounters. Each attribute has a specific score, which you will record on the *Character Sheet*. There are four core attributes critical to your journey: LIFE, POWER, MANA, PROTECTION.

LIFE LIFE represents your stamina or hit-points. It is vital as it keeps you alive in the game. Every Necromancer begins with 20 points, which is the maximum LIFE score. It decreases when you take damage and increases when you receive healing, but it cannot exceed 20.

Your max LIFE score can only be extended beyond 20 when you attain a higher level, or due to blessings and certain items. **Record 20 in the LIFE section of your Character Sheet**.

POWER POWER represents your vigour or strength. It is the primary factor that influences your outcome in combat with Opponents, by affecting the OFFENCE scores which in turn contribute to DAMAGE on the LIFE scores of the Opponent. While it stays fairly constant, it can still be affected under specific circumstances (e.g. decrease due to draining by ghosts).

The maximum POWER score in the beginning is 10 for every necromancer, and it may not be restored beyond 10. The max POWER score can only be extended beyond 10 when you gain a higher level, or due to blessings and certain items. **Record 10 in the POWER section of your Character Sheet**.

MANA   MANA represents your magical force or spiritual force. Spellcasting costs MANA, hence it is the reserve that you can use for magic work before it gets depleted, potentially going down to 0. However, there are means to restore MANA scores (e.g. via potions).

Every NECROMANCER begins with 10 MANA points, which is the max score. Your max MANA score can only be extended beyond 10 when you attain a higher level, or due to blessings and certain items. **Record 10 in the MANA section of your Character Sheet**.

PROTECTION   PROTECTION represents your security and luck (halo). It is the primary factor that influences your outcome in combat with opponents, affecting the DEFENCE scores, which in turn deflect OFFENCE to minimize the DAMAGE to your LIFE scores. While it stays fairly constant, it can still be affected under specific circumstances (e.g. decrease due to draining by ghosts).

The maximum PROTECTION score in the beginning is 5 for every necromancer, and it may not be restored beyond 5. The max PROTECTION score can only be extended beyond 5 when you gain a higher level, or due to blessings and certain items. **Record 5 in the PROTECTION section of your Character Sheet**.

2. Items

There are seven categories of items you will find in the course of the game: WEAPON, FOCUS, ARMOUR, QUEST ITEMS, MISC, REAGENTS and GOLD.

All items, excluding QUEST ITEMS and REAGENTS, have a value, indicated by Gp, which stands for Gold piece.

All of them, except REAGENTS and GOLD can be placed in the *Inventory* section of the *Character Sheet*.

There are additional slots on the *Character Sheet*: PRIMARY WEAPON for Weapon, FOCUS for Focus Gems, PRIMARY ARMOUR for Armour, REAGENTS for Reagents and GOLD for Gold pieces. All items, except QUEST ITEMS and REAGENTS can be sold/barter traded or discarded. You can only fill up 12 of the *Inventory Slots*- you may need to discard some items to make space. Note: Multiples of MISC items can fit in one slot.

WEAPON

WEAPON is used to inflict damage on opponents during close combat. All of them have a modifier, indicated by "+ *numeral*", which can be added up with the POWER score to derive the OFFENCE (MELEE) points.

Only one WEAPON can be the PRIMARY WEAPON in the *Character Sheet* at a time, but it can be interchanged with other WEAPON, except during combat. WEAPON not placed in PRIMARY WEAPON will be stored in the *Inventory* slots.

NECROMANCERS are most fond of Staffs, because these WEAPON can be affixed with a FOCUS to provide ranged attack (shooting missiles from a distance). Other WEAPON like Swords for example do not have this function though.

In your Character Sheet, under PRIMARY WEAPON, add a Birch Staff (Dmg: +2, Gp: 5). This Birch Staff has a modifier of +2 that can contribute to OFFENCE (MELEE), can be sold/barter traded for 10 Gold Pieces, and can allow any type of FOCUS to be added.

FOCUS

FOCUS are gems that are set at the top of Staffs, for the purpose of ranged attack against opponents who are from a distance during combat. All of them have a modifier, indicated by "+ *numeral*", which can be added up with the POWER score to derive the OFFENCE (RANGE) points. Only one FOCUS can be used at any time, but it can be interchanged with other FOCUS, except during combat. Focus Gems not placed in FOCUS will be stored in the *Inventory* slots.

FOCUS can only be set on Staffs, not other WEAPON. If you are having a non-Staff WEAPON as the PRIMARY WEAPON, you cannot use the FOCUS, have to leave it in the *Inventory* and cannot use OFFENCE (RANGE) attack.

Beside damage modifier and Gp, it also has a *Radius* (Rd) which indicates how wide it can hit the opponents. Rd is calculated based on the number of *Combat Squares* deviating from the straight path between yourself and the opponent.

In your Character Sheet, under FOCUS, add an Emerald (Dmg: +1, Gp: 5, Rd: 1, Type: Magic Missile). This Emerald has a modifier of +1 that can contribute to OFFENCE (RANGE), can be sold/barter traded for 5 Gold Pieces, has a radius of 1 *Combat Squares* (which is essentially a projectile in a straight line), and can be fixed on any Staff.

ARMOUR

ARMOUR, as the name implies, is gear used to protect against the opponents during combat. All of them have a Shield (Shd) modifier, indicated by "+ *numeral*", which can be added to the PROTECTION score to derive the DEFENCE points.

Only one ARMOUR can be the PRIMARY ARMOUR in the *Character Sheet* at a time, but it can be interchanged with other ARMOUR, except during combat. ARMOUR not placed in PRIMARY ARMOUR will be stored in the *Inventory* slots. **In your Character Sheet, under PRIMARY ARMOUR, add a Cloak (Shd: +1, Gp: 2).** This Cloak has a modifier of +1 that can contribute to DEFENCE, and can be sold/barter traded for 2 Gold Pieces.

QUEST ITEMS

QUEST ITEMS are artefacts that the player will find in the game that are significant to its progress. When you do find them, record them in one of the available slots in the *Inventory* section of the *Character Sheet*.

MISC

MISC refers to all items that are not assigned to the other categories. When you do find them, record them in one of the available slots in the *Inventory* section of the *Character Sheet*. If there are multiples of same items, they can fit in 1 slot in *Inventory* but the qty needs to be indicated. Items with one time use are to be removed from *Inventory* after use, or qty reduced.

In your Character Sheet, under Inventory, add a Healing Potion (LIFE: +5, Gp: 5), Rations (LIFE +2, Gp: 2) and 2x Torches (Gp: 1). 1x Healing Potion can be used anytime ONCE except during combat, to restore +5 to LIFE, and can be sold/barter traded for 5 Gold Pieces. 1x Rations is used anytime ONCE except during combat, to restore +2 to LIFE, and is sold/barter traded for 2 Gold Pieces. 2x Torches are used to illuminate the dungeons for your navigation and can be sold/barter traded for 1 Gold Piece each.

REAGENTS   REAGENTS are used for concoction of necromantic spells. There are six known REAGENTS, namely *Bones, Ghost Caps, Nightshade, Charnel Ash, Grimwood Bark,* and *Ectoplasm.* Slots for these REAGENTS are found under the *Spells* section on the *Character Sheet.* Refer to Page 19 for more information on spellcasting.

In your Character Sheet, under the Spells section, add 2x each in the Quantity slots corresponding to Bones, Ghost Caps, Nightshade, Charnel Ash and Grimwood Bark- except Ectoplasm. There will be 10x REAGENTS in total when the game begins.

GOLD   GOLD is short for Gold Pieces that you will use as currency for purchasing items during trading. They can also be accumulated by selling your items for their Gp's worth, when you are not doing a barter trade (which you can of course).

There are generally two modes of commerce in the game. The first involve buying and selling of goods with GOLD as a medium. The second is barter trade, which involves exchanging an item for another with similar Gp value. You can also sell/barter something, and make up for the balance with buy/barter.

In your Character Sheet, under GOLD section, write 30 in the slot. You will begin the game with 30 Gold Pieces.

3. Combat Attributes

Combat Attributes are what the NECROMANCER will use to gauge the strengths and weaknesses and determine the outcome of ensuing combat with opponents. The *Combat Attributes* are combinations of the *Core Attributes* and *Item Modifiers*. There are two types of *Combat Attributes*: OFFENCE and DEFENCE. OFFENCE is further subdivided into MELEE and RANGE.

MELEE   OFFENCE (MELEE) is used during close combat, ONLY when the Opponent is next to you on the *Combat Squares*, either vertically or horizontally, but not diagonally. It is a sum of POWER + Dmg modifier from the PRIMARY WEAPON. It is used to offset against the DEFENCE of the Opponent to derive the amount of DAMAGE hit on its LIFE score.

Sum your POWER score (10) + Primary Weapon Dmg (+2) to get 12, and record it under OFFENCE (MELEE) section on the Character Sheet. When you change out a PRIMARY WEAPON with a new *Dmg* modifier or when your POWER score changes, take note to update the OFFENCE (MELEE).

RANGE

OFFENCE (RANGE) is used during ranged combat when the FOCUS is active, when the Opponent is at least 1 square from you on the *Combat Squares*, either vertically or horizontally, but not diagonally. It is the sum of POWER + Dmg modifier from the FOCUS. It is used to offset against the DEFENCE of the Opponent to derive the amount of DAMAGE hit on its LIFE score. RADIUS is how wide a projectile can hit. It is derived from the Rd of the FOCUS.

Sum your POWER score (10) + FOCUS Dmg (+2) to get 11, and record It under OFFENCE (RANGE) section. Also write 1 under RADIUS on the Character Sheet. When you change out a FOCUS with a new *Dmg* and *Rd* modifier and when your POWER score changes, take note to update the OFFENCE (RANGE) and RADIUS.

DEFENCE

DEFENCE is basically the opposite of OFFENCE. It is how much you can ward off the OFFENCE from the Opponent, to minimize the DAMAGE to your LIFE score. It is a sum of PROTECTION + Shd modifier from the PRIMARY ARMOUR.

Sum your PROTECTION score (5) + PRIMARY ARMOUR Shd (+1) to get 6, and record it under DEFENCE section on the Character Sheet. When you change out a PRIMARY ARMOUR with a new *Shd* modifier or when your DEFENCE score changes, take note to update the DEFENCE.

4. Levelling Up

As the NECROMANCER gains more experience, it can be accumulated for levelling up. When you begin, there's nothing in the EXPERIENCE section on the *Character Sheet*, but you will add up those *Exp* points as you gain them.

You will also keep track of the *Exp* points, because once they hit a certain amount, you will attain a higher level. You begin at *Level 1*, and the highest attainable for any NECROMANCER is at *Level 5*.

The benefit of levelling up is simply to increase your chances of hitting an Opponent. At Level 1, you have 1/3 chance of *Missed Hit*, 1/3 chance of *Exact Hit*, a 1/6 chance of a *Reduced Hit* and a 1/6 chance of a *Critical Hit*.

Go to the Levels section on the Character Sheet, indicate that you are Level 1, and fill the Probability Table with the descriptors along the Outcomes row as indicated below.

Next, fill up the cells in the Dice Number row a sequence of 1 to 6 in any order on the table. They will be essential in Combat later on Page 12.

Outcomes	Missed Hit	Exact Hit	Exact Hit	Exact Hit	Reduced Hit	Critical Hit
Dice Number						

Take note of the *Levels* below, the *Exp* points to reach them, as well as the *Outcomes* for updating the *Probability Table*. As you can see, the likelihood of inflicting a better hit on your Opponent goes up as you reach a new *Level*.

Level 2 100 Exp	Missed Hit	Exact Hit	Exact Hit	Exact Hit	Reduced Hit	Critical Hit
Level 3 300 Exp	Missed Hit	Exact Hit	Exact Hit	Exact Hit	Exact Hit	Critical Hit
Level 4 600 Exp	Missed Hit	Exact Hit	Exact Hit	Exact Hit	Critical Hit	Critical Hit
Level 5 900 Exp	Exact Hit	Exact Hit	Exact Hit	Critical Hit	Critical Hit	Critical Hit

5. Skills

Certain *Skills* can be learnt and acquired from the outset or during the game. Some *Skills* are also bestowed upon by Deities. Regardless of it, all NECROMANCERS have a choice of beginning the game with one of the two *Skills*, namely: *Swimming, and Climbing*. **From SWIMMING or CLIMBING, choose ONLY one and write it into the Skills section in the Character Sheet**.

6. Blessings (Enhanced Attributes and Skills)

In the *Realms of Thorns*, five elemental deities, known as the *Ancient Ones*, govern the realms. These deities are often at war with one another, vying for supremacy through the devotion of their followers. The NECROMANCER will align with one of the five *Ancient Ones*, who shall bestow blessings upon you in the form of enhanced attributes or new skills. While attributes like POWER and MANA usually cannot exceed their max scores by default, it is exceptional to devotees of certain Deities. **From the list below, choose only one Deity and register it under the Deity section in the Character Sheet, then adjust the Core Attributes or Skills sections accordingly.**

Hish — Also known as the Wise One. He bestows +2 to overall MANA score. **Add +2 to MANA score (which should reflect 12 MANA)** if you choose Him as your Deity. Hish is ally of Barat, and enemy with Zakl, Taph and Ked.

Zakl — Also known as the Gloomy One. He bestows **PERCEPTION (add to the Skills Section)** if you choose Him as your Deity. Zakl is ally with Taph and Ked, and enemy with Hish and Barat.

Barat — Also known as the Bloodied One. He bestows +2 to overall POWER score. **Add +2 to POWER score (which should reflect 12 POWER)** if you choose Him as your Deity. Barat is ally of Hish, and enemy with Taph, Ked and Zakl.

Ked — Also known as the Beautiful One. She bestows **CHARM (add to the Skills section)** if you choose Her as your Deity. Ked is ally with Zakl and Taph, and enemy with Hish and Barat.

Taph — Also known as the Quick One. He bestows **THIEVERY (add to the Skills section)** if you choose Him as your Deity. Taph is ally with Zakl and Ked, and enemy with Hish and Barat.

Engaging in Combat

1. **Combat Rules**

   a) **The Attributes**- During combat, the Opponent's *Combat Attributes* and *Probability Table* will be shown. The attributes are primary LIFE, OFFENCE (MELEE), DEFENCE and, sometimes OFFENCE (RANGE) and *Radius* if Opponents have ranged weapons.

Orc	
Life	15
Offence (Melee)	9
Offence (Range)	8
Defence	4
Radius	1

   Also take note of the Opponent's *Probability Table*. It indicates the *Outcomes* that will correspond to the Dice Rolls when it takes *Action*.

Outcomes	Missed Hit	Exact Hit	Exact Hit	Exact Hit	Reduced Hit	Critical Hit
Dice Number	5	3	4	6	2	1

   b) **Combat Squares**- When combat commences, the initial positions of both yourself (depicted by hooded figure) and the Opponent (depicted by skull) will be indicated on the *Combat Squares*- see example below.

   Both parties will make a series of moves known as *Turns*, with the objective of advancing closer, and reducing the other's LIFE score to 0, to kill it. The game section will indicate which party should initiate the first *Turn*. Each *Turn* consists of a *Move* and *Action*.

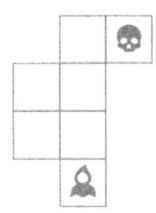

   A *Move* consists of placing yourself or the Opponent to an adjacent and available *Combat Square*, closer to each other by ONE SQUARE. You can indicate this by using a pencil to mark the current position, starting from the default position.

   Later in the Game, you may encounter some items that will help you move more than ONE SQUARE.

   In a *Move*, you can choose to go in any direction (advance towards or away from Opponent), or not to move at all (pass a *Move*; *Action* can be performed should a *Move* be passed in a *Turn*), on the *Combat Squares*.

However, when it comes to the Opponent's *Turn*, you are obliged to ONLY advance the Opponent towards you, where you are currently situated. Once it is beside you, no more *Moves* are made, unless you *Move* away from it.

Neither party can move diagonally. *Action* will be further explained in the following subsection.

c) **Combat Rolls**- *Action* is performed to deliver hits whenever possible. Even when a *Move* is possible, yet further *Action* is not available (either blocked, or no OFFENCE (RANGE)), *Action* will be passed in that *Turn*.

An *Action* consists of only one activity below:

Melee Attack- This *Action* is performed when both parties are adjacent to each other, vertically or horizontally but not diagonally. A *Melee Attack* consists of the following steps:

i) Roll a dice. Take note of the number. Track the number to the corresponding *Outcomes* on the *Probability Table*.

i) If it is *Missed Hit*, this *Action* misses the other party, and the *Turn* will end. If it is an *Exact Hit*, the OFFENCE (MELEE) will be used in full. If it is a *Reduced Hit*, the OFFENCE (MELEE) will be divided in half, and rounded down. If it is a *Critical Hit*, roll a dice, and add this number to the full OFFENCE (MELEE) to give a temporary score that is only used during the *Turn*.

ii) Once the *Outcomes* of the OFFENCE (MELEE) are determined, this number will be used to subtract against the other party's DEFENCE. The result from this subtraction will be the DAMAGE. Note: If the outcome is 0 or negative number, the DAMAGE is deflected.

iii) Take the LIFE of the other party and subtract it with the DAMAGE. This will be the updated LIFE score and will the combat will be concluded when it reaches 0 (the other party is dead).

Ranged Attack- This *Action* is performed when both parties are at least ONE SQUARE away from each other, have OFFENCE (RANGE)/Radius in place, and are positioned in a line of sight (unless the Radius can affect the nearby squares), vertically or horizontally but not diagonally. A *Ranged Attack* consists of the following steps:

13

ii) Roll a dice. Take note of the number. Track the number to the corresponding *Outcomes* on the *Probability Table*.

iii) If it is *Missed Hit*, this *Action* misses the other party, and the *Turn* will end. If it is an *Exact Hit*, the OFFENCE (RANGE) will be used in full. If it is a *Reduced Hit*, the OFFENCE (RANGE) will be divided in half, and rounded down. If it is a *Critical Hit*, roll a dice, and add this number to the full OFFENCE (RANGE) to give a temporary score used during the *Turn*.

iv) Once the *Outcomes* of the OFFENCE (RANGE) are determined, this number will be used to subtract against the other party's DEFENCE. The result from this subtraction will be the DAMAGE. Note: If the outcome is 0 or negative number, the DAMAGE is deflected.

iv) Take the LIFE of the other party and subtract it with the DAMAGE. This will be the updated LIFE score- the combat will be concluded when it reaches 0 (the other party is dead).

v) RADIUS is reflective of *Rd* from FOCUS, and can affect adjacent Opponent in *Multiple Opponents Combat*.

No Action- You can choose to take no *Action* during a *Turn*. But you are obliged to have the Opponent take *Action* in their *Turns* whenever possible- a *Ranged Attack* when available and in line of sight, and a *Melee Attack* when close enough.

d) **Important Points**- During combat, swapping PRIMARY WEAPON, FOCUS, ARMOUR, using an item (e.g. drinking a Healing Potion) and casting/making any spells are **not allowed**.

2. Combat Sequence

Two examples of combat sequences are shown below.

a) Single Opponent

i) You encounter an Orc (armed with bow and arrows). Below are the *Combat Attributes*, the *Probability Tables* and the *Combat Squares* positions of both Parties. You will initiate the *Turn*.

Orc		You	
Life	15	Life	20
Offence (Melee)	9	Offence (Melee)	12
Offence (Range)	8	Offence (Range)	11
Defence	4	Defence	6
Radius	1	Radius	1

Your Probability Table (Prefilled)

Outcomes	Missed Hit	Missed Hit	Exact Hit	Exact Hit	Reduced Hit	Critical Hit
Dice Number	6	1	5	2	4	3

The Opponent's Probability Table

Outcomes	Missed Hit	Exact Hit	Exact Hit	Exact Hit	Reduced Hit	Critical Hit
Dice Number	5	3	4	6	2	1

ii) Your *Turn-Move*: Not made. *Action*: Not made.

Orc		You	
Life	15	Life	20
Offence (Melee)	9	Offence (Melee)	12
Offence (Range)	8	Offence (Range)	11
Defence	4	Defence	6
Radius	1	Radius	1

iii) Opponent's *Turn-Move*: Made. *Action*: Initiate Ranged Attack. Roll dice for 6, corresponding to Exact Hit. Its OFFENCE (RANGE) of 8 subtracts your DEFENCE of 6, and you receive 2 DAMAGES. Your LIFE is deducted of 2, reducing it to 18 points.

Orc		You	
Life	15	Life	18
Offence (Melee)	9	Offence (Melee)	12
Offence (Range)	8	Offence (Range)	11
Defence	4	Defence	6
Radius	1	Radius	1

iv) Your *Turn-Move*: Not made. *Action*: Initiate Ranged Attack. Roll dice for 1 corresponding to Missed Hit.

Orc		You	
Life	15	Life	18
Offence (Melee)	9	Offence (Melee)	12
Offence (Range)	8	Offence (Range)	11
Defence	4	Defence	6
Radius	1	Radius	1

v) Opponent's *Turn-Move*: Made. Action: Initiate Ranged Attack. Roll dice for 2, corresponding to Reduced Hit. Its OFFENCE (RANGE) of 8 halved into 4, subtracts your DEFENCE of 6, and you receive NO DAMAGE.

Orc		You	
Life	15	Life	18
Offence (Melee)	9	Offence (Melee)	12
Offence (Range)	8	Offence (Range)	11
Defence	4	Defence	6
Radius	1	Radius	1

vi) Your *Turn-Move*: Made forward. *Action*: Initiate Melee Attack. Roll dice for 3, corresponding to Critical Hit. You roll the dice again for 6, and add up to OFFENCE (MELEE) of 12 for 18 points, which subtracts its DEFENCE of 4, and it receives 14 DAMAGES. Its LIFE Is deducted of 14, reducing it to 1 point.

Orc		You	
Life	1	Life	18
Offence (Melee)	9	Offence (Melee)	12
Offence (Range)	8	Offence (Range)	11
Defence	4	Defence	6
Radius	1	Radius	1

vii) Opponent's *Turn-Move*: Not made. *Action*: Initiate Melee Attack. Roll dice for 5, corresponding to Missed Hit.

Orc		You	
Life	1	Life	18
Offence (Melee)	9	Offence (Melee)	12
Offence (Range)	8	Offence (Range)	11
Defence	4	Defence	6
Radius	1	Radius	1

viii) Your *Turn-Move*: Made backward. *Action*: Initiate Ranged Attack. Roll dice for 2, corresponding to Exact Hit. Your OFFENCE (RANGE) of 11, subtracts its DEFENCE of 4, and it receives 7 DAMAGES. Its LIFE Is deducted of 7, killing it. **You win the Battle**.

Orc		You	
Life	0	Life	18
Offence (Melee)	9	Offence (Melee)	12
Offence (Range)	8	Offence (Range)	11
Defence	4	Defence	6
Radius	1	Radius	1

b) Multiple Opponents

i) You encounter a normal Rat, and a fast Bat who can move *Two Squares* in a Turn. You are equipped with a FOCUS that gives you *Rd* = 2. Below are the *Combat Attributes*, the *Probability Tables* and the *Combat Squares* positions of the three Parties. The Opponents will initiate the *Turns*.

Rat (A)	
Life	5
Offence (Melee)	4
Defence	2

Bat (B)	
Life	5
Offence (Melee)	4
Defence	3

You	
Life	20
Offence (Melee)	12
Offence (Range)	11
Defence	6
Radius	2

Your Probability Table (Prefilled)

Outcomes	Missed Hit	Missed Hit	Exact Hit	Exact Hit	Reduced Hit	Critical Hit
Dice Number	6	1	5	2	4	3

Opponent A's Probability Table

Outcomes	Missed Hit	Missed Hit	Exact Hit	Reduced Hit	Reduced Hit	Critical Hit
Dice Number	4	2	1	5	3	6

Opponent B's Probability Table

Outcomes	Missed Hit	Missed Hit	Exact Hit	Reduced Hit	Reduced Hit	Critical Hit
Dice Number	3	1	4	2	6	5

ii) Opponent A's *Turn*- *Move*: Made. *Action*: Not made.

Rat (A)	
Life	5
Offence (Melee)	4
Defence	2

Bat (B)	
Life	5
Offence (Melee)	4
Defence	3

You	
Life	20
Offence (Melee)	12
Offence (Range)	11
Defence	6
Radius	2

iii) Opponent B's *Turn- Move*: Made (2 Squares). *Action*: Initiate Melee Attack. Roll dice for 1, corresponding to Missed Hit.

Rat (A)	
Life	5
Offence (Melee)	4
Defence	2

Bat (B)	
Life	5
Offence (Melee)	4
Defence	3

You	
Life	20
Offence (Melee)	12
Offence (Range)	11
Defence	6
Radius	2

iv) Your *Turn- Move*: Made backward. *Action*: Initiate Ranged Attack. The direct target is Opponent B (Bat). Roll dice for 4, corresponding to Reduced Hit. Your OFFENCE (RANGE) of 11 halved into 5 (rounded down), subtracts Bat's DEFENCE of 3, for a DAMAGE of 2. Its LIFE is deducted of 2, reducing to 3 points. Due to Radius 2, Opponent A (Rat) is also affected. Roll dice for 5, corresponding to Exact Hit. Your OFFENCE (RANGE) of 11, subtracts DEFENCE of 2 of Opponent A (Rat), and Rat receives 9 DAMAGES. Its LIFE is deducted of 9, killing it.

Rat (A)	
Life	5
Offence (Melee)	4
Defence	2

Bat (B)	
Life	5
Offence (Melee)	4
Defence	3

You	
Life	20
Offence (Melee)	12
Offence (Range)	11
Defence	6
Radius	2

v) Opponent B's *Turn- Move*: Made. *Action*: Initiate Melee Attack. Roll dice for 1, corresponding to Missed Hit.

vi) Your *Turn- Move*: Not made. *Action*: Initiate Melee Attack. Roll dice for 2 corresponding to Exact Hit. Your OFFENCE (MELEE) of 12, subtracts DEFENCE of 3 of Opponent B (Bat), and Bat receives 9 DAMAGES. Its LIFE is deducted of 9, killing it. **You win the Battle.**

Bat (B)	
Life	0
Offence (Melee)	4
Defence	3

You	
Life	20
Offence (Melee)	12
Offence (Range)	11
Defence	6
Radius	2

Spellcasting

Magic is widespread in the *Realms of Thorns*. As someone schooled in the Dark Arts of Necromancy, you wield magical powers over the dead and the undead, and with the aid of REAGENTS, you could cast *Spells* to assist you in your quest. You currently know four *Spells* in your *Spellbook*, and they have specific requirement for each one of them. In your quest, you also have the chance to learn new *Spells*.

You should look out for the symbol ✪ which indicate the opportunity to cast a *Spell* in the Section. You can always choose not to cast any *Spell*.

First, decide on that one *Spell* you want to cast; look at its *Function*, *Reagents Used* as well as the *Mana Cost* in the *Spellbook*. Check the REAGENTS on the *Character Sheet*, and determine the MANA cost to cast that *Spell*. Once you cast the *Spell*, refer to *Add to Section* for that *Spell* and add this number to the Section number, and turn to the new Section for the outcome. For example, at Section 50, where you can cast a *Spell*, and you want to cast a *Séance Spell*, you will deduct 1x *Bones*, 1x *Nightshade*, 1x *Grimwood Bark* from REAGENTS, and deduct 4 points from MANA, then add 22 to 50, which gives 72- the new Section you will turn to for the Outcome.

Spellbook

Spell	Function	Reagents Used	Mana Cost	Add to Section
Repel Undead	Turn undead away for duration of the spell.	1x *Bones* 1x *Ghost Caps* 1x *Charnel Ash*	3	18
Dispel Magic	Remove magic field, protection and trap for duration of spell.	1x *Ghost Caps* 1x *Charnel Ash* 1x *Grimwood Bark*	3	45
Séance	Communicate with undead for the duration of the spell.	1x *Bones* 1x *Nightshade* 1x *Grimwood Bark*	4	22
Familiar	Summon a familiar to do your bidding for duration of the spell.	1x *Ghost Caps* 1x *Nightshade* 1x *Ectoplasm*	4	51

Character Sheet

Name: _____

Class: Necromancer

Deity: _____

Core Attributes

LIFE	POWER	MANA	PROTECTION	LEVEL	EXPERIENCE

Combat Attributes

OFFENCE (MELEE)	OFFENCE (RANGE)	DEFENCE	RADIUS

Skills

Probability Table

OUTCOMES					
DICE NUMBER					

Inventory

Primary Weapon

Name	Dmg	Gp

Armour

Name	Shd	Gp

Focus

Name	Dmg	Type	Rd	Gp

Gold

Gp

Inventory Slots

Reagents

NAMES	Bones	Ghost Caps	Night Shade	Charnel Ash	Grimwood Bark	Ectoplasm
QUANTITY						

Notes

The Story So Far...

The relentless pursuit of *Æther* has driven you to the farthest reaches of *Thorns*, into the barren, unforgiving expanse known as *Krator*. This wasteland, with its shifting sands and lifeless dunes, harbours the legendary *Necropolis*, the final resting place of the ancient *Regii* and the lair of *Mortis*, the dreaded Great Lich. Access to this elusive catacombs lies through the *Deathspires*, a daunting series of isolated inselbergs that pierce the desolate landscape like ancient sentinels in the middle of the desert.

Your journey to *Krator* has been fraught with peril and misfortune. After countless failed attempts to secure a reliable guide, you were left with no choice but to rely on *Sladder*, a man whose reputation for deceit is as notorious as the desert viper. Yet, he was your only hope, offering clandestine passage through the perilous desert. The days were a relentless blur of heat and sand, while the nights provided little solace, the cold seeping into your bones as you meticulously planned your course. Your thoughts remained steadfastly fixed on the prize that lay ahead. As dawn breaks on the final day of your journey, the cool morning air offers a fleeting respite from the oppressive heat. The first light of day casts long shadows across the bleak landscape. A sharp kick to your tent jolts you awake. *Sladder*, with his greasy hair and perpetual smirk, stands impatiently at the entrance.

"Oi, adventurer, wake up! We've arrived," he snarls, his voice grating on your ears. "Time to be on your way and find that cursed *Necropolis*. Ahead lies the *Deathspires*. My part of the bargain ends here." You rise, fixing *Sladder* with a cold, piercing stare. "You're awfully eager to be rid of me, *Sladder*," you say, your voice a low, menacing growl. "Our agreement was that you would guide me to the *Necropolis*, through the *Deathspires*."

Sladder's grin widens, malice glinting in his eyes. "Our agreement was to get you to *Krator*. The *Deathspires* are no place for a mere caravanner like me." You step closer, your presence a tangible threat. "You misunderstand, *Sladder*. You will guide me through the *Deathspires*, or you will never leave this wasteland alive."

For a moment, fear flickers in *Sladder's* eyes, but he quickly masks it with bravado and responds with a quick-witted reply. "Listen, NECROMANCER, when you're done with your foolish games in the *Necropolis*, who will bring you out of *Krator*? The *Deathspires* will surely spell my demise, hence I think you are not thinking right, you wretched thing that molest corpses in the cemetery, your mind must be clouded and muddled by all that unholy filth. But I'll give you some advice: wait until nightfall and observe the *Behenian* stars. These celestial guides will lead you like beacons through the *Deathspires* to the *Necropolis*."

"I will return here in fifteen days to retrieve you- not because I like you, but there's a chance that you might return with good loots to pay the premium, and if you're not here, I'll assume you're dead." With a dismissive wave, *Sladder* turns back to his caravan, his voice carrying a final taunt. "Good luck, NECROMANCER. You'll need it!"

You are left standing alone as *Sladder* and his caravan vanish into the desert. You suddenly realize that you could have asked *Sladder* to at least send you to the edge of the *Deathspires*, but it is too late. You curse his name under your breath and swear to get back at him after you succeed. The cool dawn air fills your lungs as you take a deep breath, bracing yourself for the heat that will soon engulf the wasteland. You estimate that your journey to the *Deathspires* will take you until late afternoon.

As the day wears on, the burning sun beats down on you, each step through the arid desert sapping your strength. By the time you reach the *Deathspires*, fatigue has set in, and your water supply is depleted. The *Deathspires* rise before you, a formidable series of isolated mountains jutting out of the desert sands like the jagged teeth of some ancient beast. Their sharp, foreboding peaks seem to pierce the sky. The terrain is harsh, the path narrow and winding, littered with loose rocks and treacherous drops. As you begin your ascent, the air grows thin and the temperature drops, a stark contrast to the scorching desert below. Night is falling. Each step is a battle against the elements. The wind howls through the narrow passes, carrying with it the eerie cries of unseen creatures. Your cloak flutters around you, offering little protection from the biting cold. Yet, your resolve remains unshaken. The *Behenian* stars, including the ominous *Evil Eye*, guide you through the treacherous paths under the night sky.

Finally, after what feels like an eternity, you crest the final ridge and behold the entrance to the *Necropolis*. As dawn breaks, the ancient ruins lies shrouded in mist in a hidden valley, its towering spires and crumbling walls barely visible in the dim light. A palpable sense of dread hangs in the air, the very ground seeming to pulse with dark energy (which of course intrigued someone as dark as you). You descend into the valley, where the air grows thick with the scent of decay and forlorn, the oppressive silence broken only by the occasional rustle of unseen creatures. Each step brings you closer to your goal, the promise of the *Æther* propelling you onward.

At last, you stand before the entrance to the *Necropolis*, The megalithic masonry of this stronghold suggests a very ancient origin; it emits an ominous aura of eldritch evil, and you can feel the chill running down your spine. A massive stone archway adorned with cryptic runes and symbols. It is sealed. You must determine how to enter the *Necropolis*. But first you'll want to set up camp here, though it's morning, and take a good, long rest, before anything else. Turn to **1**.

1

You awaken to the rays of dawn the next day, filtering through the narrow opening of your makeshift camp, and you welcome its sight. After the gruelling journey and the frustrating encounter, the rest has revitalized you. You stretch, feeling the stiffness in your limbs ease, and take a moment to gather your thoughts. The massive sealed stone archway looms before you, its cryptic runes and symbols seemingly mocking at you. The barrier remains as impenetrable as ever, but you are determined to enter the *Necropolis*, remembering the rumours of secret passages in the surrounding.

You begin your search, navigating the rocky outcrops and narrow passes that encircle the *Necropolis*. Hours pass as you meticulously explore the area, your eyes scanning every shadow and crevice for signs of an opening. The terrain is unforgiving, the rocks sharp and the ground uneven. At last, your perseverance is rewarded. Nestled between two towering rock formations, partially obscured by overgrown shrubs and tangled vines, you find a narrow opening. It is unassuming, easily overlooked by the untrained eye, but you recognize it for what it is: a hidden entrance, a pathway into the depths of the *Necropolis*. The opening is just wide enough to admit you, a dark tunnel leading into the heart of the hill. The air here is cooler, the shadows deeper. With bated breath, you step into the cavern. Turn to **167**.

2

You step onto the pressure plate, holding your breath in anticipation, but nothing happens. The silence is deafening. The walls remain unmoving, the gate steadfastly shut. Panic sets in as the reality of your situation sinks in- you shall be trapped here forever. The thought of endless days in this dark, claustrophobic space, with no escape and no hope, fills you with dread. Misery and despair threaten to overwhelm you as you contemplate the grim fate of wasting away in this part of the *Necropolis*. Your quest ends here.

3

You've successfully climbed out of the underground cavern, back into the *Necropolis*! You are in a small chamber, and you see a corridor ahead towards north, and it seems to be lined up by rather impressive-looking majestic columns. Turn to **87**.

4

If you have codeword **POISON** and have passed by here for the first time, you will **deduct 1 count.**

You are at a north-south tunnel. The walls are hewn roughly from dark stone. Do you want to head north (turn to **264**) or head south (turn to **485**)?

5

The tunnel ends in a small chamber, and a new corridor opens ahead. From here, you can already see that the corridor beyond is lined up by rather impressive-looking majestic columns. Turn to **87**.

6

As you dig away at the burial ground, you catch a cloud of black miasma escaping the crevices of the ground and a whiff of its pungent vapour. Suddenly, you feel your throat tightening and you start asphyxiating, rolling about on the ground, before you cease to move again. Your quest ends here.

7

The tunnel ends at a T-junction. You can either head right eastward (turn to **184**) or left westward (turn to **246**).

8

The passageway abruptly terminates in a dark alcove, with a towering statue, its imposing presence immediately commanding your attention. The statue depicts a strange humanoid figure with dog-head, stretching its mouth open in a gaping maw, dark and cavernous, and probably serving a sinister purpose, as it seems to be pointed towards you. It stands atop a pedestal, which is cracked and weathered. Do you wish to explore the statue (turn to **69**), or leave immediately, returning to the T-junction to continue east (turn to **115**)?

9

You are as the southside of the *Grand Hall* near the entrance. Do you move north (turn to **305**), west (turn to **15**) or east (turn to **114**)?

10

As you touch the lever, the skeleton is suddenly jolted to life. Turn to **445**.

11

You rush out of the room and slam the door shut behind you. A faint but creepy cackle can still be heard on the other side of the door. Not wanting to risk the wrath of a dire spirit, you decide that it is wiser to leave it as it is and continue on your journey. Turn to **508**.

12

Nothing happen in this sector. You are at the north-western corner of the *Grand Hall*. A wall is on the north and west-side. Do you move east (turn to **291**) or south (turn to **151**)?

13

You arrive at a clearing in the cave where the walls glisten with moisture, and the floor grows soft underfoot, covered with a thin layer of decaying organic matter. Your eyes scan the area, taking in the rich tapestry of fungal growth. Vibrant clusters of golden chanterelles, deep crimson blood caps, and delicate, fan-shaped oyster mushrooms cover every available surface. Amidst this fungal forest, something catches your eye—a patch of ethereal, almost translucent mushrooms standing out from the rest. You found the Ghost Caps, important ingredients for your spellcasting! **Add +2 to Ghost Caps** under Reagents. Strangely enough, you also find an interesting artefact amongst the undergrowth. You figure someone lost a key here. If you want to, **add Silver Key** to your inventory.

At this point, you can choose to retreat back north (turn to **117**) or continue your southward exploration (turn to **152**).

14

You are in a passage surrounded by black stone walls. There is a path that opens to the west along the north-south tunnel. Do you want to head west (turn to **560**), head north (turn to **500**) or go south (turn to **41**)?

15

Nothing happen in this sector. You have come to the south-western corner of the *Grand Hall*. A wall is on the south and west-side. Do you move north (turn to **224**) or east (turn to **9**)?

16

Do you have the codeword COBB? If you do, you've already explored this sector and there's nothing left for you to do here (turn to **243**). Next, check if you have the codeword HOBBS? If you have, turn to **483**. Otherwise, read on.

You notice a shoreline and move towards it from the river. The shoreline leads north to a dark, rocky cavern, its mouth yawning like a black void. From the edge of the cavern, you can hear the distant sound of metal clanging, echoing faintly through the cavern. Do you step into the cavern (turn to **105**), or return to the confluence to the south (turn to **243**)?

17

Leaving the 'mirror-room' behind you, you continue your passage eastward. Turn to **440**.

18

The book titled "*Book of Prophecies*" is authored by *Dracegy Cae* the *Sleeping Prophet*, and set in a heavy volume. The text within details the fate of *Krator*, foretelling that there will be thirteen *Regii*, beginning with *Kralj* and concluding with the untimely demise of *Caduccus*. The prophecy states that these *Regii* shall be interred within a *Necropolis*, specially designed by a *Preceptor*, the *Great Wizard*, to access the *Æther*. The *Æther* must be accumulated during the *Regii's* lifetime, as a substantial amount will be required from the Repository during *'The Reckoning'* for the *'Final Battles'* at the *'End of Times.'* These battles are to be fought against a *Master of Dark Arts*, who is prophesied to infiltrate the ruins, seizing power, and obliterating the last remnants of the *Regii's* legacy.

The prophecy also hints at a glimmer of hope—the possibility for all the *Regii* to be awakened with the help of the *Preceptor*. This awakening would occur through a process of resurrection, wherein the *Regii* would merge into a single entity within the *Æther*. This fusion would grant them God-like powers necessary to combat the *Master of Dark Arts* and that the ultimate fate of dominion remains unclear- if it is in favour of the *Regii*, *Krator* will thrive again, ruled by *The One God-King*, an amalgamation of all the *Regii*. However, the prophecy also warns that the identity of this dark master remains elusive, as he may assume many forms, obscuring his true nature until it is too late.

There is a poetry within the book, which is cryptic but also chilling. '*Necromancer- Dead's invoker; Wrath, odious, desire, in my corpus is born. The fates last, terror's spread, for a necros creature of the crypts.*' You wonder if this is referring to you, **NECROMANCER- Master of Dark Arts**? Perhaps you are thinking too much. When you are done reading, turn to **396**.

19

In the following order, if you have codeword QUORK, turn to **450** immediately. Next check whether you have the codework KRECK? If you have it, turn to **361**. Otherwise read on.

Obviously you wouldn't knock on the door, fearing there might be an unfriendly occupant on the other side. You can attempt to pick at the lock (turn to **56**). Since this is a wooden door, you can also attempt to break it open (turn to **109**). Otherwise you will abort the attempt (turn to **93**).

20

Do you have the codeword GRIM? If so, turn to **53**. Otherwise turn to **96**.

21

You press onward to the north, the carefully constructed walls of the passage gradually giving way to raw, jagged rock. The air grows cooler and damp as you delve deeper into the tunnel. The confined space begins to open up slightly, and you sense a broader area ahead. You feel a faint draft, hinting at a cave clearing just beyond your current position. Turn to **81**.

22

You continue down the tunnel westward, until it leads to a sharp turn that veers to the right, changing its course towards the north. Turn to **73**.

23

As you flip open the black book, titled "*Umas Fimus*", a book with no apparent authorship stated, you feel a strange sensation. As the pages part, your eyes are met with bizarre and grotesque illustrations—twisted forms that defy reason, accompanied by cyphers that pulse with a sinister energy. A wave of dread washes over you, gripping your heart. Before you can react, an unseen force seems to latch onto your very soul, pulling it toward the dark pages. Your vision blurs, the world around you fades, and with a final, desperate gasp, you collapse, the book still clutched in your lifeless hands. Your quest ends here.

24

You are hit by a column of lightning that crashes down from the ceiling! **Deduct 5 LIFE** points. If you are still alive, you have to move on. Do you move north (turn to **291**), east (turn to **129**), west (turn to **151**) or south (turn to **305**)?

25

As you approach the sarcophagus, a faint, ghostly light begins to shimmer in the air. The light gradually takes shape, forming into a translucent, ethereal figure. You realize it's a disembodied spirit, floating just above the ancient stone coffin. The spirit loiters around, its form flickering like a candle in the wind, with hollow eyes that seem to stare into the abyss. You realize that there is also no body in this open sarcophagus. On the wall opposite of the sarcophagus is a large symbol of *Mesa*.

You can **cast a spell** ⛤

If you don't want or can't cast a spell, you can choose to leave the spirit alone, and leave in the direction of east (turn to **497**) or west (turn to **563**).

26

As the fading figure of *Miriam* drifts closer to you, you ask, "Is there anything else you can tell me to help on my journey?"

Miriam pauses, her spectral form flickering with a faint glow. "Yes," she replies, her voice tinged with urgency. "It is crucial that you find the grave of the *Great Wizard*. It lies somewhere along the underground river in the catacombs. The waters can be navigated by a skiff, which was last seen in the possession of a paladin who ventured here a while ago. Seek out this skiff, and it will guide you through the treacherous currents to the *Great Wizard*'s resting place. Only there will you find the knowledge and power necessary to complete your quest." **Gain 10 Exp points**.

With a final, sorrowful sigh, *Miriam's* form dissipates, leaving you alone in the cold, dark room. Turn to **331**.

27

A sense of unease coils in your gut. Something about his demeanour feels off, his words carrying an undertone of desperation that doesn't quite match the wisdom and calm you'd expect from a *Great Wizard*. Your instincts scream caution, and you withdraw your hand slightly, eyes narrowing as you scrutinize his features more closely.

"Why were you trapped here, to begin with?" you ask, your voice steady but wary. "What dark sorcery imprisoned you in this mirror?" The old man's expression falters, a flicker of irritation flashing across his face. He quickly masks it with a look of profound sorrow.

"A powerful enemy, envious of my abilities, cursed me. I've been trapped here for a long time, unable to escape. You are my only hope." Your hesitation grows, and the old man's impatience becomes more pronounced. He leans closer to the glass, his hands pressed against the inside of the mirror as if trying to push through by sheer will. "You don't understand the urgency of this!" he snaps, his voice losing its pleading tone and taking on a harsher edge. "Pull me out, now! Do not waste time with questions."

You notice a sizeable rock on the floor. Do you take the opportunity to teach this liar a lesson by hurling the rock at the mirror, in an attempt to break it (turn to **204**), or continue to talk to this old man (turn to **272**)?

28

You rotate the statue right, back to its original position. But all of a sudden comes a stream of scorching red flame again, shooting out from the mouth of the dog-head towards you, and this time much more intense! **Deduct 5 LIFE** points. If you are still alive, you notice that the statue is stuck at this point and you cannot rotate it anymore. Realizing that there's nothing more you can do, you decide to turn back towards the eastern tunnel instead (turn to **115**).

29

You are at a corner of the *Library*. You see a large tapestry of a Lion wearing a Crown on the northside wall. You can either head east (turn to **320**) or head towards south (turn to **158**).

30

Suddenly, you notice that the jade figure's eyes seem to glint with sharp awareness, focusing intently on something in your possession. A voice start to piece through your head.

"Ah, what have we here?" *Taph's* voice murmurs, smooth and serpentine. "Lockpicks, I see. Quite the resourceful guest, aren't you?" You instinctively reach for the lockpicks in your inventory, feeling a twinge of vulnerability under the god's scrutinizing gaze. The atmosphere grows tenser, the green light flickering as if in response to *Taph's* piqued interest.

"Do not be in such a rush to leave my shrine," *Taph* chides, his tone now taking on a greedy, calculating edge. "You see, there are certain... skills that I could impart upon someone of your apparent appreciation of my craft. THIEVERY, for instance, is an art I have taught over countless eons. It is the most important craft for surviving in the dungeons, as well as in any social situations."

"Without this skill, you won't even know how to use the lockpicks properly!" He pauses, letting the tantalizing offer sink in before continuing, "But, of course, such knowledge comes at a price, especially for non-follower such as yourself. Nothing in this world is free, and yet, no offer is impossible, as I am, after all, a God of trade as well as thievery. And I am happy to sell my art to those who pay." *Taph* added, "All you need to do is to simply deposit a certain amount of gold on the altar to gain access to this skill." You wonder why a deity like *Taph* would covet over your mere pittance, but greed is limitless and inexplicable.

Followers of *Hish* and *Barat* can learn THIEVERY for a price of **15 Gp**.
Followers of *Ked* and *Zakl* can learn THIEVERY for a price of **8 Gp**.

Once you pay the price, you, will feel a strange sensation overcoming you, as if knowledge has been downloaded into your head, and you shall record **THIEVERY** as one of your Skills. You can choose not to pay of course, to forfeit this offer. When you are done, turn to **22**.

31

As you step into the *Grand Hall*, you are immediately struck by the imposing presence of giant statues lining the vast chamber. These stone effigies of former *Regii* tower above you, their expressions stern and commanding, immortalized in their regal splendour. However, the grandeur of the hall is overshadowed by an ominous atmosphere. The air is heavy with a sense of foreboding, and as you glance around, you realize that the hall is divided into different sectors. This arrangement is a grim reminder that some sectors might be hidden with traps. You have to proceed cautiously, each step measured and deliberate. Turn to **9**.

32

You see a stone artifact with occult symbol etched on its surface. This item may be useful in your quest.

If you want this item, **add the ▽ Stone with an associated number 3** to your inventory. You have **gained 50 Exp points**. There's nothing else for you to do in the cave and you shall take leave. Turn to **207**.

33

As you carry out the final step of the ritual, a form begins to materialize from the ground before you. Slowly, it rises, taking on the ethereal shape of a wizard. The apparition emits a greenish hue, casting an eerie glow around the area, yet its features remain strikingly vivid. Once fully emerged, it stands motionlessly beside its grave, its spectral eyes fixed upon you with a look of mild annoyance. You can feel the weight of its presence, and you think that it is likely the ghost of *The Great Wizard*.

You can **cast a spell** ✪

Otherwise, you can choose to address the apparition (turn to **360**), attack it (turn to **45**), or leave him alone, retreating back to the river (turn to **282**).

34

You arrive at a door, and there seems to be some activity from the inside. You realize the door is not locked. Do you enter the door (turn to **490**), retrace back to head north (turn to **36**)?

35

If you have codeword **POISON** and have passed by here for the first time, you will **deduct 1 count.**

You are situated somewhere in an east-west tunnel. Do you want to head east (turn to **135**) or head west (turn to **313**)?

36

The tunnel leads north for some distance before ending at a T-junction. Do you turn left-side west (turn to **482**) or right-side east (turn to **527**)?

37

You quickly raise your hands, palms outward, and speak in a calm, soothing, yet persuasive tone, explaining that you mean no harm and only want to explore this part of the dungeon. The paladin's eyes, once aflame with fury, slowly soften. His breathing steadies, and he lowers his broken long-sword. With a weary nod, he takes a step back, signalling that the immediate danger has passed. Turn to **283**.

38

The iron gates clanged shut behind you, their echo resonating through the corridor, reminding you that you have no option but to move forward. As you walk down the marbled passageway, you notice that in the distance, there's a silverish door to the right, its surface gleaming faintly in the dim light. It stands out starkly against the otherwise uniform corridor. Do you wish to open the door (turn to **212**), or do you want to continue walking down north along the corridor (turn to **508**)?

39

After you drop the liquid, you see the eye of the *Homunculus*, blinking at you, as if confused by what you are doing. If you want to try other potion on the *Homunculus*, turn to **257**. If you are done with it and want to leave, turn to **29**.

40

The blindfish tastes horrible! You retch as you feel the putrid innards of the fish run down your throat. You could have at least cooked it instead of doing it the Gollum-way. Not surprisingly, now you are not just nauseated, but also feeling rather sick in the stomach. The pale nasty thing is working its ill effects on you and you think that you are poisoned.

Deduct 5 from LIFE. Turn to **198**.

41

After walking along the dark stone-walled tunnel for a while, you arrive at an L-junction, with a passage to the east. You can move north (turn to **14**) or south (turn to **135**) along the same passage, or explore the east-side (turn to **159**).

42

As you approach the shoreline, the familiar earthy smell of the tunnel mingles with the brackish scent of the river. With your steps sinking slightly into the ground, you make your way back to the dungeon complex. Turn to **485**.

43

Your spell seems effective. Upon the incantation, the spirit's features seem to show panic and it quickly dissipates into the nothingness. You are now left absolutely alone in the tombs. Turn to **339**.

44

The corridor leads to a stonegate, with an outstretched stony palm on its surface. The hand appears almost lifelike, fingers splayed wide as if commanding you to halt. It seems like you are not authorized to venture further into this section of the *Library*. Left with no other choice, you have to retrace your steps. Turn to **457**.

45

You see the gloomy visage of the *Great Wizard* transition into amusement as you try to wield your weapon against it. Without warning, the ghost poof into thin air, disappearing without a trace. You might not have the chance to invoke the *Grand Wizard* again. Since there's nothing left for you to do here, you will retreat to safer waters. Turn to **282**.

46

Deciding not to waste any more time, you swiftly draw your weapon and lunge at *Kolgrim*. The element of surprise fuels your strike, but before you can land a blow, *Kolgrim* quickly sidesteps the blow and retreat, his eyes widen in shock. "What the—" he exclaims. In an instant, his surprise turns to anger, and he quickly brings a silver whistle to his lips. He blows it hard, the shrill sound cutting through the air. "Intruder!" he shouts.

The echoes of the whistle haven't even faded before you hear the heavy footsteps of approaching brigands. *Kolgrim's* face twists into a sneer as he brandishes his sword, ready to defend himself. "You'll regret that, paladin!" he snarls, and in moments, the corridor fills with the sound of steel as *Kanwulf's* crew rushes to the scene. Turn to **417**.

47

As you cast the spell, the air around you grows cold, and a faint blue light emanates from your fingertips, reaching out toward the lingering spirit. The ghostly figure begins to shimmer, its form becoming more defined as it responds to your call. Slowly, the spirit turns to face you, its hollow eyes filled with a mixture of sadness and resolve.

"I am the servant of *Taleh* the Second, once a guardian of these sacred tombs," the spirit whispers, its voice echoing softly in the chamber. "I have waited here for an eternity, bound to this place, hoping for someone like you to arrive. But my strength wanes... soon, I will be no more."

The spirit pauses, its form flickering, before continuing with urgency. "When *Mortis*, the Great Lich, breached the *Necropolis*, he discovered a way to penetrate the *Tombs of the Regii*. He and his foul servants defiled these hallowed grounds, plundering their riches and desecrating the resting places of the kings. The bodies of the *Regii* were removed, scattered, disposed of with haste, lest anyone attempt to resurrect them."

The spirit's voice grows faint, its energy dwindling. "To the east of these tombs lies a stairwell... it descends into the chasms below, where the *Repository of Æther* is situated. *Mortis* is there, gathering his undead legions, preparing for something... something terrible. You must stop him before it's too late."

As the spirit's form wavers, its ethereal glow dimming with each passing moment, it looks at you with a solemn expression. "My time is nearly spent," it murmurs, its voice barely above a whisper. "But before I fade into the nothingness, I can answer one question. Choose wisely, for it shall be the last knowledge I can offer."

What do you want to ask the ghostly servant? You only have one choice. If you want to ask him how to defeat *Mortis*, turn to **543**. If you want to ask him how to access the *Repository*, turn to **492**.

48

As you prepare to draw your weapon, a sudden clamour of footsteps echoes from behind. You spin around, instinctively reaching for your weapon, only to find a familiar face charging towards you. It's *Sir Elandor*, his armour gleaming in the dim light, his (new) sword already drawn! "Hey!" he calls out, his voice filled with determination. "I promised I'd return to help you, and here I am!"

Kanwulf, who had been readying himself for the fight, freezes in shock. His eyes widen as he stares at *Sir Elandor*, disbelief etched across his face. "How can you be alive?" *Kanwulf* roars, his voice tinged with both anger and fear.

But there's no time for explanations. With a surge of adrenaline and a renewed sense of hope, you rush forward, ready to meet the oncoming foes. *Sir Elandor* charges past you, his blade aimed directly at *Kanwulf* and *Kolgrim*. The two brigands, caught off guard by *Elandor's* sudden appearance, scramble to defend themselves. "Leave these two to me!" *Sir Elandor* shouts, his voice full of conviction. "You handle the others!" You nod, turning your attention to the rest of the gang as they close in, weapons raised. Turn to **254**.

49

You arrive at a junction. Do you want to head south (turn to **264**), head north (turn to **100**), or go east (turn to **228**)?

50

Sir Elandor approaches you, his armour scratched and dented from the fierce combat, yet his expression is one of deep gratitude. He sheathes his sword and extends his hand towards you.

"Thank you," he says, his voice filled with sincerity as he grips your hand firmly. "You saved my life when I was poisoned, and now, because of you, I've finally put an end to *Kanwulf* and his brigands. This would not have been possible without your help." He releases your hand and steps back, his gaze steady and full of respect. "The *Order of Solaris* will be forever grateful for your bravery and assistance. You have proven yourself a true ally, and I will make sure that your deeds are known among my brethren."

With a final nod, *Sir Elandor* turns to leave, his footsteps echoing as he makes his way out of the chamber. "May the light of *Solaris* guide you on your journey," he says over his shoulder, before disappearing into the shadows beyond, leaving you alone in the aftermath of the battle. Turn to **382**.

51

The spell works, though you see the apparition hurriedly disappears into thin air. You might not have the chance to invoke the spirit of the *Great Wizard* again. You can only leave this place and go back to the river. Turn to **282**.

52

If you've met *Brutal Brutus* before, turn to **530**. Otherwise read on.

You cautiously approach the burly man resting by the fire, his massive form casting a looming shadow over the room. As you get closer, his piercing eyes lock onto you, assessing you with a cold, calculating stare. His face looks primitive, like a caveman, oversized and rugged with a low forehead, marked by scars, and his muscles bulge beneath his worn leather armour.

"So, you've got the look of a squealer," he says with a rough chuckle, his voice deep and gravelly. "Think you can handle a little secret? Or will you run off with your tail between your legs?" He sits up straighter, cracking his knuckles loudly as he eyes you from head to toe. "Name's *Brutal Brutus*. I've crushed skulls and snapped necks like twigs. But you… you look like the type who'll squeal the moment things get tough."

He leans forward, his face inches from yours, his breath hot, heavy and rather foul. "I know something that could be of use to you. A little secret that's worth more than gold. But everything comes at a price. Are you willing to pay the cost?" He gives you a menacing grin, waiting to see how you'll respond to his challenge. "This secret costs 20 gold pieces."

Do you agree to buy the secret? If you do and can afford it, **deduct 20 gold pieces** and turn to **148**. If you don't want to, or can't afford, turn to **498**.

53

You have exhausted all viable options to get out of the underground caverns. You shall stay here till the day you expire, that is if the *Gnagers* do not get to you first. Your quest ends here.

54

Do you also have the codeword HLAGA? If you do, turn to **293**. If not, turn to **499**.

55

As the spell takes hold, the ghostly figure steps forward and starts addressing you, in a solemn manner. *The Great Wizard's* spectral eyes narrow as he surveys you, his gaze probing and suspicious. "Who are you, why do you summon me and what is your business here?" he demands, his voice carrying an edge of authority and wariness.

You introduce yourself as an adventurer, and the reason you summon the *Great Wizard* is to aid you in your quest. However, you have to state your intention.

If you reply that you are after the *Æther*, turn to **454**.
If you reply that you are here to slay *Mortis*, the Great Lich, turn to **412**.
If you want to attack the *Great Wizard*, turn to **45**.

56

Do you have lockpicks? If you do turn to **430**. Otherwise you have no mean to pick on the lock. Turn to **93**.

57

Do you also have CLIMBING skill? If you have, you manage to swing the grappling hook to a good spot above and successfully climb out of the hole. If not, you fall several times in your attempt to get out of the pit, which costs you **2 LIFE** points. After you succeeded, you retrieve the rope and the grappling hook back into your inventory. Turn to **3**.

58

As you draw closer to the grave, you notice a stick firmly planted in the ground, its surface etched with the mysterious *Xenochian* scripts, which reads: *Askir Ustuk Arcanas*. If you know what to do at this point, turn to the relevant section. Otherwise, read on.

Do you have a shovel? If you do, and would like to try to see if you can exhume the content of the grave, turn to **6**. You may also opt to leave here, perhaps to return next time when you are more prepared, and navigate your way towards the safer part of the river. Turn to **378**.

59

"Come on, now. Time to meet the *Huntsman*," *Ornias* says, beckoning you forward. Watching the goblin with caution and apprehension, you follow *Ornias* through the gate, which opens into a large chamber. A purple swirling teleporter stood on the other side of the chamber.

Ornias gestures toward the teleporter with a crooked finger, "This is where it gets tricky. To reach the *Huntsman*, you'll need to step onto these teleporters. They'll take you deeper into the lair. But they may also bring you to your eternal prison- or your tomb if you're not careful! So navigate cautiously, hehehe..." You barely have time to process his words when, with a sudden cackle, *Ornias* steps back. "Good luck," he says as he turns back suddenly towards the stone gate, which slams shut behind you with a resounding thud, leaving you alone here, or trapping you here within the chamber. You shouted and cursed *Ornias'* name but your voice merely becomes a mild echo in this chamber, before silence envelops you, where the only sound is the soft hum of the teleporter.

Do you have SCRYING skill? If you do, turn to **369**.
Otherwise, you have no choice but to step forward into the teleporter **582**.

60

As you step away, you see the ghost stretch out her hands in despair and disappointment. With a deep sigh, the apparition of *Miriam* fades away. Turn to **331**.

61

By the blessings of *Ked*, you manage to manipulate *Thokk* into giving you an item for free! Turn back to **359** and pick an item of your choice before returning to this section. Once you are done, turn to **289**.

62

As you advance towards the colossal gate, the realization dawns upon you that this is the entrance to the *Inner Chambers*. The motifs carved into the gate depict the *Kralj*, the First of the *Regii* of *Krator*, locked in an epic battle with the fearsome *Draak*, the mighty black dragon of the underworld. Suddenly, you hear a grinding sound behind you—the walls close in, creating a small, claustrophobic space. The sensation is unnerving, and far more stifling than the iron gate that sealed behind you earlier in the corridor, as you are now trapped within a rather narrow, claustrophobic confine. Before you, just in front of the imposing gate, you notice a pressure plate embedded in the floor. With no other options, you step on the plate, hoping that it will open the gate.

If you have the codeword ZARAS, add the associated number to this section, and turn to the new section. If you do not have the codeword, turn to **2**.

63

This must be the secret location hinted by *Ahmes* in his cryptic riddle, with an ornate pedestal in the centre of the room. Resting upon the pedestal is a magnificent suit of black armour, gleaming with an eerie lustre despite the darkness around it. The craftsmanship is exquisite, every curve and edge polished to perfection. The intricate detailing along the breastplate and gauntlets suggests a design of ancient origin, yet the armour remains as flawless as if it had just been forged. This can only be the legendary **Draco**, the fabled armour fashioned from the skin of the Black Dragon *Draak*. **Add 50 Exp points** and codeword **DRACO**.

If you want to take this armour, **add Draco (Shd: 20)** to your inventory. This suit will make any wearer pretty much impenetrable to any damages.

When you are done, you head back to the corridor to the west (turn to **513**).

64

You appear in a room, painted entirely in greyish hue. Within this room are two teleporters, placed in different directions. Do you take the one to the east (turn to **511**), or the one to the west (turn to **582**)?

65

You choose a spot away at the corner of the quarters, away from the rest, and the fireplace, and you remind yourself to be vigilant even though you are resting. But soon you doze off into a rather deep sleep, satiated and contented from the feast. Unbeknownst to you, the brigands were robbing you of your belongings as you slumber through the night, before plunging their merciless blades into your defenceless body, which promptly woke you up in great pain before you lose consciousness again. Your quest ends here.

66

You carefully close the door behind you. Record codeword **KRUZ**. You can head north (turn to **36**). You can also head east only if you do not have the codeword **MERZ** (turn to **34**).

67

After you drop the liquid, you notice a disturbing reaction- the *Homunculus* inside the tank begins to twitch violently, its misshapen limbs thrashing with newfound energy.

The grotesque mass of flesh starts to swell, its giant eye bulging unnaturally, the blood vessels within it pulsing as if under immense pressure. The flesh stretches and contorts, pressing against the confines of the cylindrical glass tank. The glass groans under the strain, hairline cracks forming and spider-webbing across the surface.

With a sudden, deafening pop, the glass shatters, sending shards flying in all directions. A wave of viscous liquid, gushes out, splashing against your body. You stagger back, feeling the liquid seeping through your clothes. The remnants of the *Homunculus*, now a grotesque mess of flesh and ooze, slump to the floor, twitching in its final throes. You start to feel great pain all over your body, as the liquid seems to eat into your skin, corroding away your tissues. In no time, you are also reduced to a similarly formed grotesque mess of flesh and ooze. Your quest ends here.

68

The northward corridor comes to a dead-end at an unyielding wall. Scattered across the dusty floor are rat droppings. If you've been here before, you should turn back south (turn to **207**). If not, read on.

Your gaze falls upon a small mousehole at the base of the wall, barely noticeable amid the shadows. A flicker of curiosity stirs within you. What secrets could be hidden inside this tiny opening? Is it worth the risk to investigate further?

You can **cast a spell** ⛧

Otherwise, you can ignore this place, and retreat back south (turn to **207**).

69

Do you have the THIEVERY skill? If you do, turn to **510**. Otherwise turn to **415**.

70

Nothing happens. But the spirit seems to get the hint and its form slowly fade away into the nothingness. You have wasted a spell. Turn to **339**.

71

"Take this as a parting gift!" shouts the *Demonomancer*. With a flick of his wrist, he shoots a fireball, its flames crackling with deadly intent, at your back. **Roll a dice**. This number will be the damage. **Minus** accordingly from your **LIFE score**. If you are still alive, record the codeword **DEMONOS**. With desperation, you dash out of this corridor back to the junction. Turn to **403**.

72

The path veers sharply to the right, changing course north. After witnessing what happened earlier, you tread with extreme caution and apprehension. Turn to **594**.

73

The air grows cooler and the darkness thickens, your footsteps echoing through the stone floor, as you walk through the tunnel. After a while, you come across a wooden door to the left, which doesn't seem to be locked. Do you open the door to see what's in the room (turn to **410**), or do you continue your journey north (turn to **552**)?

74

Are you on a skiff? If you are, turn to **524**. Otherwise, turn to **337**.

75

You arrive at the south-eastern corner of the lair, frantic and panting. You can either dash up along the northern corridor (turn to **260**) or hurry back west where you came from (turn to **358**).

76

You call forth your familiar and you direct it toward the disembodied spirit still lingering near the sarcophagus. As your familiar approaches the ghost, it reaches out, attempting to interact with the ethereal figure. The spirit's form flickers, its hollow eyes narrowing as though irritated by the presence of your summoned companion. It shudders and begins to fade, its transparent figure growing thinner and less defined.

Before you can react, the spirit disappears completely, vanishing into the air. But something unexpected happens—your familiar, too, begins to flicker and fades away entirely, leaving you standing alone in the silent tomb once again. You think you have wasted a spell. Turn to **339**.

77

You return to the south-western corner of the lair, where you first arrived. As soon as you turn your head right towards north, you see a massive net falling onto you, sprung from a figure that is standing just right before you in the northern passage. The coarse ropes tangle around you, pulling tight and knocking you to the ground. Panic floods your senses as you struggle against the net, but your movements only seem to make it tighter.

Your eyes widen in horror as you spot this figure, advancing slowly towards you, his slim built, black skin and an unholy looking spear in his hand looking menacing as it casts a silhouette against the dim lights. You have no doubt— this must be the legendary *Huntsman*. Without a word, the figure hurls the spear at you with deadly precision, aiming at your heart. The spear closes in, and you only feel an instantaneous piercing pain before your consciousness fades. You are immediately killed by a weapon what many referred to as a 'Godkiller'- *The Spear of Signonul*. Your quest ends here.

78

You cast the spell, but there's no effect on the apparition. The spirit frowns and you suddenly, without warning, you see the spirit poof into thin air. You might not have the chance to invoke the spirit of the *Great Wizard* again. All you can do is leave this place, and get to a safer area of the river. Turn to **282**.

79

You are between walls, with paths leading north and south. Do you want to go north (turn to **344**), or south (turn to **411**)?

80

Between you is a decorated wall to the south with a large symbol of *Capricornus*, and a wall at the north that recedes into an alcove, which houses an open sarcophagus made of the finest mahogany wood. This sarcophagus must have belonged to one of the deceased *Regii*. However, you realize the sarcophagus is empty! The body of the *Regii* seems to have been removed. There's nothing you can do here, except to move on towards east (turn to **116**) or west (turn to **436**).

81

Do you have codeword VORNH? If you do, there's nothing left for you to explore ahead and you shall turn back. Turn to **122**. If you do not have the codeword, turn to **179**.

82

You lunge at *Ornias* but the goblin doesn't flinch. Instead, with a flick of his wrist, a rusty cage appears out of nowhere and falls from the ceiling, crashing onto the floor, trapping you on the spot. *Ornias* mocking laughter fills the room, echoing off the stone walls. "I knew this would happen," he sneers, his eyes glittering with vengeful glee. ". Stupidity has a price. And now, you'll pay yours. I'll pass you to my master, the *Huntsman*. He always needs new practice targets." His laughter grows louder as the reality of your predicament sinks in, leaving you to ponder your fate. Your quest ends here.

83

As you attempt to force open the door, it unexpectedly swings wide, revealing a wounded paladin, who was visibly upset by your attempt. Clad in a royal standard mail and clutching a broken long-sword, he charges at you with fierce determination, his eyes burning with desperate fury.

Do you have CHARM skill? If you do, turn to **37**. Otherwise, the battle will ensue, and you shall turn to **123**.

84

A familiar is summoned but the spirit simply swipe it away, and before you can act, both entities dissipate into thin air. You might not have the chance to invoke the spirit of the *Great Wizard* again. All you can do is leave this place, and get to a safer area of the river. Turn to **282**.

85

With a deep breath, you call out, "Heads." The coin begins to slow down, before coming to a stop on the altar stone. The obverse coin face shows 'Heads'. A heavy silence fills the chamber, and then the voice of *Zakl* echoes through your mind once more, this time with a note of approval. "Well done." And the voice sounds no more. You watch the coin on the altar with a profound sense of contemplation, and realize it is your lucky coin, imbued with a great significance. If you wish to take it, **add Lucky Coin (+5 to PROTECTION possible to upgrade default core attribute)** to the inventory. You leave this place feeling rather philosophical after the sobering experience. Turn to **459**.

86

The spell fizzes in the air, but the wall remains cold and unyielding. You have wasted a spell. Turn to **207**.

87

A sense of awe fills you as you walk down the grand corridor, your senses heightened by the sheer magnitude of the colossal marble columns that rise from the stone floor, stretching upward to the shadowy ceiling far above. This corridor, with its pristine elegance and artistic splendour, suggests that it will lead to a place of great significance, far removed from the dark and foreboding passages you've traversed before. However, your exhilaration is suddenly interrupted by a huge clang behind you! Turn to **38**.

88

Suddenly, you notice a green wisp of light darts through the air and enters *Grobb's* body. His eyes instantly glow with an eerie green hue, and a palpable wave of hostility emanates from him. Without warning, he turns towards you, a menacing snarl twisting his features.

"You... traitor! Proselytes of *Hish* shall not be spared!" *Grobb* growls, his voice distorted and filled with malice. Before you can react, he lunges at you. He may have been weakened from the imprisonment, but the newly possessed *Grobb* has grown immensely strong with his newfound supernatural strength. *Grobb* will begin the turn.

Grobb
Life   10
Offence (Melee) 13
Defence   5

Grobb's Probability Table

Outcomes	Missed Hit	Exact Hit	Missed Hit	Exact Hit	Reduced Hit	Critical Hit
Dice Number	2	1	3	4	6	5

If you win the battle, **gain 20 Exp points** and turn to **280**.

89

You are on a north-south corridor with an opening to the west. Do you want to dash towards west (turn to **548**), north (turn to **234**) or south (turn to **375**)?

90

You try to have a meaningful conversation with the wall, but all you hear is silence. You have wasted a spell. Turn to **207**.

91

Your body tingles as the spell takes effect, and in an instant, you shrink down to a diminutive size. The world around you seems to expand, the towering sarcophagus and looming walls of the tomb now appearing even more imposing. Looking up, you see the spirit hovering above you. Its hollow eyes gaze forward, seemingly disinterested in your sudden transformation, as if it doesn't even register your presence in this tiny form.

A few moments later, you feel the spell's energy begin to wane, and your body starts to grow, returning to its original size. As you regain your normal stature, you glance back at the spirit, only to see it slowly beginning to fade, its outline blurring as it drifts toward nothingness. The ghostly figure dissolves into the air, leaving behind only a faint, cold breeze that sends a shiver down your spine. Turn to **339**.

92

After you rotate the statue to the left again, you're suddenly roasted by the same stream of scorching red flame shooting out from the mouth of the dog-head, this time much more intense! **Deduct 5 LIFE** points. If you are still alive, you that the statue is stuck at this point and you cannot rotate it anymore. Realizing that there's nothing more you can do, you decide to turn back towards the eastern tunnel instead (turn to **115**).

93

You are along a dark passage, with a locked door to the south. Do you attempt to open the door (turn to **19**)? Otherwise you can move east (turn to **122**) or head west (turn to **159**).

94

Taking a deep breath, you kneel before the imposing statue of *Hish*, the Wise One. "I accept your offer, *Lord Hish*, the Wise One, the Grand Benefic, Eldest of All Elementals," you declare, your voice steady but your heart racing. As the words leave your lips, the shrine begins to glow with a warm, golden light. The cold air dissipates, replaced by a comforting warmth that envelops you. The voice of *Hish* echoes once more in your mind, now filled with approval. "Welcome, my reborn child. Embrace the path of wisdom and fortune." You feel a surge of energy flow through you, blessed by the benevolent god.

By the blessings of your Patron Deity, you are healed. Restore your **LIFE** and **MANA** to their maximum values. You also find 20 Gold pieces materialize before you! **Add 20 Gold pieces.** At the same time, you feel a heaviness weighing on your mind. Your action may have alerted your previous Patron Deity and you may be marked. Record codeword **PROSE**. There's nothing else to do here and you shall take leave. Turn to **122**.

95

The southern path leads shortly to a large cavern, and before you, stretching as far as the dim light allows you to see, are countless skeleton warriors. Each one is armoured and armed, and they are no ordinary group of undead- it is a legion, an army amassed for purposes you can only begin to imagine.

For a brief moment, you are frozen in place, taking in the sheer scale of what you have stumbled upon. Then, as if sensing the living among them, the skeletons turn their empty gazes towards you. A low, rattling sound rises from the mass as they begin to move, weapons clanking and bones creaking. The ground trembles beneath their march, and within moments, they are charging in your direction, an unstoppable tide of death.

Instinct kicks in, and you prepare yourself to fight, drawing upon every skill and weapon at your disposal. You might have the means to "kill Gods", to wield powers beyond mortal comprehension, but as the wave of skeletal warriors crashes down upon you, their numbers prove too overwhelming. They swarm over you, a relentless flood of bones and blades. You strike out, taking down many, but for every one you destroy, two more take its place. Their sheer volume is inescapable, and soon you find yourself engulfed in a sea of armour and bone, the darkness closing in as their weapons tear into you from all sides. Your quest ends here.

96

After travelling a considerable distance north, the tunnel veers sharply to the left, changing course towards the west. You eventually arrive at a dead end, but you notice a hole in the cave ceiling, about 12 feet high. You figure that this is another hole that lead you back to the main dungeons of the *Necropolis* above.

If you have CLIMBING skill and decide to use it, turn to **501**.
If you have a Rope + Grappling Hook and decide to use it, turn to **57**.
If you have none of the above, turn to **387**.

97

You dash northward and the passage soon splits into a junction, with paths leading in three directions—north, west, and east. You pause for a brief moment, trying to decide which way to go, but your decision is made for you.

As soon as you reach the junction, a massive net shoots out from the eastern passage, catching you off guard. The coarse ropes tangle around you, pulling tight and knocking you to the ground. Panic floods your senses as you struggle against the net, but your movements only seem to make it tighter. You turn to your right, eyes widening in horror as you spot a slim, menacing figure emerging from the shadows. His skin is as black as night and he is holding an unholy looking spear. You have no doubt—this must be the legendary *Huntsman*. Without a word, the figure hurls the spear at you with deadly precision, aiming at your heart. The spear closes in, and you only feel an instantaneous piercing pain before your consciousness fades. You are immediately killed by a weapon what many referred to as a 'Godkiller'- *The Spear of Signonul.* Your quest ends here.

98

Ked's voice suddenly breaks into a laughter, which makes you grow increasingly uneasy. "Ah, you're that little traitorous grave-worm they told me about. Your previous master was not pleased, and they had told me about you, little turncoat. Remember this, NECROMANCER: justice is not always swift, but it is inevitable. Your newfound loyalty to *Hish* The Fool will not shield you from the consequences of your treachery. Be afraid, the worst is yet to come."

You shudder and spring to your feet, leaving the shrine in haste back to the shoreline, while you the maniacal cackle of *Ked* ring in your head. Turn to **243**.

99

Within moments, you find yourself dwarfed by your surroundings, and you are now barely the size of a rat. You see the grave and the apparition looms before you in colossal proportion, the latter seemingly amused. Then without warning, the spirit poofs into thin air. After a while, you find yourself reverting back to your original size after the spell wears off. However, you might not have the chance to invoke the spirit of the *Great Wizard* again. All you can do is leave this place, and get to a safer area of the river. Turn to **282**.

100

You are walking along a long north-south passageway. Do you want to go up north (turn to **554**) or head down south (turn to **49**)?

101

The opening leads into a narrow rock passage, with uneven rocky ground which is challenging to walk on. After much struggle, you arrive at a colossal stone gate, which towers above you. There doesn't seem to be any visible mechanism nor handles or levers that might suggest a way to open it, and it appears to be sealed shut, its weight and insurmountable by any means you possess. Sensing that there's no way through, you have to return to where you come from. Turn to **404**.

102

You step cautiously into the room, the air thick with the scent of age and decay. Your eyes flicker as it catches the sight of a skeleton sprawled on the cold stone floor in the middle of the room, its bony fingers wrapped around a rusted lever protruding from the ground. The skeleton, clothed in tattered remnants of once-fine garments, seems eerily undisturbed by time. Dust has settled in thick layers, indicating it has lain here for countless years.

You can **cast a spell** ⛤

Otherwise, you can inspect the skeleton (turn to **218**), pull the lever (turn to **10**), or leave the room (turn to **66**).

103

After you cast the spell, you expect to see the disembodied spirit transform back into its original body. But something unexpected happens.

The ghostly figure begins to waver and ripple, its ethereal form trembling as if struggling against the force of your magic. Instead of reanimating into a living being, the spirit starts to condense, growing denser and more tangible. Before you can react, the once-insubstantial ghost solidifies and collapses to the ground with a soft thud, transforming into a puddle of thick ectoplasm. Soon it dawns on you that this spell only works on physical dead bodies, instead of incorporeal beings. Nevertheless, you have access to one of the rarest reagents for your spellcasting. **Add +2 Ectoplasm** into Reagents. Turn to **339**.

104

You appear in a room, painted entirely in fern-green. Within this room are three teleporters, placed in different directions. Do you take the one to the north (turn to **434**), to the east (turn to **352**), or to the west (turn to **208**)?

105

As you venture deeper into the cavern, the metallic clanging grows louder, followed by frantic shouts. Suspended from the cavern ceiling by a thick chain is a rusted iron cage. Inside, a dishevelled figure frantically bangs against the bars, and cries for help, his eyes wide with desperation. He spots you and beckons urgently.

"Over here! Please, come over!" the man calls out. As you approach, he introduces himself. "My name is *Grobb*. I've been imprisoned here by *Kanwulf* and his brigands just three days ago. They left me here to rot.."

He explains, "I was working as a runner for *Kanwulf*, gathering intelligence throughout the *Necropolis* to aid in his quest. But after a disagreement, he had me locked up. I know a lot about the *Great Wizard*, the *Tombs of the Regii*, where *Mortis* and the access to the *Æther* are. I've kept this information from *Kanwulf* as leverage, but now it can help you. These are information vital to your success!" *Grobb* looks at you with pleading eyes. "Please, open this cage and free me. I promise to share everything I know to ensure your success."

You notice that the iron cage, while heavily rusted, is actually firmly locked and that the bars are strong and steady and will not give in to any attempts to break them by weapons. You also find it unusual to encounter such a character in the depths of a dungeon.

If you have PERCEPTION and want to use it, turn to **449**.

Do you have a Black Key? If you do, **remove the Black Key** from the inventory and turn to **163**. Otherwise, you can try to pick open the lock if you have lockpicks (turn to **366**). You can also leave this area, maybe to come back again at a later date when you have the right key (record codeword **HOBBS** and turn to **243**), or even… try to kill him (turn to **551**)!

106

Steeling yourself, you plant your feet firmly on the ground, determined to face the *Huntsman* head-on. Your breath is steady now, and your hand tightens around your weapon, ready to strike. The black figure races closer, its menacing presence growing with every step. But as the figure nears, you soon realize this is a wrong move. You find a massive net cast from his hand, unfurling through the air with terrifying speed, and you barely have time to raise your weapon before it ensnares you, the thick cords wrapping around your body and pinning your arms to your sides.

Struggling against the net, you barely notice as the *Huntsman* calmly steps forward. His black skin seems to absorb the surrounding darkness, his eye filled with savage malice. With chilling precision, he hurls his spear. It cuts through the air with deadly accuracy, and you have no time to evade. The sharp pain pierces your chest, and you are instantaneously killed by the legendary opponent, with a legendary weapon- the *Spear of Signonul*, also known as the "Godkiller". Your quest ends here.

107

As you step onto the pressure plate, a deep rumbling reverberates through the chamber. To your astonishment, the giant gate slowly begins to lift, creaking and groaning as ancient mechanisms spring to life. The once-immovable barrier rises, revealing a vast hall beyond. The first place that awaits you in the *Inner Chambers* is the infamous *Grand Hall*, known far and wide for its treacherous traps. The grandeur of the hall, with its towering columns and intricate carvings, belies the deadly perils that lie in wait. You take a deep breath and step into the hall. Turn to **31**.

108

You sense that *Kanwulf* is likely up to no good, and that you will be put into a very dangerous predicament should you stay. But the choice is still yours. Do you want to agree to *Kanwulf's* offer and participate in the feast, and to stay overnight (turn to **487**), or outright refuse him (turn to **562**)?

109

Do you have codework BRAKK? If you do, turn to **83**. Otherwise turn to **428**.

110

If you've been here before, there is nothing more you can do here anymore, except to return to the cavern junction. Turn to **576**. Otherwise, read on.

You proceed cautiously along the southern path and eventually, the tunnel comes to an abrupt stop, and you find yourself at the edge of a large, gaping hole in the ground. Peering into the darkness, you see a shallow pit below, littered with the remains of many skeletons. Bones are scattered haphazardly, some partially buried in the loose earth, others lying fully exposed. The sight is unsettling, but something about it strikes you as odd. This doesn't feel like a proper charnel ground where the dead are laid to rest with respect, but rather a place of hurried disposal. Perhaps magic will unravel this mystery?

You can **cast a spell**

If you don't want to do so, or you are unable to do so, you can walk back to the cavern junction where you came from. Turn to **576**.

111

How do you even cast this spell? Cheaters must die. Your quest ends here.

112

As the crimson gate creaks open when you unlock it, you step beyond and behold a vast, cavernous *Repository*, the air thick with ethereal energy. Before you lies a giant lake, its surface shimmering with a silverish liquid that seems to pulse with life. This is it—the *Æther*, the wellspring of omnipotence, the source of the power you have sought for so long.

The sight is mesmerizing, the liquid swirling in patterns that defy logic, as if it holds the very essence of creation itself. But your awe is interrupted by the sound of heavy footsteps and a deep, guttural voice. The *Abomination*, the monstrous fusion of the *Regii*, lumbers into view, but its massive form is too large to pass through the gateway to the *Repository*. It thrashes and struggles, its many faces twisted in rage as it curses at you, calling you intruder, a thief.

Ignoring its vile outbursts, you fix your gaze on the shimmering lake. Without hesitation, you sprint towards it and plunge into the silvery depths. The liquid envelops you, and you begin to drink and bathe, the *Æther* filling your body with a warmth that quickly turns into a blazing inferno of power. Every cell in your body ignites with raw energy, and you feel your mortal limitations shatter as you transcend into something far greater. Your mind expands, your senses sharpen, and your very soul becomes intertwined with the fabric of the universe.

You emerge from the lake, no longer the person you once were. Now, you are something more—an entity of pure power, beyond mortal comprehension. The god-killing weaponry in your hands hums with the same energy that courses through your veins, and you turn your gaze toward the *Abomination*, still struggling at the gateway, its curses now tinged with fear.

With a single step, you close the distance between you and the monstrous being. It flails in desperation, but you are far beyond its reach. With effortless grace, you strike it with a weapon. The *Abomination* lets out a final, pitiful wail as you strike it down. The blow cleaves through its amalgamated form, and you watch as it releases a torrent of black gusts that dissipate into the air.

The once-mighty creature deflates like a punctured balloon, its grotesque form collapsing in on itself until nothing remains but a withered, empty skin on the floor. The chamber falls silent, the echoes of its demise lingering for a moment before fading into nothingness.

You stand tall, surveying the scene before you. The last hope of *Krator*, the monstrous fusion of the *Regii*, has been destroyed. The *Æther* still swirls in the lake behind you, a testament to the power you now wield. You have transcended mortality, and with the defeat of both the *Abomination* and *Mortis*, you are now a force beyond reckoning. **Gain 200 Exp points**. Turn to **600**.

113

The spell fizzes in the air, but the wall remains cold and unyielding. You have wasted a spell. Turn to **207**.

114

Nothing happen in this sector. You have come to the south-eastern corner of the *Grand Hall*. A wall is on the south and east-side. Do you move north (turn to **357**) or west (turn to **9**)?

115

The passageway stretches endlessly before you, but soon it veers to the left, towards north. Turn to **5**.

116

You are at row one of the tombs, on the central side, and in a junction where you can travel in all directions. The sarcophagi are situated in the walls along east and west. Do you want to go north (turn to **525**), south (turn to **248**), east (turn to **486**), or west (turn to **80**)?

117

You are back at the L-junction. Record the codeword **GARM**. You can continue to press north (turn to **20**) if you want to. If you do not have the codeword GROM, you can also turn right into a tunnel in the east (turn to **569**).

118

This way will lead you back to the *Black Serpent* corridor and the *Grand Hall*, and you wouldn't want to do so. You'd need to consider your option again. Turn to **135**.

119

You summoned a familiar, directing it to enter the mousehole (it is small enough to enter), to retrieve any interesting item it can find. About a minute later, the familiar emerges from the mousehole and presents you with a startling find. Turn to **32**.

120

You see the sprawled skeleton ever moving so slightly to the side, away from you, but it has also released its grip on the lever. Do you pull the lever (turn to **402**), or do you wish to examine the skeleton, perhaps to take some of its bones as your necromantic ingredient (turn to **322**)?

121

As you follow the north passage, the cold draft seems to get chillier, until a point where it feels freezing cold. It opens into an east-west tunnel where you are taken aback by a surreal and macabre sight. Emerging from the shadows, a ghostly procession winds its way across the tunnel before you.

There are many of them—pale, translucent figures that drift forward in a slow, solemn march. The faces of these apparitions are expressionless, hollowed by death. These spirits seem lost in their own world, oblivious to your presence, their focus solely on the path ahead.

At the head and alongside the procession, some ghosts also serve as shepherds, guiding the spectral throng with deliberate steps. Their spectral hands hold funerary bells and every few moments, one of the undead shepherds strikes a bell, sending a mournful chime echoing through the tunnel. The sound reverberates with a haunting resonance, adding to the unsettling atmosphere.

You can **cast a spell** ⭐

You can also try to get up close to the undeads (turn to **202**), or ignore them for now, retreating back to the 'relative' safety of the dungeons (turn to **588**).

122

You are at the end of the east-west passageway, which lead to a T-junction. A faint golden light is emanated from the south. Do you head up north (turn to **21**), head south (turn to **475**), or retreat westward (turn to **93**)?

123

Even though this paladin, *Sir Elandor* is wounded and using a broken blade, he prove to be a formidable opponent. **Row a die**. If **1, 3, 5, you will begin your turn**. Whereas for **2, 4, 6, he will begin his turn**.

Sir Elandor
Life 3
Offence (Melee) 20
Defence 11

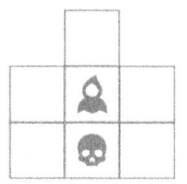

Sir Elandor's Probability Table

Outcomes	Exact Hit	Exact Hit	Exact Hit	Critical Hit	Critical Hit	Critical Hit
Dice Number	2	1	4	3	6	5

If you win the battle, **gain 20 Exp points**, record codeword **QUORK** and turn to **476**.

124

"I am the Steward of the Inner Chambers," the skeleton intones, its voice echoing with a hollow, spectral timbre. "None shall pass the threshold. I am bound by duty to protect the sanctity of the place." You meet the skeleton's warning, unflinching. "I seek passage to the inner chambers," you declare, your voice steady and resolute. "The Æther lies beyond, and I will not be deterred." The skeleton's bony fingers tighten around the lever, its reply assertive. "I am bound by ancient oaths, and my duty is clear. None shall pass. Or you shall die!"

Do you back out the room (turn to **66**) or challenge the skeleton (turn to **445**)?

125

You find yourself in a confluence of the underground river, its waters flowing with a quiet persistence through the subterranean landscape. The cavern walls rise high above you, adorned with stalactites that glisten in the dim light. Shadows dance on the surface of the water, creating an eerie yet mesmerizing scene. To the north and south, narrow passages beckon, while the eastern path leads back to the shoreline. Do you go north (turn to **350**), head south (turn to **395**) or head back to shore to the east (turn to **42**)?

126

If you have the codeword GYARG, there is nothing much for you to do here, except to find *Ornias* later in the lair, and you shall leave here. Turn to **135**.

If you have the codeword HLAGA, turn to **425**.
If you do not have HLAGA, but have the codeword VLAGR., turn to **154**.
If you do not have any, turn to **593**.

127

As you step away from the forcefield, it suddenly shimmers with an intense, blinding light. The electrifying sound fills the cave, crackling and buzzing with fierce energy. You shield your eyes, feeling the hairs on your arms stand on end as the powerful light intensifies.

In a moment, the light vanishes, leaving behind an eerie silence. The forcefield (and whatever is inside) is gone, leaving the cave feeling strangely empty. The once vibrant hum of energy is replaced by a deafening stillness, making the cavern seem even more foreboding. You glance around, half-expecting something to emerge from the darkness, but nothing stirs.. There's nothing else here in this cave. Turn to **470**.

128

Nothing happens. You have wasted a spell. There's nothing much you can do here but leave this place. Turn to **576**.

129

Nothing happen in this sector. A wall is on the east-side. Do you move north (turn to **397**), west (turn to **24**) or south (turn to **357**)?

130

You hesitated, and finally decided not to eat the blindfish, releasing it back into the underground stream. Feeling not much else to do at the stream, you decide to move on. Turn to **225**.

131

The paladin's appear enraged and ridiculed, his eyes widen and bulge with fury and intensity. "Then you shall taste my blade!" shouts the paladin. A battle shall commence. Turn to **123**.

132

After you cast the spell, the air around you thickens, growing cold as a faint, otherworldly light begins to emanate from the scattered bones. The pit, once silent and still, now comes alive with the sounds of moans and groans, as if the very ground itself is lamenting. Suddenly, a distinct voice rises above the others, commanding your attention. It is deep and resonant, filled with ancient authority. "You have awakened us from our slumber," the voice intones. "And it is at an opportune time."

You scan the darkness, searching for the source of the voice, and then you see it—a faint, ghostly figure slowly coalescing from the swirling mist above the bones. The figure is tall and imposing, clad in ethereal armour that glows faintly with a dim, otherworldly light. He is crowned with a regal helm, and his eyes hollow and deathly.

"I am *Kralj*, first of the *Regii*," the voice continues. "Once, I ruled with honour and strength. But now, I have been reduced to this...a mere shadow, condemned to the pits by the dark forces that now plague this land. But vengeance will be mine," he declares, his voice filled with an unyielding resolve. "And you, stranger, have the power to restore us to our former glory. Cast the spell, and resurrect our forms. With your aid, we shall rise once more to reclaim what is ours and to end the reign of the one who defiled our tombs." The other voices, still moaning and groaning, seem to echo *Kralj's* plea, urging you to act. The air is thick with anticipation, the spirits restless and yearning for their return to the world of the living.

Kralj extends a ghostly hand toward you, his expression one of grim expectation. "Do this, and you shall have the allegiance of the *Regii*. Together, we will bring an end to the darkness that threatens all."

Do you still have enough reagents and mana to cast the *Zilaq Fimus* spell? If you do, turn to **188**. If not, you hear the haunting scorns and curses of the *Regii* before they fade away once more into obscurity. Turn to **576**.

133

You manage to stabilize yourself on the skiff, despite the whirlpool that is forming below the boat. Do you want to head north (turn to **288**), south (turn to **125**) or west (turn to **243**)?

134

After casting the spell, you feel a strange tingling sensation wash over your body as you rapidly begin to shrink. The walls around you grow taller, and the once small mousehole now looms before you like the entrance to a cavern. You step into the darkness, your now tiny form navigating through the narrow, twisting passage.

After about a minute of searching within the cramped confines, your fingers brush against something smooth and solid. You tug at it, slowly dragging the object out of the mousehole. It's surprisingly heavy for your shrunken form, but you manage to pull it into the open.

As the spell's effects begin to fade, you feel yourself expanding back to your normal size, as you watch both he mousehole and the item revert back to their miniscule forms. As you hold up the curious item, you are startled by what you've found. Turn to **32**.

135

You are at a cross-junction. The walls are hewn roughly from dark stone. A carpet of dust muffled your footsteps. South is the direction which leads back to the *Grand Hall*. From a distance, you can see that the east-side leads to an open chamber. Do you go north (turn to **41**), east (turn to **126**), west (turn to **35**) or south (turn to **118**)?

136

Ked's voice drops to a lower, more sinister tone, dripping with a chilling courtesy. "Ah, I see we have a traitor among us," she intones with a terrifying calmness. "How quaint that you would seek refuge in the arms of *Hish*. But do not think you can escape my gaze so easily. Bad things have a way of finding those who betray their true masters, and they will come for you in no time."

Her words send a shiver down your spine, each syllable a promise of impending doom. "Remember this, NECROMANCER: justice is not always swift, but it is inevitable. Your newfound loyalty to *Hish* the Fool will not shield you from the consequences of your treachery, and of course my little lovely tantrum. Be afraid, for the worst is yet to come."

You shudder and spring to your feet, leaving the shrine in haste back to the shoreline, while youcthe maniacal cackle of *Ked* ring in your head. Turn to **243**.

137

By the blessings of *Taph*, you find yourself an opportunity to pilfer an item from *Thokk*. If you want to do so, turn back to **359** and pick an item of your choice before returning to this section. Once you are done, turn to **289**.

138

You have to get out of this area fast, before the *Nyx* return to try to drown you again. There's only a straight river passage towards either east or west. If you decide to head east, turn to **243**. If you prefer to head west instead, turn to **522**.

139

After the spell is cast, you witness the ghostly apparitions, once moving steadily in their solemn march, suddenly scatter in every direction. Their hollow eyes widen with fear, their forms flickering like candle flames in a strong wind. The shepherds through their silent authority, falter and hesitate, though not loosening their grips on the funerary bells.

But as the spell begins to fade, the undead slowly regather, reforming their ranks with eerie precision. The procession resumes its march, as if nothing had happened, the spirits drifting forward with the same monotonous trudging. The funerary bells once again toll in rhythm, and the shepherds resume their duty, guiding the lost souls. It is time for you to retreat back to the 'safety' of the dungeons (turn to **588**).

140

With the fallen *Chelonoth* beneath your feet, you remember the high value of its carapace and how it is sought after by many merchants. Carefully, you pry away sections of the tough shell, stowing them away for later. If you want to, **add Carapace (Gp: 20)** into your inventory. As you search the clearing, your eyes fall upon tattered clothes—remnants of an unfortunate victim who met their end here. The *Chelonoth* may have consumed their flesh, even their bones, but the clothing remains.

Amidst the fabric, you uncover a curious artifact: a library pass. This may come in handy. If you want to, **add Library Pass** into your inventory. When you're done, you decide to leave this place and continue with your river navigation (turn to **125**).

141

As you move closer to the stonegate, the details of the pentagram become clearer. Each of the five points is marked with a unique symbol and a slot that can be affixed with small stone, and there's a larger sixth symbol in the middle of the pentagram. You figure that it is an alchemical puzzle, the symbol in the middle depicts the *Philosopher's Stone* associated with transmutation, and that solving this puzzle might possibly open the stonegate.

Do you have all the Five Stones with symbols corresponding to the ones on the pentagram, as well as the solution to this puzzle? If you do, **add the final number** from the transmutation **to number of this section**, and **turn to the new section** corresponding to the **summed number**.

If you do not have all the Five Stones, and do not know the solution to this puzzle, you are not prepared to open the stonegate, and should return to the main tunnel (turn to **313**).

142

After you drop the liquid, you see the *Homunculus* forming a wide-grin, as if appreciative of this liquid. If you want to try other potion on the *Homunculus*, turn to **257**. If you are done with it and want to leave, turn to **29**.

143

After the spell is cast, you sense that the ghosts become more acutely aware of your presence. You call out to them, and one of the spirits, a figure with hollow eyes and tattered robes, turns its gaze toward you, acknowledging your call. "We are part of *'The Reaping'*," the spirit whispers, its voice hollow and distant, like the rustling of dry leaves. "We are drawn to the *Necropolis*, compelled to serve *Mortis*. Our energy fuels the production of the *Æther* in the repository, a vast reservoir of power for both himself and his undead armies.

Then, with a final, mournful glance, the spirit turns away and rejoins the procession. Having find the purpose of their death-march, it is time for you to retreat back to the 'safety' of the dungeons (turn to **588**).

144

You feel the water fill your lungs, as the *Nyx* pulls you deeper into the depths. And soon, you lose consciousness, as you are immersed in a surreal state of stupor, in the dark depths where unimaginable horror takes place without your knowledge. Your quest ends here.

145

Upon return to the guard-post, you find the place eerily silent, with an unsettling quiet coming from the bodies where they fell. You survey the quarters once more, but there's nothing left to claim—no hidden treasures or overlooked trinkets. The once-bustling den of brigands is now a desolate, empty space. You decide it's better to turn back. Turn to **49**.

146

The spell fizzes in the air, but the wall remains cold and unyielding. You have wasted a spell. Turn to **207**.

147

The spell fizzes in the air. There seems to be no effect. You can choose to leave the room (turn to **66**), inspect the skeleton (turn to **218**) or pull on the lever (turn to **10**).

148

If you have CHARM and want to use it, turn to **245**. Otherwise turn to **566**.

149

You hesitate, still unconvinced. "Why should I trust you? Anyone could claim to be a *Great Wizard*."

His expression softens, taking on a look of profound sadness. "I understand your hesitation," he says, his voice now gentle and soothing. "But consider this: would a mere trickster have such knowledge?" He raises his hands, and you could feel magic enveloping your surroundings, casting the room in a soft, otherworldly glow. "My abilities are a mark of my power, and my imprisonment." The old man sighs, a look of wearied resignation crossing his face. "I see you are not easily swayed, and I respect that. But look into my eyes and see the truth. Feel the magic that binds me here, and understand the burden I carry."

He presses his hand against the glass, and you feel a wave of raw, potent magic emanate from it, brushing against your senses. It's powerful, undeniably so, and hints at a depth of knowledge and experience far beyond that of an ordinary sorcerer. "Please," he whispers, his voice cracking with emotion. "Help me reclaim my freedom. Together, we can achieve what you seek and more."

You can attempt to reach out into the mirror to help him (turn to **164**), step away from the mirror (turn to **367**), or wait and see what else he has got to say (turn to **255**).

150

You arrive at an area where an embankment to the west forms a shoreline, along the north-south channel you are currently in. Do you wish to head west towards the shoreline (**533**), head north (turn to **481**) or head south (turn to **288**)?

151

You are hit by a column of lightning that crashes down from the ceiling! **Deduct 5 LIFE** points. If you are still alive, you have to move on. A wall is on the west-side. Do you move north (turn to **12**), east (turn to **24**) or south (turn to **224**)?

152

The chattering has become much louder. You sense that there might be a colony of *Gnagers* close by in the vicinity. However, you also notice something glowing in the soil, which you instantly bend over and pick up. To your surprise, this is actually a Sapphire, which you can use as a FOCUS on your staff! If you want to, **add Sapphire (Dmg: +2, Rd: +2, Type: Fireball, Gp: 10)** to your inventory. Pleased with your find, you can choose to turn back up north (turn to **117**) or continue further south (turn to **231**).

153

How do you even cast this spell? Cheaters must die. Your quest ends here.

154

You find yourself back to *Ornias'* peculiar establishment. As you step inside, *Ornias* greets you with a knowing smirk, his beady eyes glinting with amusement. "Back so soon?" he scoffs. "I knew you'd return."

If you haven't seen the wares *Ornias* has to offer, turn to **383**.
If you came back to discuss his service again, turn to **250**.
If you want to attack him, turn to **82**.
If you decide to leave again, turn to **135**.

155

Nothing happens. You have wasted a spell. There's nothing much you can do here but leave this place. Turn to **576**.

156

The southerly passage eventually lead into an alcove, and you are immediately captivated by a stunning painting of a white serpent hung on the wall. This painting exudes an air of ancient regal. Despite its allure, you soon realize there's nothing else of interest here, and you reluctantly decide to move on. Turn to **407**.

157

After around half an hour or so, your patience pays off. You chance upon a remarkable oak staff hidden within the dirt pile. This weapon is a significant upgrade over your current staff! If you want to, **add Oak Staff (Dmg: +3, Gp: 8)** to your inventory. Pleased with this find, you decide to leave the room. Turn to **552**.

158

Shelves line up on both sides of the walls, alongside a corridor that leads north and south. Amongst the books, a red book stands out, with the title "*The Black Dragon of the Underworld*". Do you want to read this book (turn to **316**), or head either north (turn to **29**) or south (turn to **557**)?

159

You are in a dark, narrow passage, extending to east and west. Heading west will return you to the main L-junction, while moving further east will bring you deeper into the other end of the passage. Do you move west (turn to **41**) or move east (turn to **93**)?

160

Do you have the coderword KRECK? If you do not have it, you do not encounter anything in this area, which leads to a dead-end, forcing you to turn back. Turn to **403**. Otherwise, read on.

Do you have the codeword DEMONOS? If you do, you will not come back here again. Turn to **403**. Otherwise, read on.

Within moments down the path, you hear shouting from a distance. "Halt right there!" which makes you stiffen and stop your steps. From the shadows ahead, a figure steps forward, his form slowly emerging into view. Cloaked in red robes, the hooded figure stands at the edge of a giant pentagram drawn on the ground, with lit candles placed on the diagram, and seems ready to cast a spell at you. "Declare your purpose!" shouted the figure. You shout back at the figure, telling him that you are just another adventurer here to seek out the *Æther*, after which the figure in red robes lets out a low, menacing laugh that echoes through the dark passage.

"The *Æther*, you say?" he sneers, his tone dripping with amusement. "How quaint. It seems we share a common goal, then, NECROMANCER." He steps closer, his presence becoming more imposing as he reveals more of himself. "I am the DEMONOMANCER," he declares, his voice filled with haughty airs. "Master of the infernal arts, wielder of fire, and summoner of demons." He raises a hand, and for a moment, you feel the air around you grow heavy with heat, as if the very atmosphere is threatening to ignite at his command. "I could send a fireball your way to incinerate you, or call forth horrors from the abyss to tear you apart," he continues, his voice calm yet filled with menace.

"But I am not here to destroy... not yet, at least. I have figured out the elemental puzzles that guard the *Æther*, but the final piece of the puzzle eludes me." He pauses, his gaze piercing through the shadow of his hood. "I seek the elemental stones. Tell me, do you have any of them?"

If you say yes, turn to **519**. If you would rather say no, turn to **591**.

You can also attack the *Demonomancer* (turn to **452**), or back away from him (turn to **71**).

161

You summoned a familiar but you are not sure what to do with it here. You stare blankly at it, and it returns your blank stare before it goes poof into the air. You have wasted a spell. There's nothing much you can do here but leave this place. Turn to **576**.

162

You begin to feel an oppressive energy enveloping you. Suddenly, a voice pierce your mind, with an ancient and powerful baritone, reverberating within your skull.

"You dare stand before me, yet your heart belongs to others," the voice of *Zakl* whispers. "You have trespassed into a shrine that is not yours to claim, seeker. Fate does not smile upon a heretic." A sense of dread grips you as the voice continues. "Let this coin toss decide your fate," it declares, and before you can react, something materializes before your eyes, on the altar—a spinning coin. The voice asks, "...What's the most you've ever lost on a coin toss?" You protested, "I got to know what I stand to win" to which the voice replies, "You stand to win everything. Call it."

Zakl speaks again, more commanding this time. "Call it," it demands, the words echoing through your mind, heavy with finality, as you watch the spinning coin gradually slows down. **Roll a dice**. If the result is **1, 3** and **5**, you call 'Heads' (turn to **85**). If the result is **2, 4** and **6**, you call 'Tails' (turn to **278**).

163

With hardly any effort, you hear a satisfying click echoes through the chamber. The cage door swings open with a creak. *Grobb*'s eyes widen in disbelief and then joy, as he steps out of his confinement.

"Freedom at last!" *Grobb* exclaims, his voice brimming with relief and elation.

Do you have codeword PROSE? If you do, turn to **88**. Otherwise, turn to **574**.

164

The moment your fingertips make contact with the mirror, a strange sensation washes over you. The glass, cool and solid a moment before, now feels like a viscous, almost living substance. Your hand sinks into the mirror as if plunging into a pool of quicksilver.

You push your arm deeper, feeling a resistance that yields slightly to your determined effort. The old man's eyes lock onto yours, a glimmer of hope mingling with the desperation in his gaze. "That's it," he encourages, his voice resonating with a new strength. "Pull me through." Turn to **259**.

165

If you are on a skiff, turn to **133**. Otherwise, turn to **196**.

166

The spell fizzes in the air, and nothing has changed, the procession still goes on. You realize you have just wasted a spell. It is time for you to retreat back to the 'safety' of the dungeons (turn to **588**).

167

The passage opens into a larger cavern, its ceiling lost in the gloom above. Stalactites hang like ancient teeth, and the floor is uneven, littered with loose rocks and debris. The air is thick with the scent of earth and stone, a welcome change from the arid desert outside.

You come across a small, clear stream running through the cavern. The water, cool and pristine, sparkles slightly from the gentle rays of light from outside. As you kneel to inspect it, you notice small, pale fish swimming just below the surface. Their eyes are vestigial, covered by a thin layer of skin, rendering them blind. Suddenly you have a strange notion- if these fishes have the gift of 'sight' despite their blindness, will they bestow you the ability to see in the dark if you consume one of them?

As you move your hand gently, back and forth in the water, you instinctively feel the urge to catch a blindfish to eat. Your hand movement becomes more aggressive and sudden, as you try to grab them, and that frightens the blindfishes, causing them to disperse and swim away from your hand rapidly. After repeated attempts, you manage to catch one!

Do you want to eat the blindfish (turn to **40**), or release it back into the water (turn to **130**)?

168

How do you even cast this spell? Cheaters must die. Your quest ends here.

169

You are at the shoreline, the scent of brackish water fills the air, mingling with the cool, damp atmosphere of the underground tunnel. The sound of waves lapping against the rocky shore reaches your ears, gentle but foreboding. To the west lies the dark, murky waters of the subterranean river. To the east, a gradient slope back up to the walled-dungeon complex.

In order to travel on the river, you need either SWIMMING skill or a skiff. If you have either or both of this and wish to explore the underground river complex, turn to **125**. If you have neither of these to access water travel, or do not wish to explore the river, you can head back into the dungeon. Turn to **485**.

170

You find yourself accelerating as you are swept down towards the waterfall, the current growing stronger with each passing second. The roar of the cascading water drowns out all other sounds. Suddenly, you plunge over the edge, crashing a significant distance down. For a moment, you feel your body suspended in mid-air, a brief sensation of weightlessness, before you slam into a jagged rock below. Your quest ends here.

171

After the brutal skirmish, the imps lay vanquished at your feet, their grotesque forms now motionless. You wipe the sweat from your brow and turn your attention to the eerie glow ahead. As you approach, you see it's a magical forcefield, shimmering with an ethereal light that pulses gently.

Within the forcefield, something faintly glimmers, though the exact shape remains obscured by the arcane energy surrounding it. The air around the barrier is charged with an ineffable sense of power, and you can feel a faint hum emanating from it, vibrating through your bones.

You take a step closer, cautiously extending your hand. The forcefield thrums in response, sending a tingling sensation up your arm but not allowing you to pass through. It's clear this barrier is more than a simple obstacle; it's a protective cage, designed to keep whatever is inside both hidden and safe from intruders.

You can **cast a spell**

Alternatively, you can ignore or avoid this forcefield. Turn to **127**.

172

You summon a familiar, and instruct it to get something from the ghostly procession. With a silent nod, your familiar takes flight, its movements swift as it swoops down toward the procession. The undeads pay no heed as the creature weaves through their ranks, and in one fluid motion, it snatches a Funerary Bell from the ghost's spectral grasp. The ghost notices too late, its spectral hand closing on empty air as the familiar ascends, clutching the stolen bell. The procession continues unabated, unaware of the loss. Your familiar glides back to you, the bell clutched tightly in its claws. As it lands, it presents the bell, its mission completed.

The moment you take the bell, your familiar fades. This Funerary Bell is made of brass and seems cold to touch. If you want to keep this item, **add Funerary Bell**, with **associated number 13** to the inventory. **Add 50 Exp points**. It is time for you to retreat back to the 'safety' of the dungeons (turn to **588**).

173

You are inside a cave tunnel, a dark, musty one with the scent of earth and ancient, subterranean mysteries, distinctly different from the dungeon walls of the *Necropolis*. You figure that you are in the middle of a passageway that is heading from north to south. You can either head north (turn to **20**) or go south (turn to **192**) along this tunnel.

174

Knowing what hides behind the tapestry, you tug at the painting and the wall slides open, revealing a secret room. You step forward into this secret location. Turn to **257**.

175

Upon intoning the correct answer to the riddle, the wall lifts up, revealing a secret room. If you have codeword DRACO, you have already explored this area and you shall turn to **513**. Otherwise, you step into the secret room. Turn to **63**.

176

As the spell takes hold, you feel a sudden sensation of lightness, and the world around you seems to expand. The walls of the chamber stretch upward and you lose sight of the skeleton-filled pit. After the spell wears off, you go back to the normal size again. You have wasted a spell. There's nothing much you can do here but leave this place. Turn to **576**.

177

If you used to worship *Ked*, turn to **136**. Otherwise turn to **98**.

178

With the brigands lying motionless around you, you steady yourself and begin to search the fallen brigands and their quarters. You rifle through their belongings, turning over worn leather pouches, rifling through pockets, and prying open small crates scattered throughout the quarters. Your efforts yield several useful items:

Items	Quantity	Property	Price
Healing Potion	2x	LIFE +5 (1 use each)	5 Gp each
Rations	2x	LIFE +2 (1 use each)	2 Gp each
Short Sword	3x	Dmg: +3	5 Gp each
Leather Vest	3x	Shd: +3	8 Gp each
Obsidian Staff	1x	Dmg: +8	30 Gp
Wizard's Robe	1x	Shd: +4	20 Gp
Poison	1x	Cause poisoning	10 Gp

Most importantly, you found their secret stash of gold. **Add 100 Gold pieces**.

You also found a stone artifact with esoteric symbol etched on it.

If you want this item, **add the △ Stone with an associated number 23** to your inventory. You have **gained 50 Exp points**.

When you are done, add the codeword **GNASHER** and turn to **49**.

179

With great caution, you walk slowly to the edge of the cave clearing. You see a magical glow from a distance, perhaps hinting at some arcane activities. The light illuminates the otherwise pitch-black clearing. The air is thick with the humming and buzzing of unseen wings, creating a constant, unsettling din.

As you peer deeper into the cave, the faint outlines of flying beings become apparent, their movements swift and erratic. An almost palpable sense of hostility fills the space, as if these creatures are collectively warning you to back off from whatever lies ahead. Do you want to back off from the cave (turn to **470**), or press on ahead (turn to **517**)?

180

How do you even cast this spell? Cheaters must die. Your quest ends here.

181

After walking a considerable distance from the clearing, you feel the passage narrowing. As you walk closer to the point, you see a small opening leading into a distinctively different area from the cavern, where the interior is laid with flat stones and bricks, thereby indicating that this is most likely one of the chambers within the *Necropolis*.

Without further ado, you climb through the opening into the room. Huge pillars with carvings of imposing figures decorates the large room, which is otherwise littered by extensive rubble (likely from the breaching of the wall from the cavern by those who came before). A huge metallic gate stands shut at one end of the large room, corroded by rust and age yet unyielding. This is the sealed entrance.

This area is most likely the antechamber used to serve as the gateway between the *Necropolis* and the outside world, which had since fallen to disrepair from neglect and inaccessibility. You see a tunnel at the other end of the antechamber, and decide to move through it. Turn to **220**.

182

Sir Elandor figured that you are going to carry out the acts of malicious intent and quickly brandished his broken long-sword, while simultaneously uttering a bitter exclamation. "What treachery! I know your morbid kind are the worst of the lot, NECROMANCER. I shall send you to the grave, where you rightfully belong!" And thus a fight will ensue. Turn to **123**.

183

You are inside another secret section of the *Library*, with shelves that are filled with the more exquisite collection of arcane texts. A particular book caught your attention, titled *"Necromantic Spells Compendium,"* and you also notice several potions carefully arranged on a lower shelf, each contained in a glass vial. If you want to read the book, turn to **528**.

With the potions at your disposal, and if you haven't done so, add **1x Spirit Potion (Restores Mana, 10 Gp)**, **1x Strength Potion (Restores Power, 20 Gp)** and **2x Healing Potions (LIFE +5, 5 Gp each)** to your inventory as you wish. Note: you can only take them once. Once you are finished with your business here, turn to **457**.

184

The tunnel comes to a dead end, with no further path except a large hole on the ground. As you peer through the hole, you notice that it leads down into a cavern underneath. You can either try to go through the hole to explore this new area (turn to **348**), or return to the T-junction to head west (turn to **287**).

185

As you approach the gate, you notice the stone eye scans you from head to toe, before three consecutive blinks that trigger the opening of the gate, and you quickly step out without hesitation. Once you are outside the *Library*, you notice the gate shuts, and the mouth on the facing side is slightly ajar, as if gagging while regurgitating something from within. In a moment's notice, the a tongue slides out from the mouth, presenting your library pass. If you want to, **add Library Pass** back into your inventory. You shall head back to the main tunnel. Turn to **14**.

186

The stonegate slowly begins to lift, revealing a dark, yawning opening. Cold air wafts through, carrying with it the faint, musty scent of earth and age-old dust. Beyond the gate, a flight of stone stairs descends into the shadows, leading deep underground. Each step is worn and uneven, carved long ago by unknown hands. The walls on either side are rough-hewn. You take a deep breath and step forward, the stairs creaking slightly underfoot as you begin your journey into the depths below. Turn to **489**.

187

After the spell is cast, the world around you expands as you dwindle to a minuscule size. You see from a distance, the towering forms of the ghosts and spirits loom like giants, their ghostly procession continuing, oblivious to your small presence. And watch is all you can do, until the spell's effect begins to wear off, and you return to your normal size. You have wasted a spell. It is time for you to retreat back to the 'safety' of the dungeons (turn to **588**).

188

As the spell takes effect, a ripple of dark energy pulses through the pit, and the once-still remains begin to stir. The sight is eerie and unsettling: skeletons clatter as they rise from this shallow mass-grave, their bones creaking and snapping back into place. Even the smallest fragments of bone twitch and jerk, compelled by the necromantic force. Some of the more intact skeletons manage to stand, moving with a disjointed grace, the bones scraping against each other as they begin to climb out of the pit.

Those with missing limbs or broken bodies are not hindered; they drag their fractured parts along, or in some cases, other skeletons pause to hoist them up, helping them ascend from the depths.

Even the smallest fragments, like disembodied hands, crawl along the ground in a grotesque display of macabre animation. Fingers curl and uncurl as they scuttle forward, determined to follow the rest of the reanimated dead. The entire scene is one of coordinated chaos, as the undead make their way toward the edge of the pit.

Once they reach the top, they continue their march with a sense of purpose, moving northward out of the pit. Their collective movement creates a rattling symphony of bones against stone, echoing through the corridors. They reach the junction, and without hesitation, head toward the northern path. As you watch, you realize that they have specific reasons to travel there- perhaps to regain or even grow their lost powers. Add the codeword **ANIMA**. And also **add 100 Exp points**.

There's nothing much you can do here but leave this place. Turn to **576**.

189

Despite your effort to cast a spell to repel it, the forcefield did not budge. You have wasted a spell. Turn to **127**.

190

If you've been here before, you will not get an audience with the elemental deity again, and you should leave, by going back to the river confluence (turn to **243**). Otherwise, read on.

The southern river passage leads to a narrow shoreline. As you set ashore on the beach, the landscape immediately transitions into a beautifully marbled alcove. The walls and floor are of the purest pristine white, polished to a mirror-like sheen, and the entire alcove glows with a soft, white, ethereal light. At the centre of this majestic space stands a statue of *Ked*, the Beautiful One, the Goddess of Desires. The figure is exquisitely sculpted, embodying feminine characteristics with flawless grace, the geometrically balanced face framed by flowing hair that seems to ripple like water (amidst the real sound of water from the distant background), and her eyes are half-closed in an expression of beauty and seduction. Draped in delicate, almost translucent garments that hint at, but do not fully reveal, the divine form beneath, she holds an aura of eroticism and mischief. Her outstretched hand seems to beckon, inviting you to come closer and partake in the desires she may provide.

Are you a follower of *Ked*? If you are, turn to **451**. If you are a follower of *Taph* or *Zakl*, turn to **406**. Otherwise, turn to **362**.

191

Despite the powerful current, you are determined to swim against the flow. Each stroke feels like a battle, but you push forward, fighting the rapids with all your might, your resolve remains steadfast. Slowly, agonizingly, you make progress, inch by inch. You can see from a distance, a shoreline to the west. To the north, is where the rapids lead to. Do you want to take the risk and head north (turn to **170**), head west towards the shoreline (turn to **325**), or retreat south towards safer waters (turn to **590**)?

192

As you walk in this direction, the fetid smell of rat-droppings grow strong and overwhelming. The tunnel leads south for some distance before you arrive at an L-junction. There's a new path to the left but it seem to emanate a faint red glow from that direction. Do you turn east to where the glow is (turn to **569**), or continue south (turn to **469**)?

193

The forcefield is neither an undead nor a living thing, therefore you do not get a response. Your spell is wasted. Turn to **127**.

194

You sense a piercing pain in your eardrums and an intense palpitation in your head as the graven voice of *Zakl* appears within. "I see deeper into your past than you might wish," *Zakl* intones, his voice carrying an unforgiving tone of judgement. "You have strayed into the embrace of the Fool to your lack of better judgement. That can only lead to perdition. Betrayal does not go unnoticed in the eyes of fate." Before you can react, the atmosphere around you shifts violently. The statue's eyes flare with a dark, malevolent light, and the air crackles with electrifying energy.

"Betrayal," *Zakl's* voice thunders, "can only lead to death!" In that instant, you feel your soul leaves your chest through your wide-opened mouth, extracted by an unseen force from the statue. Your quest ends here.

195

Record the codeword **VLAGR** if you do not have it earlier. Turn to **135**.

196

You hear a chilling cackle echoes through the cavern and you can feel an increasing ripple on the water. It is unmistakably the voice of *Ked*. Suddenly, the water around you begins to churn violently, forming a powerful whirlpool. Panic seizes you as the force of the vortex pulls you into its swirling depths. The current is relentless, dragging you down into the cold, dark abyss below. Your quest ends here.

197

You are travelling in a north-south tunnel. Do you want to head north (turn to **442**) or head south (turn to **554**)?

198

Although you are still weak from the effects of the blindfish poison, you are surprised by what you can see in the cavern. You are able to make out details of the dark crevices between the cave ceiling and the stalactites- the movement of bats which were otherwise hidden from plain sight before. Indeed, you feel like you are able to see clearly at the different dark spots of the cavern. You will be able to see in the dark, later on in places where the light doesn't shine.

Add NIGHTVISION to Skills. You need not use your torches anymore throughout the rest of the adventure (you might want to just sell them/trade them off later). You sheepishly count your luck in this otherwise horrible experience. **Gain 10 Exp points**. Turn to **181**.

199

How do you even cast this spell? Cheaters must die. Your quest ends here.

200

If you've visited the Shrine of *Zakl* before, you will not find further audience from the deity, and shall return to the main tunnel (turn to **459**). If not, read on.

The blue light casts a long ominous shadow along the stone walls, and the effect becomes more intense, the further you walk down this southern passage. This path eventually lead to a small alcove at the end of the passage.

In the centre of the alcove stands a black statue dressed in black hood, and revealing a solemn face, bathed in the ethereal blue light. The figure is imposing and stoic, carved with intricate detail from a dark, almost obsidian-like stone. This is *Zakl*, the Gloomy One, God of Fate, the Timelord.

His expression is stern, his eyes hollow, seeming to pierce through the veil of time itself. In one hand, he holds an hourglass, which connotes the kind of power he wield, which transcends time and space. This is no ordinary deity. He is the *Black Sun* powerful enough to contend with *Hish* the *Grand Benefic* and even the *Eldest Father- Solaris*, and he is also the Leader of the Three Damned Ones- which include Ked and Taph. You realize you are at the Shrine of Zakl- a place where this Elemental Deity can manifest its will.

Are you a follower of *Zakl*? If you are turn to **579**. If you are instead, a follower of *Taph* or *Ked* or have no patron deity, turn to **547**. If you are worshipper of *Hish* or *Barat*, turn to **507**.

201

You are at the entrance of the *Library*. Its interior is a labyrinth of towering shelves, each crammed with books of every imaginable size and age. The smell of aged parchment and ink fills the air, mingling with the faint scent of dust that has settled over centuries.

To the east, the gate with the eye, through which you entered looms ominously. A corridor extends both north and south. Do you head east (turn to **438**) to where the gate is, walk up north (turn to **396**) or go south (turn to **586**)?

202

With a mixture of bravery and recklessness, you decide to approach the ghostly procession. As you step closer, the cold, ethereal air grows heavier around you. The undead continues to ignore your presence, but then, as you cross into their midst, a sudden and terrible fatigue washes over you. Your legs grow weak, your vision dims, and an unbearable heaviness pulls at your very soul. The air thickens, as if laden with invisible chains, and your strength drains away in an instant.

Before you can comprehend what's happening, your body crumples to the ground, an empty shell. Your consciousness, untethered from the physical form, is drawn into the ranks of the procession. Your spirit, now disembodied, joins the other spectres, taking its place among the lost souls marching forward in eternal silence. Your quest ends here.

203

Kanwulf and his whole contingent of brigands are here. You have to battle all of them yourself. You realize that there's a spellcaster in the gang, *Lorelei*, who can cast Lightning ranged attack. You will begin the turn.

Kolgrim (A)	
Life	15
Offence (Melee)	12
Defence	8

Kanwulf (B)	
Life	20
Offence (Melee)	15
Defence	8

Lorelei (C)	
Life	15
Offence (Melee)	10
Offence (Range)	20
Defence	8
Radius	2

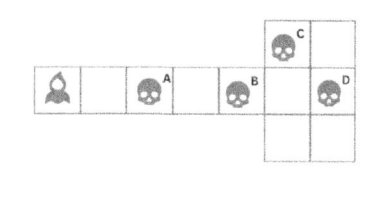

Brutus (D)	
Life	20
Offence (Melee)	20
Defence	10

Kolgrim (A)'s Probability Table

Outcomes	Missed Hit	Missed Hit	Exact Hit	Exact Hit	Reduced Hit	Critical Hit
Dice Number	6	5	4	3	1	2

Kanwulf (B)'s Probability Table

Outcomes	Missed Hit	Reduced Hit	Exact Hit	Exact Hit	Critical Hit	Critical Hit
Dice Number	1	2	4	6	3	5

Lorelei (C)'s Probability Table

Outcomes	Missed Hit	Exact Hit	Exact Hit	Exact Hit	Reduced Hit	Critical Hit
Dice Number	3	5	6	4	2	1

Brutus (D)'s Probability Table

Outcomes	Missed Hit	Exact Hit	Exact Hit	Reduced Hit	Critical Hit	Critical Hit
Dice Number	3	2	6	4	5	1

If you win the battle, **gain 100 Exp points** and turn to **382**.

204

You grab a rock from the floor, its weight solid and comforting in your hand. The old man's eyes widen in horror as he realizes your intent.

"No!" he screams, his voice shrill and desperate. "Don't do it!" Ignoring his pleas, you hurl the rock with all your strength. The impact is immediate and catastrophic. The mirror shatters into a thousand pieces, the shards catching the light as they explode outward in a dazzling, crystalline storm. The old man's scream is cut short, his image splintering and disappearing into the void. As the last fragments settle, an eerie silence falls over the room, broken only by the soft tinkle of glass settling. You step forward cautiously, surveying the wreckage. Amidst the scattered shards, something catches your eye—a small, rolled-up piece of parchment tucked into the base of the mirror's frame, now exposed by the destruction.

Carefully, you retrieve the note, unrolling it with trembling fingers. The parchment is aged and brittle, the ink faded but still legible. It reads: 'Blind the eyes of the Black Serpent to stop its fiery wrath.' While it does not make sense for now, this clue might come in handy later. Record codeword **MARAS** and associated number **14**. **Gain 20 Exp points**. Turn to **17**.

205

Your body fall through the hole and land at the bottom of the cavern with a loud thud. Unfortunately, you are also hurt in the process. **Deduct 5 LIFE** points. If you are still alive, you grimace in pain as you have sprained your leg and struggle to get up to continue the exploration. Turn to **173**.

206

As you reach down to search the man's body, your fingers inadvertently brush against the black slime. Before you can pull away, the slime clings to your skin, spreading rapidly over your body. Panic surges through you as the slime snakes up your arm to the rest of your body. Your skin bubbles and warps, melting away like wax. You try to scream, but your voice is lost in the horror as your body begins to collapse in on itself, muscles, and bones liquefying into a viscous, black ooze. Soon, your form merges with the same grotesque puddle that claimed the man before you. Your quest ends here.

207

You arrive at a junction. This section of the dungeon seems to hum with an enchanted energy, where remnants of magical aura lingers in the air. Do you wish to head north (turn to **68**), head east (turn to **513**), or south (turn to **599**)?

208

You appear in a room, painted entirely in metallic sheen. Within this room are three teleporters, placed in different directions. Do you take the one to the north (turn to **511**), to the east (turn to **104**), or to the west (turn to **409**)?

209

Your keen sense hones in on subtle inconsistencies about this person. His eyes flicker with an unnatural gleam, shifting hues imperceptibly. The texture of his skin seems to ripple, almost as if it struggles to maintain a consistent form. A fleeting glimpse of a non-human silhouette in the dim light confirms your suspicion: He is not what he appears to be.

He is likely a changeling, a creature of deception and disguise, blending into the shadows of the *Necropolis* with a guise designed to fool unsuspecting adventurers. You know that you cannot trust him, but pretend as if nothing happened. **Gain 10 Exp points.** Turn to **289**.

210

Because you revere enemy deities, you can sense that the warm glow of the shrine turns cold, and an oppressive silence falls. Suddenly, through the statue of *Hish*, you hear a voice resonating in your mind. "I am *Hish*, the Wise One and the Grand Benefic, Eldest of the Elementals and Heir Apparent to *Solaris*. Though you follow other wrong paths, I offer you redemption, by chance of conversion and embracing my rule, righting your follies with wisdom. Accept my benevolence, and you shall be blessed as one of my followers. Reject me, and mercy may not be yours to claim." The voice carries both a promise of salvation and a subtle threat, leaving you to ponder your next move.

This may be a very critical test of faith. Do you wish to convert (turn to **94**)? Or do you deny *Hish* (turn to **400**)?

211

You hesitated, before taking a sip. "Chug it!" shouts the crew. In which case you did, and you have to admit this is really good stuff. The merriment lasts into the night, and it is time to take a rest. Turn to **65**.

212

The silver door appears locked. Do you have a Silver Key? If you have it, you will be able to unlock the door (turn to **456**). If not, do you have Lockpicks? You can attempt to use it to unlock the door (turn to **564**). If you do not have any of them, you have no choice but to move on (turn to **508**).

213

The passageway leads north for a while, until you see a junction ahead. Turn to **135**.

214

Sir Elandor approaches you, his armour scratched and dented from the fierce combat, yet his expression is one of deep gratitude. He sheathes his sword and extends his hand towards you.

"Thank you," he says, his voice filled with sincerity as he grips your hand firmly. "You saved my life when I was poisoned, and now, because of you, I've finally put an end to *Kanwulf* and his brigands. This would not have been possible without your help." He releases your hand and steps back, his gaze steady and full of respect. "The *Order of Solaris* will be forever grateful for your bravery and assistance. You have proven yourself a true ally, and I will make sure that your deeds are known among my brethren."

With a final nod, *Sir Elandor* turns to leave, his footsteps echoing as he makes his way out of the chamber. "May the light of *Solaris* guide you on your journey," he says over his shoulder, before disappearing into the shadows beyond, leaving you alone in the aftermath of the battle. Turn to **178**.

215

Kanwulf and his whole contingent of brigands are here. You have to battle all of them yourself. You will begin the turn.

Kolgrim (A)	
Life	15
Offence (Melee)	12
Defence	8

Brutus (B)	
Life	20
Offence (Melee)	20
Defence	10

Lorelei (C)	
Life	15
Offence (Melee)	10
Offence (Range)	20
Defence	8
Radius	2

Kanwulf (D)	
Life	20
Offence (Melee)	15
Defence	8

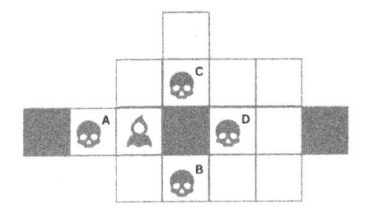

Kolgrim (A)'s Probability Table

Outcomes	Missed Hit	Missed Hit	Exact Hit	Exact Hit	Reduced Hit	Critical Hit
Dice Number	6	5	4	3	1	2

Brutus (B)'s Probability Table

Outcomes	Missed Hit	Exact Hit	Exact Hit	Reduced Hit	Critical Hit	Critical Hit
Dice Number	3	2	6	4	5	1

Lorelei (C)'s Probability Table

Outcomes	Missed Hit	Exact Hit	Exact Hit	Exact Hit	Reduced Hit	Critical Hit
Dice Number	3	5	6	4	2	1

Kanwulf (D)'s Probability Table

Outcomes	Missed Hit	Reduced Hit	Exact Hit	Exact Hit	Critical Hit	Critical Hit
Dice Number	1	2	4	6	3	5

If you win the battle, **gain 100 Exp points** and turn to **178**.

216

After you cast the spell, a low rumble echoes through the cave. The forcefield, once shimmering with a bright and electrifying light, begins to waver and distort. You watch in anticipation as the magical barrier flickers and then suddenly dissipates, leaving a deafening silence in its wake. Before you, where the forcefield once stood, lies an artifact, a stone adorned with an intricate symbol. This item will be important in your quest.

If you want this item, **add the ▽ Stone with an associated number 17** to your inventory. You have **gained 50 Exp points**. There's nothing else for you to do in the cave and you shall take leave. Turn to **470**.

217

You sprint after *Ornias* as the goblin darts ahead, his small figure barely visible in the dim light as he scurries northward.

Suddenly, as you reach an area where the path opens up to the east, your heart skips a beat. Before you can react, a massive net unfurls towards you from the eastern passage, ensnaring you in its thick, coarse ropes. The force of the trap knocks you off your feet, and you crash to the ground, struggling desperately against the net's tight grip. Your eyes dart to the right, where you catch sight of a slim, menacing figure emerging from the shadows. The figure's black skin glistens with a sinister sheen, and its eyes gleam with a predatory hunger. It stands tall and imposing, holding a long, wicked-looking spear in its hands. You think this is very well the legendary *Huntsman*.

Without a word, the figure hurls the spear at you with deadly precision. The weapon slices through the air, aimed directly at your heart. The spear closes in, and you only feel an instantaneous piercing pain before your consciousness fades. You are immediately killed by a weapon what many referred to as a 'Godkiller'- *The Spear of Signonul.* Your quest ends here.

218

You examine the skeleton and figure that it might serve some purpose as a protector. Its grasp on the lever is very firm and it seems almost impossible to pry it away from the stick. Do you attempt to pull on the lever (turn to **10**) or get out of this room (turn to **66**)?

219

As you sprint towards *Ornias*, the goblin's eyes widen in confusion, unsure of your intentions. He stumbles backward, but before he can react, you brush past him, heading straight for the alcove at the dead end where the inactive portal looms. As you reach the portal, you spin around, ready to face the oncoming threat. The *Huntsman*, closes in, his hand already preparing to cast his dreaded net. Your mind races, and in a split second, you make a decision.

With all your strength, you kick *Ornias* directly into the path of the oncoming web. The goblin yelps in shock as the net ensnares him instead. The *Huntsman's* eyes narrow in confusion, but it's too late. His spear, meant for you, drives straight into *Ornias* with brutal force. *Ornias* lets out a final, pitiful scream as the spear impales him, his life ending in an instant. The *Huntsman* halts, staring down at the goblin's lifeless body, his expression unreadable beneath the shadows. The chamber falls silent, the only sound the echo of your own breath as you process what just happened. You've bought yourself a momentary reprieve, but you know the danger is far from over. Turn to **467**.

220

After walking a distance down the tunnel, you arrive at a cross-junction. Do you take a left turn to the west (turn to **311**), right turn to the east (turn to **270**) or continue heading north (turn to **36**)?

221

While you are able to scale a good portion of the jutted rocks between the hole to the bottom, you realize that there's still a large gap where there's no rock to climb. Unfortunately, your only next option is to drop to the bottom of the cavern. **Deduct 2 LIFE** points. If you are still alive, turn to **173**.

222

You summoned a familiar and instruct it to remove the forcefield. The moment it touches the forcefield, it seems to be absorbed into it, and the familiar disappears right before your eyes! You have wasted a spell. Turn to **127**.

223

You stand triumphantly before the fallen *Huntsman*, for he was indeed a formidable opponent. Your eyes are immediately drawn to the weapon that he is carrying, the legendary *Spear of Signonul*, a weapon powerful enough to be a "Godkiller". This weapon would surely aid you in your quest against powerful foe like *Mortis*, although you cannot perform anymore ranged attack with this melee weapon. If you want to keep this weapon, **add Spear of Signonul (Dmg: 20)** to your inventory. As you search through the body, you also found a stone artifact with esoteric symbol etched on it.

If you want this item, **add the ⊕ Stone with an associated number 15** to your inventory. You have **gained 50 Exp points**. When you are done, add the codeword **HLAGA** and turn to **464**.

224

Nothing happen in this sector. A wall is on the west-side. Do you move north (turn to **151**), east (turn to **305**) or south (turn to **15**)?

225

You notice pitch-black darkness engulfing you as you walk further into the cave, and realize that in no time, you will be plunged into total darkness. While you can still make out the silhouettes of your hands, it is certainly a good time to start preparing for the darkness ahead. You need to use a torch to illuminate your path ahead. **Deduct 1x Torch** from your inventory, and turn to **181**.

226

You are at the southern side of the tombs, with paths leading, north, east and west. If you want to head north, turn to **436**. If you want to head east, turn to **345**. If you want to head west instead, turn to **559**.

227

As you venture further, the path unexpectedly comes to a halt. Before you lies a solid stone wall, marking a dead end. Upon the wall, intricately carved into the stone, is a detailed engraving of magicians gathered around a grand table. The scene depicts them in the midst of a feast, where goblets and platters laden with food adorn the table. A strange message was scrawled below the carvings: ONWE IST CHEV KENI FIN VEG.

If you don't know what to do here, you shall head back west along the corridor. Turn to **513**.

228

Do you have the codeword **GNASHER**? If you do, turn to **145** immediately. Next, check to see if you have the codeword **GNAWER**? If you do turn to **550**. Otherwise turn to **364**.

229

Record the codeword **GHAST** and turn to **554**.

230

You are at the southern side of the tombs, with paths leading east and west. If you want to go east, turn to **529**. If you prefer to go west instead, turn to **315**.

231

The southern tunnel ends in an enormous cavern, with dozens of *Gnagers* scurrying about, making loud chittering. You freeze, hoping to go unnoticed, but it's too late. One of the *Gnagers* lifts its head, sniffing the air before letting out a shrill screech. The noise reverberates through the cavern, and within moments, the entire colony turns its attention to you. Panic sets in as the *Gnagers* rush forward, their clawed feet scrabbling against the rocky floor. You reach for your weapon, but the sheer number of them is overwhelming. The first wave hits you like a tidal force, knocking you off balance. Claws and teeth tear at your cloak, ripping through fabric and flesh alike. You know what comes next. Your quest ends here.

232

This corridor leads to a gate, where a once imposing stone palm now hangs limply, dangling upside down, motionless, as though the life that once imbued is gone. You press your hand against the cold stone, and the gate yields to your touch, swinging open with surprising ease. Turn to **183**.

233

Without your torch, the *Tombs of the Regii* is now an absolute darkness. You strain your eyes, hoping for a hint of light, a faint outline, but the darkness is absolute, Your quest ends here.

234

You arrive at the north-eastern corner of the lair. You hear rapid footsteps from a distance. Do you want to dash towards east (turn to **388**) or south (turn to **496**)?

235

Do you have lockpicks? If you do, turn to **30**. Otherwise, there's nothing much for you to do here at the shrine, and you'll resume your journey (turn to **22**).

236

Breath ragged and hunting pounding, you arrive again at the south-eastern corner of the lair. You pause, trying to catch your breath, but then you hear it- a faint sound, growing louder with each passing second. Footsteps. Quick, deliberate, and closing in fast. You spin around and you see a black, slim figure at a distance from the west, sprinting toward you, its movement unnaturally smooth and terrifyingly fast. The *Huntsman* is chasing after you!

Do you want to prepare to confront the Huntsman (turn to **106**), or dash north to flee from him (turn to **89**)?

237

You cast your spell, hoping for clarity. Instead, the cave around you begins to expand at an alarming rate. The walls stretch upwards and outwards, the ceiling receding into the distance. Within moments, you find yourself dwarfed by your surroundings, now barely the size of a rat. The once modest forcefield looms above you, a colossal, shimmering barrier of magical energy.

Steeling yourself, you approach the forcefield, scanning for any hint of an entry point. As you get closer, an unseen force tugs at you. Before you can react, you are sucked into the forcefield, the world around you blurring into a vortex of light and sound. You are pulled through with a disorienting rush, your surroundings shifting and warping as you are drawn deeper into the unknown. Your quest ends here.

238

You know very well not to touch the wooden chest, but you figure that you can try to use something to pry it open. First you thought of using your weapon but would not entertain the idea of holding something that could potentially melt your skin away later. Suddenly you notice that a wooden branch on the ground which can be put to good use. With careful precision and angle, you use it to knock the lid off the wooden chest and it swings open, revealing the content, which are not tainted by the black slime.

You find many reagents contained within the wooden chest, that will be useful for your spellcasting. If you want to, **add + 2 Ghost Cap, +2 Nightshade, +1 Charnel Ash, +1 Grimwood Bark and +1 Ectoplasm** to Reagents.

Satisfied with your find, you sneak a glance at the undead who offered you this, and realize that a frown develop from what used to be a smile. You shall leave this place immediately. Turn to **229**.

239

After crossing the precarious bridge that spans the dark chasm, you find yourself in a vast cavern structure, its ceiling disappearing into darkness above. The air is cooler here, but it carries an ominous stillness, as if the very stones are holding their breath. Turn to **576**.

240

Record the codeword **GROM**. Do you have the codeword GARM? If yes, you are done exploring the southern tunnels and will head up north instead (turn to **20**). If not, turn to **469**.

241

The path north soon leads to a large crimson gate looming in the distance, its massive form barely visible in the dim light. Great things might possibly lie beyond this gate- this is possibly the *Repository of the Æther*. But that excitement is quickly extinguished as a sudden, shrill sound reaches your ears.

The sharp alarm rings out, and soon a low, rumbling reverberates through the stone walls. The ground beneath your feet trembles slightly, and you hear the unmistakable sound of marching— thousands of boots, or rather, bones, moving in unison. As you turn around, you see a massive army of skeleton warriors, armed and armoured emerging from the shadows, and advancing towards you and you have no time to flee. The skeletons move with a terrifying speed, closing the distance between you in mere moments. You draw your weapon, ready to fight, but the sheer number of enemies is overwhelming.

Chelonoth- The Serpent Turtle

They surround you, pressing in from all sides, their weapons raised and ready to strike. You swing your weapon desperately, taking down several of the undead warriors, but for every one you defeat, more take its place. The skeletons press closer, their weight and numbers crushing you underfoot. You struggle to stay on your feet, but it's a futile effort. The tide of skeletal warriors overwhelms you, their bony hands grabbing at you, their weapons cutting into your flesh. Your quest ends here.

242

As you start walking up the shore, you spot a creature in the distance lumbering towards you. It has the head and neck of a serpent and the shell of a turtle, moving with a clumsy, but menacing pace. Your heart races as you recognize the beast: a *Chelonoth*, a reptilian inhabitant of forsaken waters and known for its bad temperament, hardy shell and deadly nature. This dangerous creature is now closing in on you, although you have time to prepare the first strike. You will begin the turn.

Chelonoth
Life 15
Offence (Melee) 15
Defence 8

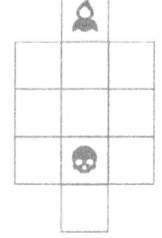

Chelonoth's Probability Table

Outcomes	Missed Hit	Exact Hit	Exact Hit	Reduced Hit	Reduced Hit	Critical Hit
Dice Number	6	5	1	2	4	3

If you win the battle, **gain 20 Exp points** and turn to **140**.

243

You are in the middle of an underground river confluence. A faint white light emanates from the south, casting a ghostly glow on the river surface. Do you want to head south (turn to **190**), north (turn to **16**), east (turn to **350**) or west (turn to **74**)?

244

As you ready yourself to strike *Ornias*, the goblin's usual sly grin fades into a look of pure terror. He backs away, his eyes darting frantically between you and the approaching *Huntsman*. Before you can make your move, *Ornias* lets out a desperate, trembling yelp, "Help me, master!" In that moment, you feel a sudden, oppressive weight press down on you. The *Huntsman's* net, cast with expert precision, ensnares you in its unyielding grip.

Struggling, you turn just in time to see the Huntsman closing in, his dark, slim figure moving with a relentless, predatory grace.

With cold, calculated precision, the *Huntsman* drives his spear- the legendary "Godkiller" otherwise known as the *Spear of Signonul*, through your body. The sharp pain explodes through you, your vision blurring as you feel the life drain away. *Ornias*, now emboldened, cheers wickedly, his fear replaced with gleeful malice. Your quest ends here.

245

You muster your best persuasive tone, weaving your words with a charm you hope will sway *Brutal Brutus*. His stern expression softens, then, unexpectedly, he bursts into laughter. "Well, well, maybe you're not as worthless as I thought!" *Brutus* chuckles, eyeing you with newfound amusement. "Alright, I'll tell you the secret, but it'll cost you 10 gold pieces then. Here's the rest of your refund" *Brutus* tosses the excess coins back to you. **Add 10 gold pieces** to your inventory. Turn to **566**.

246

After a brief walk westward along the tunnel, you see a bend that veers sharply to the left, which changes course to the south. Turn to **495**.

247

You are at the section of a dungeon where a path to the west opens up along the north-south tunnel. Do you want to travel west (turn to **474**), head north (turn to **571**), or journey south (turn to **500**)?

248

You arrive at the centre of the southern side of the tombs. The stairs at the south will lead you back to the *Inner Chambers* on the upper levels. There's paths to the north, west and east. Do you want to head north (turn to **116**), west (turn to **345**) or east (turn to **433**)?

249

After you cast the spell, you realize that you have not only wasted a spell, but committed a grave mistake. Suddenly, you notice movement at your feet. The three imps you had previously defeated begin to stir, their grotesque faces twisting into even more nightmarish visages. Their bug-like eyes, now glazed with an eerie, lifeless glow, snap open, and they rise from the ground with an unnatural, jerky motion. Before you can react, the undead imps launch themselves at you, their claws wrapping around your limbs with a vice-like grip.

They begin biting into your flesh with an unholy ferocity, their teeth sinking deep. You struggle to fend them off, but their strength is overwhelming. And you realize, with a sinking dread, that they are far more powerful in their undead state. The world begins to blur. The last thing you hear is the triumphant screeches of the imps. Your quest ends here.

250

Ornias crosses his arms and leans backward in a confident manner. "I've got a proposition for you," he says, his voice sneaky and conniving. "For 20 gold pieces, I'll help get you into the lair of the *Huntsman*. The *Huntsman* possesses both the prized *Spear of Signonul*, a weapon of formidable power, as well as an artifact that might just be the key to your quest. This spear isn't just any weapon; it's said to be a '*Godkiller*'. And the artefact... well, let's just say it's one of the thing that you will require to access the lairs of *Mortis*.

He pauses, letting the offer sink in before continuing. "If we have a deal, you can exit this chamber and head all the way north. The *Huntsman's* lair is situated there, and it is a protected place, where no mere mortal can easily step foot into. I'll be waiting for you at the entrance and help you access the lair. Think it over carefully."

If you have the PERCEPTION skill and would like to use it, turn to **349**.
If you agree with *Ornias'* proposal, **deduct 20 Gp** and turn to **534**.
Otherwise turn to **465**.

251

Do you have codeword PROSE? If you do turn to **196**. If not, turn to **165**.

252

You close your eyes, steadying your breath as you begin to focus your mind on the scrying. The world around you fades into a blur, and soon, you are met with visions that penetrate the darkness. As you delve deeper, the images become clearer—each sarcophagus, once a resting place for the ancient *Regii*, now lies empty; the bodies have vanished.

But as you concentrate further, a presence begins to take form in your mind's eye. In the northwest corner of the tomb complex, something stirs. The entity is dark, its aura unsettling, like a shadow that refuses to fade. You sense it roaming near one of the sarcophagus in that general area. Turn to **248**.

Lorelei- The Tempest Witch

253

If you've already met *Lorelei*, turn to **530**. Otherwise read on.

You approach the heavy curtain in the northern alcove and before brushing it aside, you pause and call out softly, asking for permission to enter. There's a moment of silence before a voice, sharp and lilting, responds, "Come in." With bated breath, you brush aside the curtain. Behind it, the alcove is dimly lit, revealing a figure seated on a chair. The woman is cloaked in mage robes, and she looks like a spellcaster. Her face, oddly shaped like a fox's, is both alluring and unsettling, with sharp, angular features and eyes that glint with intelligence and malice. Her hair, dark as midnight, falls in loose waves around her shoulders, framing her vulpine visage.

She regards you with suspicion at first, her gaze narrowing as she takes in your appearance. Then, suddenly, she laughs—an unsettling kind of maniacal cackle.

"I am *Lorelei*," she says, her voice smooth and cold. "...the Tempest Witch. I find pleasure in the art of torment, in drawing out the suffering of those who cross my path. And you..." She pauses, her eyes narrowing as they sweep over you. "You are a NECROMANCER, and like a graveworm, writhing and squirming, just begging to be crushed. Perhaps I'll indulge myself... unless, of course, you have something more interesting in mind." She leans back, her laughter fading into a sly smile. "I have items to trade, if you're interested." You soon find that her items are rather overpriced.

Items	Quantity	Property	Price
Healing Potion	1x	LIFE +5	10 Gp
Rations	1x	LIFE +2	10 Gp
Poison	1x	Cause poisoning	20 Gp
Torch	1x	Illuminate dark places	20 Gp

If you have CHARM and want to use it, turn to **568**.
If you have THIEVERY and want to use it, turn to **493**.
When you are done here, turn to **530**.

254

Right behind you, *Sir Elandor* is taking care of the fight with *Kanwulf* and *Kolgrim*. But the remaining crew are no easy targets. You realize that there's a spellcaster in the gang, *Lorelei*, who can cast Lightning ranged attack. Grey squares denote blocked areas. You will begin the turn.

Brutus (A)		Lorelei (B)	
Life	20	Life	15
Offence (Melee)	20	Offence (Melee)	10
Defence	10	Offence (Range)	20
		Defence	8
		Radius	2

Brutus (A)'s Probability Table

Outcomes	Missed Hit	Exact Hit	Exact Hit	Reduced Hit	Critical Hit	Critical Hit
Dice Number	3	2	6	4	5	1

Lorelei (B)'s Probability Table

Outcomes	Missed Hit	Exact Hit	Exact Hit	Exact Hit	Reduced Hit	Critical Hit
Dice Number	3	5	6	4	2	1

If you win the battle, **gain 100 Exp points** and turn to **50**.

255

As you continue to stare into the old man's eyes, a strange, almost mesmerizing pull begins to take hold. His gaze, deep and sorrowful, seems to reach into your very soul.

His voice, now soft and melodic, weaves through your thoughts like a gentle stream. "You feel it, don't you? The connection between us, the shared destiny. I can sense your power, your potential. Together, we could accomplish so much. You have the strength to pull me out, to free me from this eternal prison." Your mind, once sharp and guarded, begins to dull under the influence of his words. The urgency of his plea, combined with the overwhelming sense of his magical presence, creates a heady mix that clouds your judgment. You find yourself nodding slowly, almost involuntarily, as if his words are a soothing balm to your doubts.

"Yes," you hear yourself say, your voice distant and dreamlike. "I'll help you." The old man's eyes shine with triumph, but the genuine gratitude in his expression draws you in even deeper. "Thank you," he whispers, his voice trembling with relief. "You don't know what this means to me." Turn to **164**.

256

Between you is a decorated wall to the south with a large symbol of *Crotus* and a wall at the north that recedes into an alcove, which houses an open sarcophagus made of the finest mahogany wood. This sarcophagus must have belonged to one of the deceased *Regii*. However, you realize the sarcophagus is empty! The body of the *Regii* seems to have been removed. There's nothing you can do here, except to move on towards east (turn to **436**) or west (turn to **393**).

257

Record the codeword **ALEX** if you haven't done so. You have entered a restricted-access area of the *Library*, and your action is surely monitored.

A low creak echoes through the vicinity as you step into the secret room concealed behind the tapestry. At the end of the room stands a medium-sized cylindrical glass tank, the surface of which is thick with condensation, making it difficult to see clearly at first. As you draw closer, you can make out a grotesque mass of flesh suspended in a viscous fluid inside the tank.

The sight is unsettling- a single, enormous eye rolls within the mass, bloodshot and twitching as though searching for something. Below the eye, a gaping mouth opens and closes rhythmically, emitting no sound. From the flesh, twisted limbs sprout haphazardly, some resembling malformed arms or legs, though none are whole or functional. The limbs writhe and twitch in a slow, grotesque dance, seemingly independent of each other, as if the creature is in a constant state of confusion and agony. This disturbing thing is likely a *Homunculus*- and it may be playing a critical role in the *Library*.

An opening is found at the top of the glass vessel which may be there to facilitate air circulation. The glass seems to be heavily reinforced, and may not break under duress or force. A mischievous thought crosses your mind- how will it affect the *Homunculus* if you drop some liquid from one of your potions through the opening of the tank? Sparing some drops will not cost you your potions either, hence you won't have to remove them from the inventory after the attempt.

If you have a Healing Potion and would like to try it, turn to **142**.
If you have a Spirit Potion and would like to try it, turn to **39**.
If you have a Strength Potion and would like to try it, turn to **67**.
If you have Poison and would like to try it, turn to **304**.
If you have an Antidote and would like to try it, turn to **401**.

If you prefer to drop the idea, you can head back to the 'normal access' areas of the *Library*. Turn to **29**.

258

Between you is a decorated wall to the south with a large symbol of *Dioscuri* and a wall at the north that recedes into an alcove, which houses an open sarcophagus made of the finest mahogany wood. This sarcophagus must have belonged to one of the deceased *Regii*. However, you realize the sarcophagus is empty! The body of the *Regii* seems to have been removed. There's nothing you can do here, except to move on towards east (turn to **444**) or west (turn to **538**).

259

As you grip the old man's hand and pull, a sudden, violent force jerks you forward. To your horror, you see the man leap over your body with vigour and agility, pulling himself out of the mirror with a triumphant, sinister grin. Your sense of reality distorts as you're yanked into the mirror, the room around you warping and twisting into a surreal, reflective nightmare. You stumble, disoriented, and find yourself in a strange, mirrored version of the room you just left. He lands gracefully on the other side, now in the real world, and you see the true depth of his deception.

"Fool," he sneers, his voice dripping with contempt. "I am no *Great Wizard*. I was like you, an adventurer seeking the *Æther*, only to be trapped here for eternity. But now, thanks to your naivety, I am free." You pound your fists against the glassy barrier, but the mirror's surface remains impenetrable, your actions echoing hollowly within the mirrored realm. The man laughs, a sound that reverberates the long periods of pent-up madness and relief. "Enjoy your new prison. You'll find it's quite the lonely, oops lovely place."

Desperation claws at your throat as the realization sinks in. You are now the prisoner of the mirror, doomed to await the next unsuspecting soul who might fall into the same trap. Now, you must wait, watching the world from behind a glass prison. Your quest ends here.

260

You are in a north-south corridor, with an opening to your left revealing another path leading west. As you cautiously peer around the corner, you catch a glimpse of the back of a figure moving away from you, heading westward. The figure's movements are fluid, almost graceful. It is the *Huntsman*.

Do you dare to take the risk, by moving west and attempting to sneak up behind the Huntsman and strike while his back is turned (turn to **558**)? Or do you choose the safer route, avoiding the encounter altogether for now, and head north (turn to **446**)?

261

You rotate the statue to the right. Nothing seems to happen. Do you wish to continue to rotate the statue right again (turn to **488**), or rotate it left (turn to **353**), or abort the attempt and turn back towards the eastern tunnel instead (turn to **115**)?

262

Before the *Nyx* make a second attempt to pull you further into the depths, you manage to deliver a good kick to its head, which causes it to back off and swims back into the depths, leaving you alone. You are now in pitch-black darkness, floating atop the underground river. Do you still have a torch? If you do, **deduct 1x Torch** from your inventory and turn to **138**. If not, turn to **545**.

263

The stairs lead you to the edge of a vast chasm, its depths unfathomable and lined with jagged igneous rocks. This area is steeped in eldritch evil and these rocks glow lightly in an ominous crimson. A narrow bridge leads ahead, to various forsaken caverns beyond. You know instinctively that *Mortis* is near, lurking in the shadows, his presence an almost tangible force in the air. This is the final part of your quest, the culmination of all your struggles. The *Repository of Æther*, the key to victory or doom, is close. You can feel its pull, mingling with the dread that fills your heart. With bated breath, your first step onto the bridge is like a leap of faith. Turn to **239**.

264

You are in the middle of a passageway. You can either north (turn to **49**) or head south (turn to **4**).

265

As *Mortis* final words echo through the cavern, the ground begins to tremble. The sound of a thousand skeletal feet marching in unison fills the air, a menacing, rhythmic rumble that sends chills down your spine. You turn to see an endless legion of skeletal warriors, their hollow eyes fixed on you, weapons gleaming in the dim light. The sight is overwhelming.

Mortis, now seated comfortably on his throne, watches you with a cruel, detached amusement. "You could have had everything," he murmurs, almost to himself. "But now, you will have nothing." You grit your teeth, and with a roar, you charge towards *Mortis*, intent on ending this nightmare at its source. But the skeletons are upon you in an instant, their bony hands clawing at you, their weapons cutting into your flesh.

You swing your weapon to fend them off, but their numbers are too great. They swarm you, overwhelming you with sheer force. Desperately, you try to push through, to reach *Mortis*, but the weight of the undead is too much. They drag you down, their relentless assault breaking your defences and soon you can feel your strength waning as the skeletal horde engulfs you, their cold, unyielding grip pulling you into darkness. Your last sight is of *Mortis*, sitting back on his throne, a smug smile on his face as he watches your struggle. Your quest ends here.

266

Do you have a Rope + Grappling Hook? If you have it, turn to **268**. If not, turn to **221**.

267

If you DO NOT have the codeword DOLORs, turn to **25**. Otherwise read on.

If you have the codeword, there's nothing much for you to do here except to move on. You can either head east (turn to **497**) or west (turn to **563**).

268

Steadily, you climb the rope into the cavern with relative ease. Once you hit the bottom, you shake the rope and the grappling hook was released, allowing you to keep the item back into your inventory. Turn to **173**.

269

You pass the antidote to *Sir Elandor* and he accepts it without hesitation, his face etched with pain but illuminated by a glimmer of hope. As he carefully drinks the potion, you help him to his feet, offering a steadying hand. An hour past as you watch the antidote take effect. Gradually, the paladin's pallor fades, and the weariness in his eyes is replaced by renewed strength. His movements become more assured, and the once-faint light of resilience begins to shine through. **Remove Antidote** from your inventory.

"Thank you," he says, his voice gaining strength with each word. "Your efforts have spared me from a grim fate. When you next encounter *Kanwulf* in the course of your adventure, know that I will stand by your side and lend you my aid. Right now, I have other matters to attend to. But I will remember your deed and be eternally indebted."

The paladin's gaze holds a deep gratitude as he prepares to leave the room. Before he departs, he pauses and turns back to you. "I've hidden a skiff in a room adorned with a painting of a white serpent. It is of great importance that you find it, if you sought to traverse the underground river passage."

He leans over to you and explain the exact location where he has hidden the skiff. Record the codeword **QUORK**, followed by **ZENGIS** and its associated number **99**. **Gain 50 Exp** points.

After he left the room, you realize that he left a pouch of gold, seemingly as an additional reward for your effort. **Add 20 Gold pieces**. There's nothing left for you to do here, and you shall leave this place. Turn to **93**.

270

The wall seems to close in around you, but soon it leads to a door, suggesting that a room lies beyond. It also seems dimly lit from the inside. You realize the door is not locked. Do you enter the door (turn to **490**), retrace back to head north (turn to **36**) or west (turn to **311**)?

271

The *Great Wizard* will not entertain you again, so it is better that you leave here. With skill and patience, you navigate out of the rapids, back to the safer portion of the river. Turn to **590**.

272

You hesitate, still unconvinced. "Why should I trust you? Anyone could claim to be a *Great Wizard.*"

His expression softens, taking on a look of profound sadness. "I understand your hesitation," he says, his voice now gentle and soothing. "But consider this: would a mere trickster have such knowledge?" He raises his hands, and you could feel magic enveloping your surroundings, casting the room in a soft, otherworldly glow. "My abilities are a mark of my power, and my imprisonment."

The old man sighs, a look of wearied resignation crossing his face. "I see you are not easily swayed, and I respect that. But look into my eyes and see the truth. Feel the magic that binds me here, and understand the burden I carry."

He presses his hand against the glass, and you feel a wave of raw, potent magic emanate from it, brushing against your senses. It's powerful, undeniably so, and hints at a depth of knowledge and experience far beyond that of an ordinary sorcerer. "Please," he whispers, his voice cracking with emotion. "Help me reclaim my freedom. Together, we can achieve what you seek and more." Turn to **255**.

273

You bow before the statue of *Taph* and feel an immense wave of halo descending upon your head. By the blessings of your Patron Deity, you are healed and even protected! Restore your **LIFE** to their maximum values. **Add +1 to your PROTECTION,** updating your default core attribute! When you are done, you leave the shrine. Turn to **22**.

274

If you had already taken the skiff, there's nothing else for you to do here, and you can turn back from the white serpent alcove. Turn to **407**. If you've not taken the skiff before, turn to **462**.

275

As the door swings open, you see a paladin, who seem to be wounded, stand up from the floor and readies his sword. "Are you sent by *Kanwulf* ?" shouts the paladin. Do you say yes (turn to **131**) or no (turn to **460**)?

276

You're a disgusting, amoral **NECROMANCER!** But you do get bones for your dark arts. **Add +2 to Bones** under Reagents. Turn to **93**.

277

You find yourself struggling to swim away from the relentless pull of the current. Each stroke feels heavy against the powerful force dragging you along. The water thrashes around you, cold and unforgiving, and you realize with growing alarm that you are in the rapids. The tumultuous flow is pulling you inexorably towards the north. The roar of water grows louder, and a sense of dread fills you as you comprehend that a waterfall likely lies ahead, waiting to claim you in its merciless descent. **Roll a dice**. If you get **2, 4** or **6**, turn to **191**. If you get **1, 3** or **5**, turn to **170**.

278

With a steady voice, you call out, "Tails." You watch with bated breath as the coin finally stops spinning on the altar, clattering against the stone. The face of the coin showing is Heads. *Zakl's* voice fills the chamber, now tinged with a cold, unforgiving tone. "Alas, you cannot escape fate." Suddenly, a chilling sensation grips your chest, as if an invisible force is reaching into your very soul. You gasp, your breath stolen away, and a searing pain courses through your body as you collapse onto the cold stone floor. Your quest ends here.

279

You hesitate, your hand hovering just inches from the shimmering surface of the mirror. "Please, you must hurry!" he urges, his voice trembling with urgency.

Do you have PERCEPTION? If you have turn to **27**. Otherwise, turn to **149**.

280

It's a pity that a potential help would end up this way. You start to contemplate if your decision to convert to *Hish* is the right one after all. Nevertheless, you realize that there's nothing else for you to do in this cavern and that you shall leave here. Record codeword **COBB**, and turn to **243**.

281

While one *Gnager* is down, there is a strong likelihood that there are many more of them further down the tunnel, as you continue to hear faint chittering. Do you dare to proceed a little bit further and see what you can find? If you want to venture further south, turn to **13**. Otherwise, you can drop the idea and turn back up north (turn to **117**).

282

Record the codeword **MAGUS**, and turn to **378**.

283

The paladin, his face pale and strained, replies, "I am *Elandor*, a paladin of the *Solaris Order*." He grimaces, clutching his side where blood seeps through his fingers. "I am wounded." His voice is filled with pain and exhaustion as he continues, "I have been tracking a gang of brigands led by a man named *Kanwulf*. They have come to this accursed place, the *Necropolis*, seeking its treasures and aiming to challenge *Mortis* for the Æther, a substance of great power."

Sir Elandor's breath becomes more laboured, and his expression tightens with each word. "I confronted *Kanwulf* and his men, but they were too many. In the fight, I was left in this dire state and I had to flee them." His eyes, once fierce with determination, now reflect a mix of desperation and fatigue. "I am gravely injured and, worse yet, poisoned. The wound festers within me, and I can feel the life draining from my body." The paladin's voice falters, and he lies on the floor, as if he is expiring soon. "I need healing, quickly. Time is running out for me. Please, help me. I cannot allow *Kanwulf* and his men to prevail. They must be stopped, and I must live to see it done."

While you have no antidote to cure of *Sir Elandor's* poisoning at the current juncture, you may try to give him food or potions to increase his LIFE points, to sustain him for a while, while the poison remain active (and will cause more damages as time goes by). He will need to be restored for an addition of at least 5 LIFE points right now.

If you have any Healing Potions or Rations that can add up to total of **5 LIFE** points, or decide to help him with this much you can give them to him now, and **deduct the quantities** from your inventory accordingly and turn to **421**.

If you are able to provide **10 LIFE** points from your Healing Potions or Rations, do **deduct the quantities** from the inventory accordingly and turn to **329**.

If you are not able to help, or refuse to help, turn to **296**. Or if you want to act like a miscreant, you may try to take his life by killing him. Turn to **182**.

284

You are at a corner of the *Library*. You can either head towards north (turn to **437**) or head towards west (turn to **396**).

285

You approach the black pool, which emits an offensive acrid scent. The dim light flickers over the surface of a black pool, its dark waters bubbling ominously. You recall the man whose body melted away, and you instinctively keep your distance, believing that he might have touched the substance in the pool. As you peer closer, you are shocked by what you see- shapes within the pool which resemble human figures, or what once were. They are naked, their skin pallid and sickly, almost translucent under the dim light. The way they move, slowly and unnaturally, betrays their true nature: these are not living beings but undead, soaking and probably bathing in the dark, bubbling liquid.

Do you want to call out to them? If you do, turn to **390**. You can also choose to circumvent the pool to see what you find (turn to **431**) or leave this place, returning to the main passage (turn to **229**).

286

As you pull the lever, it resists at first, then yields with a loud, grating sound that echoes through the room. The ancient mechanism creaks to life, shaking off centuries of dust and disuse. The ground beneath you vibrates slightly, a low rumble growing in intensity as the machinery engages. You have triggered a mechanism somewhere in the dungeon. Record codeword **ZARAS** with associated number **45**, and turn to **66**.

287

Do you have the codeword WUSS? If you do, turn to **336**. Otherwise, turn to **246**.

288

This river passage stretches for a considerable distance, with sharp and irregular rock formations lining both sides of the tunnel. Do you wish to head north (turn to **150**) or south (turn to **350**)?

289

Thokk leans in, his voice dropping to a dire whisper. "Once you pass through the *Inner Chambers*, you will encounter the *Grand Hall*, a room riddled with traps designed to snare the unwary. It's a veritable deathtrap, but I can teach you how to survive it. Upon entering, move all the way west until you hit the wall. Then, make your way north to the very end. Finally, head all the way east. Follow this path, and you might just avoid the worst of it. Tread carefully, NECROMANCER, for even the slightest misstep could be your last."

You thank *Thokk* for his advice, and take leave. Turn to **327**.

290

You have triggered a trap. A furious ball of fire was shot at you from the back. **Roll a dice**. If you get **1, 3, 6, deduct 5 LIFE** points. If you get **2, 4, 5, deduct 8 LIFE** points. If you survive the trap, turn to **555**.

291

You are hit by a succession of two columns of lightning crashing down from the ceiling! A wall is on the north-side. **Deduct 10 LIFE** points. If you are still alive, you have to move on. Do you move east (turn to **397**), west (turn to **12**) or south (turn to **24**)?

An old man, seemingly trapped in a mirror

292

As you step into the room, your eyes are immediately drawn to a large, ornate mirror mounted on the far wall, its surface pitch-black and casting a faint otherworldly glow. As you approach, the surface of the mirror shimmers, and the reflection within shifts, revealing the image of a hooded old man. His beard is a tangled mass of silver, and his eyes, deep and piercing, are filled with a mix of desperation and wisdom. His robe, once grand, now appears tattered.

"Please, hear me," he calls out, his voice echoing through the chamber with an ethereal quality. "I am the *Great Wizard*, imprisoned within this mirror by dark sorcery. My knowledge and power can aid you in your quest for, but I need your help to escape this cursed confinement."

He gestures with a gnarled hand, the reflection mimicking the movement. "Reach your hand into the mirror and pull me out. I shall be eternally grateful and will gladly be at your service, to overcome the challenges of the *Necropolis*." The room's eerie silence amplifies the gravity of his request, the only sound being your own breathing and the distant, haunting whispers of the *Necropolis*.

Do you accede to his request and reach out for his hand in the mirror (turn to **164**), or refuse him (turn to **279**)?

293

You have already slayed the *Huntsman* (and *Ornias* is dead)- there's no reason for you to go back into *the Lair*. Turn to **404**.

294

You are at row two of the tombs, on the western side, and in a junction where you can travel in all directions. The sarcophagi are situated in the walls along east and west. Do you want to go north (turn to **386**), south (turn to **374**), east (turn to **546**), or west (turn to **414**)?

295

A faint, almost imperceptible whisper begins to weave through the alcove. The voice, dripping with malice, echoes off the stone walls, growing louder and more distinct with each word: "I see infidels in my presence, one of the wretched worshippers of the three damned ones- the Harlot, the Thief and the Cursed one, I am displeased and wish ruination upon you!" The words, sting, with insult cutting deep into your soul. You feel weak and feel your energy drained. **Deduct 5 LIFE** points. If you are still alive, you hurriedly leave the shrine before suffering another assault upon you. Turn to **240**.

296

"Alas, here's to my destiny's end! Justice shall never prevail then!" laments *Sir Elandor*. As he cower on the floor, and draw his last breath, you leave the dying alone to his final moments. Record codeword **QUORK** and turn to **93**.

297

You are at the western side of the tombs, with paths leading north and south. Do you want to go north (turn to **580**), or south (turn to **393**)?

298

Ahead of you lies a meander that curves the river. Do you want to head south (turn to **473**), or go east (turn to **520**)?

299

As you are nearing the entrance of the quarters, you see *Kolgrim* coming towards it and blocking your path, and with some impatience asks, "Leaving so soon?" Suddenly, you hear the creaking sound of a wooden door, and a voice that booms from behind, which belongs to *Kanwulf*, who had just gotten out of his room and walking up to you through the quarters. "Do not be rude to our guest *Kolgrim*. Our guest must be tired, and surely deserves some good food and rest, in good company?" says *Kanwulf*. You see *Kolgrim* smiling sheepishly at you, and he gestures you to have a seat at the fireplace, while still standing firm at the entrance.

Do you agree to stay for the feast? If you do, turn to **487**. If you decline this offer, turn to **408**.

300

You kneel before the wooden door, carefully inserting your lockpicks into the keyhole. With practiced precision, you begin to manipulate the tumblers, feeling the familiar resistance give way. Just as you sense the lock nearing its release, the pick snaps, breaking off inside the mechanism. The door remains stubbornly closed. **Remove Lockpicks** from your inventory. You shall abort the attempt to lockpick the door. Turn to **93**.

301

You see a wooden door at the end of the tunnel. There's an unsettling silence in the air, which makes you feel uneasy. Intuitively, you feel that there's danger ahead. Do you enter the door (turn to **102**) or head back north (turn to **36**)?

302

As you approach the gate, you notice the once passive (but watchful) eye narrows sharply at you, and seems to be seething with anger. You try to push the gate, but it refuses to budge, remaining firmly in place. The eye glares at you, unmoving, and perhaps with the intention of trapping you within the *Library* forever to punish you for your transgressions. Exit seems impossible, but there are some things which you can try to do. Do you want to attack the eye on the gate (turn to **567**), or return to the interior of the *Library*, hoping to find some other ways to leave this place (turn to **201**)?

303

Record codeword **BRAKK**. Turn to **93**.

304

After you drop the liquid, you find the *Homunculus* seemingly disturbed by what had happened; its giant eye widens in horror, rolling wildly as if searching for a way out. The deformed limbs thrash about, banging against the glass in a desperate, futile attempt to escape. A terrible gurgling sound emanates from its grotesque mouth as the poison takes hold. The *Homunculus* writhes in agony, its flesh bubbling and hissing as the poison courses through its misshapen body. The mass of flesh begins to break down, disintegrating into a frothy, foul-smelling mess that churns within the tank. The once-vibrant eye dulls, its life extinguished as the homunculus is reduced to nothing more than a pool of thick, foaming liquid in the tank. **Add 50 Exp points**.

Record the codeword **OBFUS**. You decide to leave this area, wondering what will happen next. Turn to **29**.

305

Nothing happen in this sector. Do you move north (turn to **24**), east (turn to **357**), west (turn to **224**) or south (turn to **9**)?

306

You dash northward and the passage soon splits into a junction, with paths to all directions. Do you want to head north (turn to **589**), south (turn to **509**), east (turn to **89**), or west (turn to **427**)?

307

You secure the grappling hook on a nearby rock structure, and drop the rope into the hole. You will attempt to climb down into the cavern. Do you have CLIMBING skill? If you do, turn to **268**. Otherwise turn to **356**.

308

As you rush down the corridor south, you see a path opening up towards west before you, accompanied by rapid footsteps. The *Huntsman* seems to have changed course in his pursuit and before you can react, you see a giant net unfurled towards you; the coarse ropes tangle around you, pulling tight and knocking you to the ground. Panic floods your senses as you struggle against the net, but your movements only seem to make it tighter.

Your eyes widen in horror as you spot this figure, advancing slowly towards you, his slim built, black skin and an unholy looking spear in his hand looking menacing as it casts a silhouette against the dim lights. You have no doubt— this must be the legendary *Huntsman*. Without a word, the figure hurls the spear at you with deadly precision, aiming at your heart. The spear closes in, and you only feel an instantaneous piercing pain before your consciousness fades. You are immediately killed by a weapon what many referred to as a 'Godkiller'- *The Spear of Signonul.* Your quest ends here.

309

You enter a room surrounded by black obsidian walls, and your gaze is immediately drawn to a large black serpent statue dominating the space. Its scales are intricately carved, each one catching the dim light, but it is the eyes that captivate you—gleaming with an almost lifelike fury, and noble air. Do you have the codeword MARAS? If you do, add the associated number to this section and turn to the new section. Otherwise, there's not much to do here, and you might as well leave the room and continue up north towards the massive gate. Turn to **62**.

310

You turn around, towards the *Huntsman* to engage in combat with it. Before you can hit the opponent with your weapon, you see the figure unfurling a massive net towards you, which is to ensnare you on the spot. The coarse ropes tangle around you, pulling tight and knocking you to the ground. Panic floods your senses as you struggle against the net, but your movements only seem to make it tighter, accompanied by the shrill cackles of *Ornias*. Your eyes widen in horror as you spot this figure, advancing slowly towards you, his slim built, black skin and an unholy looking spear in his hand looking menacing as it casts a silhouette against the dim lights.

You have no doubt—this must be the legendary *Huntsman*. Without a word, the figure hurls the spear at you with deadly precision, aiming at your heart. The spear closes in, and you only feel an instantaneous piercing pain before your consciousness fades. You are immediately killed by a weapon what many referred to as a 'Godkiller'- *The Spear of Signonul.* Your quest ends here.

311

This tunnel lead leads to a wooden door. You realize the door is not locked. There's an unsettling silence in the air, which makes you feel uneasy. Intuitively, you feel that there's danger ahead. Do you enter the door (turn to **102**), or retrace back, to head north (turn to **36**) or east (turn to **270**)?

312

Between you is a decorated wall to the south with a large symbol of *Zygós* and a wall at the north that recedes into an alcove, which houses an open sarcophagus made of the finest mahogany wood. This sarcophagus must have belonged to one of the deceased *Regii*. However, you realize the sarcophagus is empty! The body of the *Regii* seems to have been removed. There's nothing you can do here, except to move on towards east (turn to **344**) or west (turn to **439**).

313

You are at a junction. A northern passage opens up along the east-west tunnel. Do you want to go north (turn to **518**), head west (turn to **407**) or head east (turn to **35**)?

314

As the skeleton crumbles to the floor, you find a good amount of bone fragments that will be useful for your necromantic spellcasting. **Add +2 to Bones** under Reagents. Now, you can pull the lever. Turn to **286**.

315

You are at the southern side of the tombs, with paths leading, north, east and west. If you want to head north, turn to **411**. If you want to head east, turn to **230**. If you want to head west instead, turn to **433**.

316

You pull the ancient tome from the shelf, its cover emblazoned with the title "*The Black Dragon of the Underworld.*" It is authored by *Ahmes*, the Scribe.

The text within tells the harrowing tale of *Kralj*, the first of the *Regii*, whose reign was threatened by an otherworldly force: *The King of the Underworld*, in the fearsome form of a black dragon named *Draak*, who rose from the depths to challenge *Kralj's* dominion.

Kralj, undeterred by this terrifying adversary, sought out the legendary weapon that was said to be capable of killing even the mightiest of gods—the *Spear of Signonul*. Knowing that no ordinary weapon could pierce the dragon's scales, he embarked on a perilous journey, descending into the underworld itself. The book describes, in vivid detail, the countless demons and foul creatures he faced along the way, each encounter pushing him to the brink of death, before finally getting the spear and encountering the black dragon. The fight that ensued was long and brutal, with the black dragon unleashing all its fury upon the mortal king. In the end, with a mighty thrust, he drove the *Spear of Signonul* through *Draak's* heart, slaying the once mighty *King of the Underworld*. *Kralj* claimed the dragon's hide as a trophy, its dark, impenetrable scales a testament to his triumph.

Returning to the world of the living, *Kralj* commanded his smiths to fashion the dragon's skin into a suit of armour. They laboured for months, crafting an impenetrable mail from the scales of the slain beast, a suit that would become known as *Draco*. This armour was said to be impervious to all harm. Fearing its power might fall into the wrong hands, *Kralj* had the armour hidden deep within the *Necropolis*, a complex he commissioned for the burial of he and his descendants.

A cryptic clue, in the form of a riddle, left in a footnote by *Ahmes* seems to suggest the location of the *Draco* armour. "Whence and whereupon you see the *Feast of Mages*, one must pronounce: '*Death to the Witchking!*' so *Draco* will not elude one in vain."

When you are done reading, return to **158**.

317

The path leads you to an alcove bathed in a shimmering greenish aura. The glow emanates from a statue at the centre of the alcove, a figure poised in mid-motion, as if caught in the act of running.

You are in the shrine of *Taph*, the Quick One, the mercurial God of Wits, much revered by thieves, merchants, and messengers alike. The statue, carved from jade, depicts a lithe, agile figure with a mischievous grin, the eyes sparkling with cunning intelligence. *Taph's* outstretched arm holds a small, ornate bag, symbolic of the wealth and tricks he bestows upon his followers. His other hand is open, fingers spread wide, as if ready to snatch an opportunity out of thin air. The greenish light pulses rhythmically, casting shifting shadows that dance across the walls, creating an almost hypnotic effect. But you sense that a presence is silently watching you.

Are you a follower of *Taph*? If you are, turn to **273**. If you are instead, a follower of *Zakl* or *Ked*, turn to **235**. If you are none of the above, turn to **514**.

318

Very soon, you reach the north-western corner of the lair, which veers sharply to the left towards south, changing your course southward. Turn to **516**.

319

You pull out the torch from the inventory, and used it in the looming darkness, casting a warm, flickering light across the vast, shadowy expanse before you. The eerie glow reveals row upon row of ancient sarcophagi, each one weathered by time, yet still imposing in its grandeur. These silent tombs stretch out in every direction, housing the remains of kings long forgotten.

Do you have SCRYING skill? If you do, turn to **252**. Otherwise, turn to **248**.

320

This section of the *Library* seems more exclusive; there are fewer books, and they look more exquisite than the other volumes elsewhere. You see a sign on the other side of the wall stating, "This is the Special Access section of the *Library*. You are not authorized to touch and read any of the books, unless permitted beforehand." A book stands out from the collection, titled "*Elemental Magick*". If you want to take the risk to read this book, turn to **504**. Otherwise you can either head east (turn to **521**) or west (turn to **29**).

321

The bodies of the *Demonomancer* and his demon, *Xaphan*, lay lifeless at your feet. The air is heavy with the lingering stench of brimstone and burnt flesh. The battle is over. You wipe the sweat from your brow and crouch beside the *Demonomancer*, carefully rifling through his tattered robes. You find a small vial filled with a shimmering liquid. It's an antidote, likely pilfered from someone else. If you want to, **add Antidote** into your inventory. **Gain 20 Exp points.** Soon, you realize this path leads to a dead-end, and it's best that you return to the junction. Add codeword **DEMONOS** and turn to **403**.

322

With the 'Repel Undead' spell in effect, the skeleton seems to back away from you as you tried to approach it, even in its unanimated state. It somehow averts you in your repeated attempts to touch it, rapidly shifting out of your grasp even when you lunged forward! At this point, you think it is futile to examine it and decide to pull the lever instead (turn to **402**).

323

You recall that you can do something with the eyes of the black serpent, to stop its fiery wrath, from the slip of parchment you found. As you examine the head of the statue, you notice that one of the eyes, though seemingly solid, have a slight give to them. You press one down, feeling it depress under your fingertip. The statue emits a low, rumbling sound, hinting at the mechanism concealed within. **Gain 20 Exp** points. Record the codeword **VRIL**. There's nothing else for you to do in this room. You shall leave this place and head towards the colossal gate. Turn to **62**.

324

With the *Shugrag* slumped on the floor dead, you are able to freely explore the room. Immediately, you gather the bones of the deceased you can find. **Add +2 to Bones** under Reagents. There are still piles of dirt littered all over the room. Would you like to continue your search (turn **379**), or leave the room (turn to **552**)?

325

Do you have the codeword MAGUS? If you do, turn to **271**. Otherwise, turn to **426**.

326

You pull a blue, weathered book from the shelf, titled "*The Xenochian Dictionary*", and written by *Torak*, the Lexicographer. The brittle pages reveal the ancient language of *Xenoch*, the tongue of the Elder Race. While you can identify most of the scripts, you still discover new words, previously unknown to you. Some of the definitions are:

Arcanas – Magick   *Askir – Rest*   *Fimus – Death*
Shekor – Lords   *Skire – Small*   *Umas – Self*
Ustuk – Great   *Zilaq – Return*

When you are done reading, turn to **457**.

327

Record the codeword **MERZ**. You can head north (turn to **36**). You can also head west only if you do not have the codeword **KRUZ** (turn to **301**).

328

Between you is a decorated wall to the south with a large symbol of *Scorpia* and a wall at the north that recedes into an alcove, which houses an open sarcophagus made of the finest mahogany wood. This sarcophagus must have belonged to one of the deceased *Regii*. However, you realize the sarcophagus is empty! The body of the *Regii* seems to have been removed. There's nothing you can do here, except to move on towards east (turn to **505**) or west (turn to **344**).

329

Your help has restored a significant amount of health for *Sir Elandor*, but he is still poisoned and will get weakened as time goes by. "I must thank you for your assistance NECROMANCER. I hope you can come back with the antidote. I am truly appreciative. I shall wait for your return."

Record the codework **KRECK. Write POISON and record 6 counts** in your notes. Do return here when you have found the antidote, or when you have more healing potions/rations to spare. Turn to **93**.

330

You find yourself in a dark, cold corner of a labyrinth. The air is thick with the metallic scent of blood, and the floor beneath your feet is littered with bones, cracked and splintered, as if many had met a gruesome end here.

To your shock, a familiar figure emerges from the gloom—*Ornias*, the goblin hustler. He grins wickedly, his eyes gleaming with malice. "Well, well, look who made it through the teleporters in one piece," he jeers. "You're one lucky fool, aren't you?" *Ornias* lets out a mocking laugh. "You're in the very LAIR now, as a play thing for the *Huntsman*. He is in the proximity and he will track you down like a prey for sport!"

His laughter grows louder, more maniacal, as he backs away, leaving you in this nightmarish place to your fate. "Run for your life, NECROMANCER!" With that, he turns and darts north, while blowing a war-horn to the *Huntsman*, announcing your arrival and commencing the *Great Hunt*!

There are two paths you can take now. You can either pursue *Ornias* to the north (turn to **217**), or run down the eastern path (turn to **424**).

331

With the ghost gone, the room falls into an uneasy silence. Glancing around, you notice slimy, translucent substances pooled on the floor—ectoplasm, remnants of the ghost's presence, an important and rather rare ingredient for spellcasting. Carefully, you gather the ectoplasm. **Add +2 Ectoplasm** into Reagents. The room, now devoid of the spectral figure, feels less menacing, but an air of mystery still lingers. Do you want to explore the room more thoroughly (turn to **463**), or leave, wary of what else might lurk in the shadows (turn to **508**)?

332

You knock on the heavy wooden door, and a gruff voice from within calls out, "Come in." As you push open the door, you are met with the sight of a tall, imposing man seated at a sturdy wooden table. His appearance is striking—his features are both handsome and ruthless. He wears a worn leather vest that clings to his muscular frame, and his eyes gleam with a sharp, predatory intelligence. Despite the menace that seems to radiate from him, he smiles at you, a gesture that feels more like a warning than a welcome.

"Ah, you must be the one causing all the commotion," he says smoothly, his voice as sharp as the blade at his side. "Welcome. I am *Kanwulf*, ex-lieutenant of *Tharach*. My crew and I are here on our own little quest, searching for the elusive *Æther* which I believe should also be your same purpose."

He gestures toward the fireplace in the centre of the room, where a succulent roasted pork slowly turns on a spit, its savoury aroma filling the air. "Why don't you stay a while? We're preparing a feast, and it would be a shame to let all this good food and wine go to waste. Besides," he adds with a smile that doesn't quite reach his eyes, "you look like you could use a good rest. Spend the night here, and we'll talk more in the morning." His invitation though polite, leaves little room for refusal.

If you have PERCEPTION and want to use it, turn to **108**.
If you agree to have the feast and stay here for the night, turn to **487**.
If you want to refuse this offer, turn to **562**.

333

Suddenly you come face to face with a sight that stops you in your tracks. A rodent-like humanoid stands before you from a distance, like a cross between a rat, a mole, a shrew and a naked human in its most grotesque form. Its eyes, small and beady, is probably blind, but it is sniffing profusely (at you) with its snout-like nose and its sharp, yellowed teeth seems to gnash with a voracious hunger. It emits an anxious, menacing chatter, its breath a rancid stench that makes your stomach churn. You recognize this creature- it is a *Gnager*, an unclean vermin that lives in the depths, gnawing and corrupting the roots that grow this deep into the earth, and an omnivore with an insatiable appetite for flesh that comes its way. The *Gnager* will begin the turn.

Gnager
Life 8
Offence (Melee) 8
Defence 3

Gnager's Probability Table

Outcomes	Missed Hit	Exact Hit	Missed Hit	Exact Hit	Reduced Hit	Critical Hit
Dice Number	4	5	6	1	2	3

If you win the battle, **gain 20 Exp points** and turn to **281**.

334

You are at the north-western corner of the tombs, with paths leading south and east. If you want to go south, turn to **597**. If you prefer to go east instead, turn to **413**.

335

You are at the northern side of the tombs, with paths leading east and west. If you want to go east, turn to **565**. If you prefer to go west instead, turn to **380**.

336

Left with no other choice, your only way to get out of here is to go back to the other end where the teleporter is, and step through it. Turn to **583**.

337

You feel something grabbing and tugging at your foot. And not before long, you are pulled into the water! Just before your torch is extinguished, you catch sight of a horrific form of a *Nyx*, the damned merman of the depths, resembling a grotesque shrivelled hag with a fish body, and notorious for dragging victims to their watery graves. **Roll a dice**. If you get **1, 3 ,5**, turn to **262**. If you get **2, 4, 6**, turn to **144**.

338

Do you have the codeword OBFUS? If you do, turn to **232**. Otherwise, turn to **44**.

339

Record the codeword **DOLORS**. There's nothing much for you to do here except to move on. You can either head east (turn to **497**) or west (turn to **563**).

340

The skiff capsizes and you are plunged into the icy cold waters! As you try to scramble to the skiff, you feel a forceful tug on your foot, and you are well aware that the *Nyx* is trying to drag you into the depths to drown you. Turn to **144**.

341

Nothing happens at the shrine, so you decide to leave the shrine and go back to the T-junction. Record codeword **HISH**. Turn to **122**.

342

Nothing happens at the shrine, so you decide to leave the shrine and retrace your steps back to the L-junction. Turn to **240**.

343

You rotate the statue to the left. Suddenly a stream of scorching red flame shoots out from the mouth of the dog-head towards you! **Deduct 2 LIFE** points. If you are still alive, do you wish to continue to rotate the statue left (turn to **92**), or rotate it right (turn to **28**), or abort the attempt and turn back towards the eastern tunnel instead (turn to **115**)?

344

You are at row two of the tombs, on the eastern side, and in a junction where you can travel in all directions. The sarcophagi are situated in the walls along east and west. Do you want to go north (turn to **377**), south (turn to **79**), east (turn to **328**), or west (turn to **312**)?

345

You are at the southern side of the tombs, with paths leading east and west. If you want to go east, turn to **248**. If you prefer to go west instead, turn to **226**.

346

Do you have the codeword ZENGIS? If you do, turn to **274**. Otherwise, turn to **156**.

347

You crouch before the door, your lockpicks in hand. With practiced precision, you insert them into the lock, feeling for the subtle resistance and gentle clicks that signal your progress. After a few tense moments, you hear a satisfying click and the lock gives way. **Gain 10 Exp points**. Slowly, you push the door open, and an ominous cold rushes out to envelop you. The chill is almost palpable, seeping into your skin and filling you with a sense of foreboding, sending an eerie whisper warning you about an impending horror ahead. Turn to **354**.

348

Based on your estimate, the distance between the hole and the pit underneath is at least 12 feet tall. You notice that there's some jutted rock between this distance that is potentially scalable. If you decide not to go through the hole and retrace back to head westward instead, turn to **287**. Otherwise you will need to figure a way down.

If you have CLIMBING skill and decide to use it, turn to **266**.
If you have a Rope + Grappling Hook and decide to use it, turn to **307**.
If you have none of the above, but wish to attempt the descent, turn to **205**.

349

Your keen perception suggests that *Ornias* may be possibly deeply linked to the *Huntsman*, perhaps even his subordinate. Despite this suspicion, you decide it might be prudent to pay him and utilize his assistance for the lair. However, you resolve to remain vigilant, aware that *Ornias* might attempt to sabotage you at some point later. With this insight, you endeavour to be especially careful with him later, and prepared to counter any treachery that may arise.

If you agree with *Ornias'* proposal, **minus 20 Gp** and turn to **534**. Otherwise turn to **465**.

350

Do you have codeword KED? If you do, turn to **251**. Otherwise read on.

The water passage north and south is wide, but to the west, the river has narrowed into a shadowy passage. Do you want to head north (turn to **288**), south (turn to **125**) or west (turn to **243**)?

351

You find yourself in the catacombs of the *Inner Chambers*, an intriguing and section of the *Necropolis* which houses the *Tombs of the Regii*. The atmosphere here is even more oppressive and darkly allure than ever before, drawing you deeper into its labyrinthine passages. Turn to **213**.

352

You appear in a room, painted entirely in swamp-green, and as soon as your legs land on a plate on the floor, it triggers an emission of toxic fume! **Deduct 5 LIFE** points. If you are still alive, read on.

Within this room are two teleporters, placed in different directions. Do you take the one to the east (turn to **330**), or to the west (turn to **434**)?

353

You rotate the statue left, back to its original position. But all of a sudden comes a stream of scorching red flame, shooting out from the mouth of the dog-head towards you! **Deduct 5 LIFE** points. If you are still alive, you notice that the statue is stuck at this point and you cannot rotate it anymore. Realizing that there's nothing more you can do, you decide to turn back towards the eastern tunnel instead (turn to **115**).

354

As your eyes adjust to the darkness from within the room, you hear a faint, eerie howl echoing from the shadows. Suddenly, out of the darkness, a ghostly apparition materializes and rushes towards you with alarming speed. Its translucent form flickers with an otherworldly glow, and its eyes, hollow and haunting, its mouth seems stretched out in an anguished gape, as if suffering great injustice and sorrow, and its ethereal hands outstretched, forming a macabre sight to behold.

You can **cast a spell** ⛤

Alternatively, you can either stand your ground (turn to **515**), or dash out of the room immediately (turn to **11**).

355

The Rabbit's Matrix: In a world where shadows whispered of conspiracies and unseen hands manipulating the fate of nations, there was a common belief among the masses: that a select few controlled the world. The powerful, the wealthy, the untouchable—they were the puppeteers pulling the strings of the grand theatre of life, or so the story went.

Every disaster, every war, every collapse was attributed to these invisible overlords. The people found solace in this belief, a comforting explanation for the chaos around them. They spoke of secret meetings, hidden agendas, and a master plan unfolding with each passing day. In their minds, everything was orchestrated, every event part of a grand design. But beneath this illusion lay a truth far more terrifying. The world was not controlled—it was careening out of control. Deep within the bowels of the earth, forces unseen and unknown to any human hand stirred. The very planet, once a beacon of life, was now on an inevitable path to doom. The balance of nature had tipped, the axis of the world itself trembling as if in a final, desperate dance.

The powerful, those thought to be the masters of destiny, were just as lost as everyone.

356

While the rope is steady, your lack of CLIMBING skill made the descent rather difficult. Midway through the climb, your hands slipped and you drop to the bottom of the pit! **Lose 2 LIFE** points. If you're still alive, you shook your head and loosen the rope and the grappling hook, retrieving it into your inventory. Turn to **173**.

357

Nothing happen in this sector. A wall is on the east-side. Do you move north (turn to **129**), west (turn to **305**) or south (turn to **114**)?

358

You retrace your steps back to this area of the lair, where a new opens up north along the east-west corridor. Do you want to dash north (turn to **306**), run all the way back west where you first arrive (turn to **77**), or hurry back again to the east side (turn to **236**)?

359

You scan the items *Thokk* has for sale, noting the quality and the prices. You can either buy them or trade them with items of equal value. You can also sell your items to him.

Items	Quantity	Property	Price
Short Sword	1x	Dmg +3	5 Gp
Mage's Robe	1x	Shd +2	5 Gp
Healing Potion	1x	LIFE +5 (1 use)	6 Gp
Rations	1x	LIFE +2 (1 use)	3 Gp
Lockpicks	1x	For lockpicking (1 use)	5 Gp
Pail	1x	For containing things	5 Gp
Shovel	1x	For digging	10 Gp
Rope + Grappling Hook	1x	For climbing	5 Gp

After you finalize your trade:
If you have CHARM, turn to **61**.
If you have THIEVERY, turn to **137**.
If you have PERCEPTION, turn to **209**.
Otherwise, turn to **289**.

360

You see the glum face of the ghost become increasingly listless and impatient as you try to converse with it. Suddenly, without warning, you see the spirit poof into thin air. You might not have the chance to invoke the spirit of the *Great Wizard* again. All you can do is leave this place, and get to a safer area of the river. Turn to **282**.

361

Review your **POISON count and deduct by 1**. If it is **0**, immediately record codeword **QUORK** and turn to **587**.

If you have the Antidote, turn to **269**.

If you have healing potions or rations, they can help sustain the life of *Sir Elandor*. Every **+5 LIFE** (do deduct the amount of healing potions or rations needed to give that, accordingly from your inventory) will contribute to **+2** to the **POISON count** (update this accordingly).

If there's nothing else you can do, you can leave the room. Turn to **93**.

362

You are acutely aware that you worship gods that are enemies of *Ked* and that you should leave immediately. But before you can do so, a melodious, yet piercing voice begins to speak in your head, dripping with charm but laced with a menacing undertone.

"I am *Ked*, the Beautiful One, the Goddess of All That is Fair and Just, desired by all in the *Realms of Thorns* and far above your kind, who is a Fool for following the other so-called gods to their graves but also afflicted with apparent ugliness, both within and without..." the voice declares with a haughty air. "To even consider punishing you here would be beneath me—I have no desire to tarnish my immaculate shrine with your filth, much less a NECROMANCER, maggoty grave-worm destined to suffer a life-long solitude because no one will fancy your kind."

Her words are laced with disdain as she continues. "Look at yourself, so wretched and pitiful. Your gaunt frame and sallow complexion are an affront to all that I embody. You are born pathetic, lacking in wisdom and grace. Even if you were to grovel at my feet in worship, I would not be bothered to acknowledge your existence." She laughs, the sound dripping with scorn. "You and your so-called gods are beneath me and my worshippers, NECROMANCER. Remember that, as you scurry about in the shadows, far from the light of my justice and beauty." Such insulting words cut at you deeply but you know that it is futile to exact any revenge here.

Record the codeword **KED**.

If you have codeword PROSE, turn to **177**. Otherwise you quickly depart the shrine, before the deity changes her mind (turn to **243**).

363

You push aside the tapestry of the painting and find a hidden compartment. Within the compartment is a skiff, a small wooden boat that is compact enough for carry. If you want to take it with you, **add a Skiff (Gp: 30)** to your inventory before you leave this place, then turn to **407**.

364

As you continue down the east-bound path, you see a sturdy guard-post ahead. A lone figure, clad in battered leather armour, steps forward, his hand resting on the hilt of his sword. His eyes narrow as he assesses you, and in a gruff voice, he demands, "What's your business here?"

You stand your ground and reply calmly, "I'm an adventurer, seeking my way through these halls." The guard grunts, his suspicion evident, but then he introduces himself, "Name's *Kolgrim*. Listen, adventurer, beyond this point lies the quarters of *Kanwulf* and his crew. We are not the kind who appreciate visitors." His hand tightens around his sword as he adds with a stern tone, "I suggest you turn around and find another path. We don't welcome you."

If you are wearing the Plate Mail of Solaris, turn to **581**. Otherwise consider other options.

If you have CHARM and would like to try it on *Kolgrim*, turn to **443**.
If you say that you have something to offer to *Kanwulf* and crew, turn to **523**.
If you want to attack *Kolgrim*, turn to **46**.
If you agree to turn back, record codeword **GNAWER** and turn to **49**.

365

You are between walls, with paths leading north and south. Do you want to go north (turn to **565**), or south (turn to **444**)?

366

Do you have both THIEVERY skill and lockpicks in the inventory, at the same time? If you have, turn to **163**. Otherwise it will likely result in a futile attempt to pick open the cage lock, and in that case, you might as well leave here and figure what to do next (record codeword **HOBBS** and turn to **243**).

367

The old man's tone grows with frustration, his calm facade crumbling. "Fool! If you do not help me, you'll regret it! The power I can offer you is beyond your imagination. Don't throw away this opportunity because of baseless doubts!" You are doubly convinced that this old man is a liar, and is up to no good.

You notice a sizable rock on the floor. Do you hurl it at the mirror in an attempt to break it and teach this old man a lesson (turn to **204**), or do you just leave the room (turn to **17**)?

368

You are at the northern side of the tombs, with paths leading, south, east and west. If you want to head south, turn to **578**. If you want to head east, turn to **419**. If you want to head west instead, turn to **413**.

369

With the chamber now eerily silent, you close your eyes, steadying your breath as you remember the skill imparted to you by *Zakl*—the gift of Scrying. Perhaps this is the moment to use it.

You calm your mind, pushing aside the anxiety that gnaws at you. Slowly, you begin to meditate, centring your thoughts on the *Huntsman*. The chamber around you fades as your consciousness delves deeper into the ethereal plane. Shapes and colours swirl in the darkness behind your closed eyelids, and then, gradually, an image forms—a fleeting glimpse of the *Huntsman*, cloaked in shadow, somewhere in the distance.

The vision lingers only for a moment, but it is enough. The *Huntsman* is to the NORTHEAST. You can almost feel his presence pulling at you from that direction. As you open your eyes, the chamber comes back into focus, the teleporter waiting ahead,. You are now aware that you should be going in the general direction of NORTH and EAST with the teleporters. With this in mind, you step forward through to the teleporter. Turn to **582**.

370

You feel the skiff rocking violently, and speeding up towards north, and you think you are now in the middle of a rapids, towards a waterfall at the northside! From a distance, you can see a shoreline to the west. Do you want to take the risk and head north (turn to **170**), move west towards the shoreline (turn to **325**), or retreat south towards safer waters (turn to **590**)?

371

Do you have the codeword ANIMA? If you do, turn to **532** immediately.

If you do not have the codeword and you've been here before, there's no more remnants of *Æther* left here for your use, except to retreat back to the main cavern junction. Turn to **576**. If not, read on.

The northern path leads only a short distance before it ends at a wall. Your gaze shifts to the wall, where a small, ancient faucet juts out, seemingly out of place amidst the rough stone.

The faucet is shut tight, locked by some kind of mechanisms. But your attention is quickly drawn to a very small pool of liquid on the ground beneath it. The substance is unlike anything you've seen before—its surface shimmers with silverish hues. Your heart skips a beat as realization dawns on you. Could this be remnants of the fabled *Æther*? Overcome with excitement, you kneel beside the puddle and carefully use your finger to scoop up what remains of the enchanted liquid and put it into your mouth.

Instantly, a wave of energy surges through your body, electrifying your senses. Your vision sharpens, the dull stone walls around you coming into crystal-clear focus and you feel that every part of your body has rejuvenated. **Restore** your **LIFE**, **POWER** and **MANA** to the **maximum scores**. You realize that the *Repository* of *Æther* must not be far from here. **Add 50 Exp points**. Once you are done, you shall leave this place back to the cavern junction. Turn to **576**.

372

As the spell takes shape, the ghost halts abruptly, its form shuddering violently as a high-pitched screech is heard. The spectral figure recoils, the mouth widens, and then, in a blur of motion, dashes in the opposite direction. It disappears into the walls, leaving an eerie silence in its wake, the room now devoid of the ghostly presence that once filled it. Turn to **331**.

373

With deft fingers and steady hands, you manage to pick the lock on the wooden door. A satisfying click echoes in the corridor, signalling your success. The door creaks open, and you step forward into the room. Turn to **275**.

374

You are between walls, with paths leading north and south. Do you want to go north (turn to **294**), or south (turn to **436**)?

375

As soon as you arrive at the south-eastern corner of the lair you see a massive net falling onto you, sprung from a figure that is situated to your right, from the west. The coarse ropes tangle around you, pulling tight and knocking you to the ground. Panic floods your senses as you struggle against the net, but your movements only seem to make it tighter.

Your eyes widen in horror as you spot this figure, advancing slowly towards you, his slim built, black skin and an unholy looking spear in his hand looking menacing as it casts a silhouette against the dim lights. You have no doubt— this must be the legendary *Huntsman*. Without a word, the figure hurls the spear at you with deadly precision, aiming at your heart. The spear closes in, and you only feel an instantaneous piercing pain before your consciousness fades. You are immediately killed by a weapon what many referred to as a 'Godkiller'- *The Spear of Signonul.* Your quest ends here.

376

As the ghost rushes toward you, you quickly cast a Séance spell. The ghost halts, its form flickering and wavering in response to the spell. **Gain 20 Exp points**. Gathering your composure, you address the apparition. "What is happening here?" you ask, your voice steady despite the lingering chill in your bones.

The ghost's expression softens, and it begins to speak in a mournful tone. "My name is *Miriam*," it says, "I was once a cleric who ventured into this *Necropolis*, seeking the *Æther*. But I was deceived by a changeling named *Thokk*. He led me astray in the Grand Hall, directing me down a path filled with deadly traps. I perished there, my soul bound to this place in eternal anguish."

You listen intently as *Miriam* continues, her voice filled with sorrow. "*Thokk* tricked me, leading me to believe that the path to the *Grand Hall* was all the way west and then up north and east. But it was a lie, a cruel ruse designed to end my life. Instead, the true path lies in the opposite direction he claimed. To reach the *Grand Hall* safely, you must go all the way east, and then continue all the way up north, then east again." *Miriam's* form flickers as she speaks, her ghostly visage a blend of despair and urgency. "Do not let my fate become yours."

As the apparition is growing weaker, it is also drifting ever closer to you. Do you want to move away to conclude the séance (turn to **60**), or do you want to stay put and ask more questions (turn to **26**)?

377

You are between walls, with paths leading north and south. Do you want to go north (turn to **444**), or south (turn to **344**)?

378

With skill and patience, you navigate out of the rapids, back to the safer portion of the river. Turn to **590**.

379

As you rummage through the dirt, you suddenly feel a sharp pain on your hand and you reel backward in shock. Upon closer examination, you see a scorpion emerging from the dirt, before disappearing into the dirt. You have been stung by a scorpion! **Deduct 2 LIFE** points. If you are still alive, do you persist with the search (**157**), or do you call it quits and leave the room (turn to **552**)?

380

You arrive at the centre of the northern side of the tombs. To the north of here is an alcove. There's also paths leading to the south, west and east. Do you want to head north (turn to **531**), west (turn to **419**), east (turn to **335**) or south (turn to **441**)?

381

When you altered the eye of the black serpent statue earlier, you have effectively switched off the fireball trap mechanism. Therefore nothing happens. Turn to **555**.

382

With the brigands lying motionless around you, you steady yourself and begin to search the fallen brigands and their quarters. You rifle through their belongings, turning over worn leather pouches, rifling through pockets, and prying open small crates scattered throughout the quarters. Your efforts yield several useful items:

Items	Quantity	Property	Price
Healing Potion	2x	LIFE +5 (1 use each)	5 Gp each
Rations	2x	LIFE +2 (1 use each)	2 Gp each
Short Sword	3x	Dmg: +3	5 Gp each
Leather Vest	3x	Shd: +3	8 Gp each
Obsidian Staff	1x	Dmg: +8	30 Gp
Wizard's Robe	1x	Shd: +4	20 Gp
Poison	1x	Cause poisoning	10 Gp

Most importantly, you found their secret stash of gold. **Add 100 Gold pieces.** You also found a stone artifact with esoteric symbol etched on it.

If you want this item, **add the △ Stone with an associated number 23** to your inventory. You have **gained 50 Exp points**.

When you are done, add the codeword **GNASHER** and turn to **49**.

383

You scan the items *Ornias* has for sale, noting the quality and the prices. You can either buy them or trade them with items of equal value. You can also sell your items to him. Reduce Quantity of Items for the amount you bought accordingly. This should also be reflected when you come back next time.

Items	Quantity	Property	Price
Spirit Potion	1x	Restores MANA (1 use)	10 Gp
Strength Potion	1x	Restores POWER (1 use)	10 Gp
Healing Potion	3x	LIFE +5 (1 use each)	5 Gp each
Rations	3x	LIFE +2 (1 use each)	2 Gp each
Ring of Haste	1x	Move 2 Squares per Turn	20 Gp
Wizard's Robe	1x	Shd +4	20 Gp
Black Opal (Focus)	1x	Dmg: +3, Rd: 3, Type: Lightning	20 Gp

If you have CHARM, and want to use it in this situation, turn to **466**.
If you have THIEVERY, and want to use it in this situation turn to **584**.
Otherwise, turn to **250**.

384

Between you is a decorated wall to the south with a large symbol of *Tauros* and a wall at the north that recedes into an alcove, which houses an open sarcophagus made of the finest mahogany wood. This sarcophagus must have belonged to one of the deceased *Regii*. However, you realize the sarcophagus is empty! The body of the *Regii* seems to have been removed. There's nothing you can do here, except to move on towards east (turn to **538**) or west (turn to **497**).

385

As you prepare to draw your weapon, a sudden clamour of footsteps echoes from behind *Kolgrim*. With a yelp, *Kolgrim* was struck by a sword on his back and he falls forward, revealing *Sir Elandor*, his armour gleaming in the dim light, his (new) sword brandishing proudly with the blood of *Kolgrim*! "Hey!" he calls out, his voice filled with determination. "I promised I'd return to help you, and here I am!" *Kanwulf*, who had been readying himself for the fight, freezes in shock. His eyes widen as he stares at *Sir Elandor*, disbelief etched across his face. "How can you be alive?" *Kanwulf* roars, his voice tinged with both anger and fear.

But there's no time for explanations. With a surge of adrenaline and a renewed sense of hope, you rush forward, ready to meet the oncoming foes. *Sir Elandor* takes on the wounded *Kolgrim* and *Brutus*, while you turn your attention to the rest of the gang as they close in, weapons raised. Turn to **506**.

386

You are between walls, with paths leading north and south. Do you want to go north (turn to **497**), or south (turn to **294**)?

387

You realize that there's no way you can get back to the *Necropolis* from that hole in the cave ceiling. Record codeword **GRIM**. Check your other options.

If you do not have either codeword GARM and GROM, you decide to explore the whole unchartered southward tunnels, turn to **192**.

If you have codeword GROM and not GARM, you will head back to continue further explorations south of the area emitting red light. Turn to **469**.

If you have codeword GARM and not GROM, you will check out the area that emits a red light, which you have missed. Turn to **569**.

If you have both codewords GARM and GROM, turn to **53**.

388

You arrive at a junction in the northern part of the lair, with paths opening to the north and south, along the east-west corridor. You hear a loud cackle coming from *Ornias*, who is now situated at an alcove in the north. Just before you can react, a massive net is cast onto you, sprung from a figure that is situated to from the south. The coarse ropes tangle around you, pulling tight and knocking you to the ground. Panic floods your senses as you struggle against the net, but your movements only seem to make it tighter.

Your eyes widen in horror as you spot this figure, advancing slowly towards you, his slim built, black skin and an unholy looking spear in his hand looking menacing as it casts a silhouette against the dim lights. You have no doubt— this must be the legendary *Huntsman*. You hear *Ornias* cheering loudly from a distance.

Without a word, the figure hurls the spear at you with deadly precision, aiming at your heart. The spear closes in, and you only feel an instantaneous piercing pain before your consciousness fades. You are immediately killed by a weapon what many referred to as a 'Godkiller'- *The Spear of Signonul.* Your quest ends here.

389

You are in an empty room, the air still but otherwise quite serene. There's nothing to do here and you shall head back to the passageway. Turn to **93**.

390

You hesitate for a moment before gathering your courage and calling out to the figures in the pool. One of the undead figures turns its head toward you, its movements slow and deliberate. The figure begins to swim toward the edge of the pool, its smile eerie and unnatural. The closer it gets, the more you can see the sickly pallor of its skin, the way the dark liquid clings to its body like a second skin. It reaches the edge and, with a grotesque grin, it places a small wooden chest on the ground before you.

The chest is small, unassuming at first glance, but as you look closer, you notice it is covered in the same black slime that seems to taint everything it touches. The undead figure, still smiling, gazes at you with lifeless eyes, waiting to see what you will do next.

Do you want to attempt to open the chest? If you do, turn to **238**.

If not, you can either ignore it and return to the main passage (turn to **229**) or circumvent the area (turn to **431**).

391

You present the Library Pass to the grotesque mouth on the gate. **Remove Library Pass** from the inventory. The mouth's lips curl into a wide grin, and in that same deep voice, it commands, "Put the pass into my mouth." Hesitating only for a moment, you push the pass towards the stone lips. As soon as the pass touches them, the mouth opens wider, revealing a dark void beyond the teeth. The pass is swiftly swallowed, disappearing into the darkness with a soft gulp. "Access authorized," the mouth declares.

The gate rumbles as it begins to slide open, stone grinding against stone. A cold draft rushes past you as the gate rises, revealing the entrance to the *Library* beyond. As soon as you're inside, the gate crashes shut behind you. Turning around, you notice something even more peculiar. On this side of the gate, a large stone eye has now formed in the centre. It blinks slowly, regarding you with an unsettling awareness. The eye follows your movements for a moment before becoming still, rotating in the stony socket, indicating the grinding sound between stones. You turn away, your steps echoing in the eerie silence of the strange *Library*. Turn to **201**.

392

Since you have taken whatever you need, there's no point in hanging around a dead body here, unless you want to take your *Necromancy* to the next level, by defiling the corpse of the paladin, hopefully to get ingredients (like bones) for your spellcasting. If you haven't done that before, you can do that (turn to **276**)? Or do you leave the dead alone and exit the room (turn to **93**)?

393

You are at row one of the tombs, with walls to the west. You can head north, east and south. Do you want to go north (turn to **297**), go south (turn to **453**) or go east (turn to **256**)?

394

Record the codeword **WUSS**. You retrace your step back to the T-junction, and decide to explore the eastern part of the tunnel (turn to **184**).

395

You find a shore littered with countless wood pieces, likely the remnants of other boats that met a grim fate. If you've met the *Chelonoth* before, there's nothing else for you to do here and you can head back north to the river (turn to **125**). If you've not met the *Chelonoth* before, turn to **242**.

396

You see shelves lining up the walls, cluttered with all kinds of books. Corridors branch off to both sides of east and west, and towards south. A book from this section caught your eye, titled '*Book of Prophecies*'. If you want to read the book, turn to **18**. Otherwise, you can choose to go east (turn to **284**), west (turn to **557**) or south (turn to **201**).

397

A wall is on the north and east-side. As you step into this sector, you realize that you have triggered a pressure plate which lifts up the wall on the east, revealing a secret exit. You step forward. Turn to **537**.

398

You bow before the statue of *Hish* and feel an immense surge of blessings and healing upon you. By the blessings of your Patron Deity, you are healed. Restore your **LIFE** and **MANA** to their maximum values. You also find 20 Gold pieces materialize before you! **Add 20 Gold pieces.** When you are done, you leave the shrine. Record codeword **HISH**. Turn to **122**.

399

After you cast the spell, the ghost is already close upon you, while the spell fizzes into the air, without causing any effect on it. Before you can gasp, the ghost passes directly through your body, and you feel an icy chill invade your very core, making you feel an overwhelming sense of weakness. Your strength drains away, leaving your limbs heavy and your breath shallow. **Deduct 2 POWER** points. The room spins around you, and you struggle to remain upright, your senses reeling from the ghostly encounter. When you look up again, the ghost is gone. Turn to **331**.

400

You straighten up and meet the unyielding gaze of *Hish's* statue. "I will not convert," you say defiantly. The golden light surrounding the shrine flickers and fades, replaced by a black cloud. The voice of *Hish* reverberates in your mind, now laced with anger. "So be it, insolent one. You shall know my wrath, for vengeance is mine! Let this be a reminder that you are following the wrong god home, you feeble worm!"

Suddenly, a searing pain courses through your body, your muscles convulsing. You struggle to stay on your feet from the overwhelming assault. **Deduct 5 LIFE** and reduce your existing **MANA by half** (round-down).
If you are still alive, you wish that you can desecrate the altar, but its sheer power overcome you. You have to leave this place in dread. Record codeword **HISH** and leave this place immediately. Turn to **122**.

401

After you drop the liquid, you see the eye of the *Homunculus*, blinking at you, as if confused by what you are doing. If you want to try other potion on the *Homunculus*, turn to **257**. If you are done with it and want to leave, turn to **29**.

402

As you touch the lever, you notice the skeleton suddenly stood up, and appears animated. However, with the spell in effect, it keeps a distance away from you. Sensing no danger, you go ahead and pull the lever (turn to **286**).

403

You are in a black stone-walled corridor, leading north and south, with a path to the west. There's a turn at the south end of the corridor, veering towards east. Do you want to follow the turn and head east from here (turn to **474**), head into the western path (turn to **160**), or head north (turn to **541**)?

404

If you have codeword **POISON** and have passed by here for the first time, you will **deduct 1 count.**

You find yourself at a north-eastern corner of the dungeon. The walls are hewn roughly from dark stone. It veers into a turn, but there's a small opening that leads up north. Do you wish to turn south (turn to **571**), turn west (turn to **541**), or enter the small opening to the north (turn to **592**)?

405

How do you even cast this spell? Cheaters must die. Your quest ends here.

406

Nothing happens at the shrine, so you decide to leave the shrine and return to the river confluence. Turn to **243**.

407

A route opens up along the east-west tunnel, leading to the south. Do you want to head west (turn to **485**), east (turn to **313**) or south (turn to **346**)?

408

You decline *Kanwulf's* invitation, shaking your head slightly. "I appreciate the offer," you say cautiously, "but I must continue on my way." You briefly turn over to look at *Kanwulf* from over your shoulder and you seem to catch him seething in rage. "You refuse?" he asks, his voice low and dangerous. "In my own quarters, you refuse? This is an affront, a blatant disrespect. Let's teach this person a lesson." Soon, you see the rest of Kanwulf's crew advancing from their positions, with weapons brandished and ready for a confrontation. You're surrounded, and likely outnumbered. Turn to **544**.

409

You appear in a room, painted entirely in jet-black, and as soon as your legs land on a plate on the floor, it triggers an emission of toxic fume! **Deduct 5 LIFE** points. If you are still alive, read on.

Within this room are three teleporters, placed in different directions. Do you take the one to the north (turn to **511**, to the east (turn to **434**), or to the west (turn to **64**)?

Shugrag- The Foul Bird

410

You step into a dirty, messy room, the stench of decay assaulting your senses. The floor is littered with bones and skulls, some cracked open and gnawed, others whole but yellowed with age. The room feels very much like a charnel house, every inch of it reeking of death and neglect, and you think that you might be able to find some reagents here for spellcasting.

However, you soon notice that at a corner of the room, perches a vulture-like creature on a mound of dirt. Its feathers are mangy and mottled, a sickly blend of black and filth. The creature's eyes, dark and beady, lock onto you with an unsettling intensity. This is no ordinary scavenger. This is a *Shugrag*, a notorious foul bird known to feast and defile the dead. Its beak, sharp and curved like a cruel hook, snaps open and shut as it regards you, a low, guttural growl emanating from its throat. It is perhaps drawn to the *Necropolis* by the prospect of many dead things to feast on, but this time, the *Shugrag* seems hungry, obviously running out of dead meat and would gladly welcome a fresh supply, with its gaze fixed on you with a predatory gleam. The *Shugrag* moves 2 squares in a turn, and will begin the turn.

Shugrag	
Life	9
Offence (Melee)	8
Defence	4

Shugrag's Probability Table

Outcomes	Missed Hit	Exact Hit	Missed Hit	Exact Hit	Reduced Hit	Critical Hit
Dice Number	1	4	3	2	5	6

If you win the battle, **gain 20 Exp points** and turn to **324**.

411

You are at row one of the tombs, on the eastern side, and in a junction where you can travel in all directions. The sarcophagi are situated in the walls along east and west. Do you want to go north (turn to **79**), south (turn to **315**), east (turn to **553**), or west (turn to **486**)?

Zathar- The Great Wizard

412

"I see that we have a hero here, questing for the great justice," acknowledges the spirit. "I am *Zathar*, whom many referred to as *The Great Wizard* the spirit intones, his voice echoing with a regal resonance. "In my time, I served the *Regii* as Preceptor, charged with procuring the *Æther* and devising mechanisms for all the *Regii* to access it in their afterlife, here in their ancestral catacombs- *The Necropolis*. Our preparations were for *The Reckoning*, a prophesy foretelling our downfall at the hands of a *Master of the Dark Arts*."

His spectral form shifts slightly, his expression growing more solemn. "I served *Caduccus*, the last of the *Regii*. However, *Mortis*, the malevolent lich from the north, infiltrated *Krator* with his agents. One such agent poisoned me, leading to my demise and leaving *Caduccus* vulnerable. With my death, the secrets of the *Æther* were lost. He was then slain by the *Tungas* during the *Battle of Permafrost* and because he left no heir, the bloodline and influence of the *Regii* was also lost. With all the *Regii* terminated and sealed in their tombs, no one knows how to prepare them for the prophecy and what becomes of the *Æther*. Soon, *Krator* fell to ruin, and the expanding desert sands engulfed what remained of it."

Zathar's eyes bore into yours. "Until the arrival of *Mortis*. He understood the power of the *Æther* and sought to use it for himself, as well as to create his own power base and army; an army of darkness wait for world domination. *Mortis* now resides deep within the *Tombs of the Regii*, where the thirteen *Regii* are interred. You must enter the *Tombs*, resurrect the *Regii*, and defeat *Mortis*. Only then can you break the prophecy that foretells the end of their reign, as well as the devastation that will be unleashed on *Thorns* during the *Reckoning*."

He pauses, allowing the gravity of his words to sink in. "Be told, that the gate to the *Tombs of the Regii* is guarded by a giant pentagram. It can only be accessed by gathering the five artifacts, and solving the *Riddle of Transmutation*. Let me give you the solution to the riddle.

Remember, this sequence: **the Spirit binds the Earth, and they obliterate the Water. The remnant binds the Air, and they obliterate the Fire. The remnant finally binds the Spirit, and thus the Great Pentagram is transmuted. When Spirit binds the Earth, it is 32, then the obliteration of Water must result in 29.** "I have here one of the artifact. You have to acquire the other four, though I know not where the rest of them lie.." says *Zathar* before he passes you an interesting stone, with etching on it.

If you want this item, **add the △ Stone with an associated number 22** to your inventory. "I have a formula to a spell that I will share with you. It is "*Zilaq Fimus*" in *Xenochian* and I want you to cast it in the room where the thirteen *Regii* are resting. They are interred in open sarcophagi."

"This will resurrect them only so slightly, but they will be too weak to carry out any attack on *Mortis*. I want you to lead them into the *Repository* where the *Æther* is stored. This will render them powerful enough to confront and defeat *Mortis*. Here is the formula." You might want to **take note of this new spell**.

Spell	Function	Reagents Used	Mana Cost	Add to Section
Zilaq Fimus	Resurrect the *Regii* at their open coffins.	1x *Bones* 1x *Ghost Caps* 1x *Nightshade* 1x *Charnel Ash* 1x *Grimwood Bark* 1x *Ectoplasm*	8	78

"Last but not least, please take this Ivory Staff. You need a good weapon to deal with the challenges ahead," stresses the wizard as he presents an item to you. If you want, **add Ivory Staff (Dmg: +5, Gp: 20)** to the inventory. "The fate of the *Regii* and the future of *Krator* rest upon your shoulders, hero, and good luck!" With a smile, the apparition dissipates into the air. **Add 80 Exp points**. Record the codeword **MAGUS**. Having completed your dealings with *The Great Wizard*, you should take leave and return to the waters. Turn to **282**.

413

You are at the northern side of the tombs, with paths leading east and west. If you want to go east, turn to **368**. If you prefer to go west instead, turn to **334**.

414

Between you is a decorated wall to the south with a large symbol of *Knem* and a wall at the north that recedes into an alcove, which houses an open sarcophagus made of the finest mahogany wood. This sarcophagus must have belonged to one of the deceased *Regii*. However, you realize the sarcophagus is empty! The body of the *Regii* seems to have been removed. There's nothing you can do here, except to move on towards east (turn to **294**) or west (turn to **580**).

415

The statue on the pedestal is set on a rotator, which can be rotated left and right, and this may trigger some hidden mechanism and activate something. Do you wish to rotate the statue left (turn to **343**), right (turn to **261**), or abort the attempt and turn back towards the eastern tunnel instead (turn to **115**)?

416

As *Mortis* begins to summon his skeletal legion, a deafening voice suddenly echoes through the corridor outside the throne room. The air seems to tremble with the sheer power of the words, and the skeletons, who were poised to charge at *Mortis'* command, suddenly halt. They stand motionless, as if frozen in time, their empty eye sockets turning towards the source of the voice.

You strain to see what is happening and catch sight of a grotesque figure emerging from the shadows of the corridor. It is the *Abomination of the Regii*, the fused remains of countless kings, their bodies grotesquely amalgamated into a single, horrifying form. You realize what had happened- the skeletons and pieces of them, which you had previously resurrected, had made their way to a source of *Æther*, which fused their bones, and grew their fleshly mass. The *Abomination* steps forward, its voice resonating with an unholy authority as it addresses the skeletons.

"We are the *Regii*, true *Kings of Krator*, and we have returned for *The Reckoning- Final Battles* in the *End of Times* !" the *Abomination* bellows, its many voices blending into a single, fearsome roar. "We have returned to reclaim my throne, and I command you, my faithful subjects to turn against this false king and usurper, this pretender to the throne known as *Mortis*!" The skeletons seem to stir, their weapons lowering as they listen intently to the abomination's proclamation. For a moment, the air is thick with tension, the skeletal army teetering on the brink of rebellion.

Sensing an opportunity, you quietly back away from the throne room, slipping into the northern path. Your heart races as you hope the skeletons will indeed mutiny against *Mortis*, buying you precious time to escape.

Behind you, *Mortis's* voice rises in anger and disbelief. "No! You will obey me!" he shouts, his tone laced with desperation. He descends from his throne, trying to reassert control over his undead minions. But the tide has turned. The skeletons, once under his command, now begin to stir, their attention focused entirely on the abomination. Without warning, a deafening clatter erupts as the skeletons rush into the throne room, their weapons raised not against you, but against *Mortis*. The air fills with the sounds of battle, bones clashing against bones, as the undead legion turns on its former master.

You continue down the northern path, not daring to look back. But as you flee, a piercing, blood-curdling shriek echoes through the cavern, sending a shiver down your spine. It is the sound of *Mortis*, caught in the midst of his downfall, his reign of terror crumbling as the very forces he commanded turn against him. **Add 100 Exp points** and turn to **570**.

417

Do you have the codeword ZENGIS? If you do, turn to **48** immediately. Otherwise, turn to **203**.

418

You are at row one of the tombs, with walls to the east. You can head north, west and south. Do you want to go north (turn to **447**), go south (turn to **529**) or go west (turn to **553**)?

419

You are at the northern side of the tombs, with paths leading east and west. If you want to go east, turn to **380**. If you prefer to go west instead, turn to **368**.

420

How do you even cast this spell? Cheaters must die. Your quest ends here.

421

Your help has restored a small amount of health for *Sir Elandor*, but he is grateful. "I must thank you for your assistance NECROMANCER. But I am still mortally wounded. If you can come back with the antidote and additional means of healing, I will be truly appreciative. I shall wait for your return."

Record the codework **KRECK**. **Write POISON and record 4 counts** in your notes. Do return here when you have found the antidote, or when you have more healing potions/rations to spare. Turn to **93**.

422

You hand the stone over to the *Demonomancer*. He snatches it from your grasp, his fingers curling around it tightly. A dark, triumphant laugh erupts from him, echoing through the chamber like a sinister wind. "I cannot believe my luck," he hisses, his eyes gleaming with malicious glee. He steps back, holding the stone up as if admiring his prize. Then, without warning, his gaze snaps back to you, and his expression twists into a sneer.

"Go to hell, fool," he snarls, raising his hand as it crackles with fiery energy.

Before you can react, a blazing fireball erupts from his palm, hurtling toward you with deadly speed. You feel the searing heat as it slams into you, sending you reeling backward. **Roll a dice**. This number will be the damage. **Minus** accordingly from your **LIFE score**. If you are still alive, read on.

The *Demonomancer* vanishes, leaving only the echo of his laughter behind. You lie on the ground, the acrid scent of scorched air filling your nostrils, as you realize he has teleported away, taking the stone—and your trust—with him. Record the codeword **DEMONOS**.

After you got up, you realize that this path leads to a dead-end, and decide to return to the junction. Turn to **403**.

423

With all your strength, you deliver a heavy kick on the head of the *Nyx*, and watches it wince in pain before it dives back into the depths of the river. Your skiff has stabilized, and you need to quickly decide your next move. Turn to **138**.

424

You ran down the eastern passage until you arrive at an area where there is a path opening to your left, leading northward. Do you want to continue east (turn to **75**) or turn left towards north (turn to **97**)?

425

You return to *Ornias'* chamber, only to find it completely cleaned out, devoid of any sign of its former occupant. The once cluttered space now feels eerily empty, with nothing remaining of the goblin trader's belongings, decorations and fixtures. While you are aware that the goblin met his end earlier at the *Huntsman's* lair, you are perplexed to find that all remnants of his former presence had mysteriously vanished along with his passing. There's nothing else for you to do here. Turn to **135**.

426

You heave a sigh of relief as you manage to extricate yourself from the rapids and make your way to the shore. The cavern around you is filled with jagged, rugged rocks, forming a treacherous path that requires careful climbing. Despite the challenge, you navigate through the rocky terrain, each step a cautious effort to avoid slipping. From a distance, you spot a grave, an intriguing sight amidst the stark surroundings. Do you want to investigate the grave (turn to **58**), or do you want to return to the river, to retreat to a safer area away from the rapids (turn to **378**)?

427

You dash westward towards the north-south corridor. As soon as you reach the corridor, you see a massive net falling onto you, sprung from a figure that is standing just right before you on the left, to the south. The coarse ropes tangle around you, pulling tight and knocking you to the ground. Panic floods your senses as you struggle against the net, but your movements only seem to make it tighter.

Your eyes widen in horror as you spot this figure, advancing slowly towards you, his slim built, black skin and an unholy looking spear in his hand looking menacing as it casts a silhouette against the dim lights. You have no doubt— this must be the legendary *Huntsman*. Without a word, the figure hurls the spear at you with deadly precision, aiming at your heart. The spear closes in, and you only feel an instantaneous piercing pain before your consciousness fades. You are immediately killed by a weapon what many referred to as a 'Godkiller'- *The Spear of Signonul*. Your quest ends here.

428

You will attempt to use brute strength on the wooden door, which may succumb to your power. Take your **OFFENCE (MELEE)**, **roll a dice** and **add up the total number**. If the number **is more than 15**, you have successfully broken into the room (turn to **275**). Otherwise, you fail to break open the door and shall abort this attempt (turn to **303**).

429

You dash southward, towards the *Huntsman* to engage in combat with it. Before you can hit the opponent with your weapon, you see the figure unfurling a massive net towards you, which is to ensnare you on the spot. The coarse ropes tangle around you, pulling tight and knocking you to the ground. Panic floods your senses as you struggle against the net, but your movements only seem to make it tighter.

Your eyes widen in horror as you spot this figure, advancing slowly towards you, his slim built, black skin and an unholy looking spear in his hand looking menacing as it casts a silhouette against the dim lights. You have no doubt— this must be the legendary *Huntsman*. Without a word, the figure hurls the spear at you with deadly precision, aiming at your heart. The spear closes in, and you only feel an instantaneous piercing pain before your consciousness fades. You are immediately killed by a weapon what many referred to as a 'Godkiller'- *The Spear of Signonul*. Your quest ends here.

430

Do you have THIEVERY skill? If you do, turn to **373**. Otherwise turn to **300**.

431

As you cautiously make your way around the black pool, you keep a wary eye on the figures within, their pallid forms shifting beneath the surface. The bubbling water hisses quietly, the air thick with an unsettling tension. Soon, you reach a shadowy corner.

But then, you notice something that makes your heart skip a beat- the figures in the pool have turned their attention towards you. Their smiles have vanished, replaced by a predatory hunger. One by one, they begin to swim in your direction, their movements disturbingly fast. Panic seizes you, and you turn on your heel, but you realize you are quite far away from the open path that led you to the pool. Before you can reach the path, cold, slimy hands grab hold of you. You struggle, but the slime spreads rapidly across your skin, its corrosive touch burning through your flesh. The pain is excruciating, your screams echoing in the chamber, but they are swallowed by the darkness as the black slime consumes you entirely.

In those final moments, as your body melts away, you realize the horrifying truth- the black slime pool are remnants of others who, like you, once lived and breathed. Now, you join them, your form dissolving into the slime, which will nourish the ghouls that fed on and bathed in them. Your quest ends here.

432

How do you even cast this spell? Cheaters must die. Your quest ends here.

433

You are at the southern side of the tombs, with paths leading east and west. If you want to go east, turn to **315**. If you prefer to go west instead, turn to **248**.

434

You appear in a room, painted entirely in jet-black. Within this room are three teleporters, placed in different directions. Do you take the one to the north (turn to **582**), to the east (turn to **352**), or to the west (turn to **409**)?

435

You bow before the statue of *Barat* and feel an immense surge of strength coursing through your veins. By the blessings of your Patron Deity, you are healed. Restore your **LIFE** and **POWER** to their maximum values. When you are done, you leave the shrine. Turn to **240**.

436

You are at row one of the tombs, on the western side, and in a junction where you can travel in all directions. The sarcophagi are situated in the walls along east and west. Do you want to go north (turn to **374**), south (turn to **226**), east (turn to **80**), or west (turn to **256**)?

437

Shelves line up on both sides of the walls, alongside a corridor that leads north and south. Amongst the books, a black book stands out, with the title "*Umas Fimus*" written in *Xenochian* scripts. Do you want to read this book (turn to **23**), or head either north (turn to **521**) or south (turn to **284**)?

438

First, check if you have the codeword OBFUS? If you do, turn to **585** immediately. If you do not have the former, but you have the codework ALEX, turn to **302**. If you do not have all the codewords, turn to **185**.

439

You are at row two of the tombs, on the central side, and in a junction where you can travel in all directions. The sarcophagi are situated in the walls along east and west. Do you want to go north (turn to **494**), south (turn to **525**), east (turn to **312**), or west (turn to **546**)?

440

The tunnel continues for a while before veering sharply to the left, which you think is now heading northward. Turn to **7**.

441

You are between walls, with paths leading north and south. Do you want to go north (turn to **380**), or south (turn to **538**)?

442

If you have codeword **POISON** and have passed by here for the first time, you will **deduct 1 count.**

You are at the north-western corner of the dungeon. The walls are hewn roughly from dark stone. Do you want to head east (turn to **503**) or head south (turn to **197**)?

443

"*Kolgrim*," you say, your voice calm and disarming, "I mean no harm. I'm merely seeking passage and perhaps a word with *Kanwulf*." You see the tension in his stance begin to ease as your words wash over him like a melody. His face softens, as if a fog has clouded his mind, and he nods slowly. "Very well," he murmurs, his voice losing its edge. "If you're truly here in peace, I suppose there's no harm in letting you through."

He turns and gestures for you to follow him. "This way," he says, his tone almost deferential. You trail behind him as he leads you into the quarters, the air thick with the scent of smoke and sweat. As you pass by the brigands lounging in the dimly lit quarters, they barely give you a second glance, their attention still fixed on their own affairs. "Go to that room at the eastern end," he instructs, pointing down the dimly lit hallway. "*Kanwulf* stays there. But be careful—he's not as easily swayed as I am." With a final nod, he steps aside, allowing you to proceed, his eyes now dull, as if your words have clouded his judgment entirely. Turn to **530**.

444

You are at row three of the tombs, on the eastern side, and in a junction where you can travel in all directions. The sarcophagi are situated in the walls along east and west. Do you want to go north (turn to **365**), south (turn to **377**), east (turn to **455**), or west (turn to **258**)?

445

With a creak of ancient bones, the skeleton becomes reanimated and stood up, assuming a battle stance. You must fight this undead steward to the death. You will begin the turn.

Skeleton	
Life	5
Offence (Melee)	7
Defence	2

Skeleton's Probability Table

Outcomes	Missed Hit	Exact Hit	Missed Hit	Missed Hit	Reduced Hit	Critical Hit
Dice Number	1	5	4	3	2	6

If you win the battle, **gain 10 Exp points** and turn to **314**.

446

You reach the north-eastern corner of the lair, which veers sharply to the left, towards west. Since you are avoiding the *Huntsman*, you cannot turn back, except to press on forward, which is to move west from here. Turn to **589**.

447

You are at the eastern side of the tombs, with paths leading north and south. Do you want to go north (turn to **505**), or south (turn to **418**)?

448

You run down north towards the corridor where *Ornias* is situated and his smirking presence is overshadowed by what seems to be an inactive portal behind him, its surface dark and dormant. The *Huntsman's* relentless approach from the south sends chills down your spine as his footsteps grow louder. Your mind races with options.

Do you want to attack *Ornias*? If you want to do so, turn to (turn to **244**). You can also choose to run past *Ornias* towards the portal (turn to **219**), or you can choose to turn back and prepare to make a stand against the Huntsman (turn to **310**).

449

You hone in at *Grobb* and intuit that he is honest and may be of great help. If you have the Black Key right now, **remove the Black Key** from the inventory and turn to **163**. Otherwise, you may have to try to pick open the lock (turn to **366**). You can also leave this area, maybe coming back here later when you get the right key (record codeword **HOBBS** and turn to **243**), or if you feel like doing so, try to kill *Grobb* (turn to **551**)!

450

Do you have the codeword ZENGIS? If you do, turn to **389**. Otherwise turn to **587**.

451

You bow before the statue of *Ked* and feel an invisible hand caressing your body, anticipating a blessing by your patron deity. But all of a sudden, you feel a tug of something from deep within you… the invisible hand of *Ked* had removed a skill she used to bestow upon you! *Ked's* voice softens to a whisper, yet her words cut deeper than ever. "You've hardly put this skill to good use," she hisses, the sound almost scraping your mind. "And you no longer shall deserve it. I find you utterly devoid of attraction now, a shadow of what you once were. I regret being your patron, NECROMANCER, for I think your kind is quite repugnant. You shall not come to me anymore, for you are now excommunicated from my patronage!"

Remove CHARM from your skills, and **remove Ked** from Deity in the characters sheet. Confounded and astonished, you hastily leave the shrine, while cursing the fickle-minded Harlot under your breath, retreating back to the river. Turn to **243**.

452

You ready yourself for the impending battle. The *Demonomancer*, sensing your determination, throws back his head and laughs, the sound echoing ominously through the corridor. "Prepare to die!" he sneers. Without giving you a moment to react, he conjures a blazing fireball, hurling it straight at you. The scorching heat sears the air as it streaks toward you. **Roll a dice**. This number will be the damage. **Minus** accordingly from your **LIFE score**. If you are still alive, read on.

But he doesn't stop there. As you regain your footing, you notice his lips moving in a rapid, dark incantation. The ground beneath the pentagram on the floor begins to tremble, a low rumble filling the air. Suddenly, the symbols on the pentagram glow with an eerie red light, and the space within it distorts and writhes as if reality itself is being torn apart.

From the centre of the pentagram, a swirling vortex of eldritch energy emerges, and with a burst of flames, a demon materializes. Its twisted form towers over you, with leathery wings, burning eyes, and claws that gleam like sharpened steel. The creature snarls, the air around it crackling with dark energy as it steps forward, eager to obey its master's command. "Behold *Xaphan!*" exclaimed the *Demonomancer*. "Now, let's see how long you last against both of us," he hisses, as the demon lunges towards you, ready to tear you apart. *Xaphan* will begin the turn.

Xaphan (A)		Demonomancer (B)	
Life	18	Life	15
Offence (Melee)	15	Offence (Melee)	10
Defence	8	Offence (Range)	15
		Defence	10
		Radius	2

Xaphan (A)'s Probability Table

Outcomes	Exact Hit	Exact Hit	Exact Hit	Exact Hit	Reduced Hit	Critical Hit
Dice Number	5	6	3	2	1	4

Demonomancer (B)'s Probability Table

Outcomes	Missed Hit	Critical Hit	Exact Hit	Exact Hit	Reduced Hit	Critical Hit
Dice Number	4	5	6	3	2	1

If you win the battle, **gain 20 Exp points** and turn to **321**.

453

You are at the south-western corner of the tombs, with paths leading north and east. If you want to go north, turn to **393**. If you prefer to go east instead, turn to **559**.

454

You take a deep breath and decide to be forthright. "I am here for the *Æther*," you declare. The ghostly form of the *Great Wizard* stiffens, his eyes flashing with anger. "The *Æther*?" he hisses, his voice rising. "You dare seek the sacred *Æther* for yourself? Begone, you insolent wretch!"

Before you can utter another word, the *Great Wizard's* form shimmers violently and with a resounding poof, he vanishes into thin air, leaving you alone in the eerie silence of the cavern. You know you may not be able to invoke the spirit of the *Great Wizard* again. There's nothing more you can do here, and you might as well retreat back to the river. Turn to **282**.

455

Between you is a decorated wall to the south with a large symbol of *Karkinos* and a wall at the north that recedes into an alcove, which houses an open sarcophagus made of the finest mahogany wood. This sarcophagus must have belonged to one of the deceased *Regii*. However, you realize the sarcophagus is empty! The body of the *Regii* seems to have been removed. There's nothing you can do here, except to move on towards east (turn to **526**) or west (turn to **444**).

456

You insert the silver key into the lock, feeling a slight resistance before it clicks. **Gain 10 Exp points**. **Remove Silver Key** from the inventory. As the door swings open, an ominous darkness greets you, and a rush of cold air envelops you, sending shivers down your spine. The chill seeps into your bones, and the oppressive blackness beyond the threshold seems to pulse with a silent, foreboding presence. You stand there, momentarily hesitating, as the icy air continues to swirl around you, whispering forsaken warnings of impending horror. Turn to **354**.

457

Shelves line up on both sides of the walls, alongside a corridor that leads east and west. Amongst the books, a blue book stands out, with the title "*The Xenochian Dictionary*". Do you want to read this book (turn to **326**), or head either east (turn to **586**) or west (turn to **338**)?

458

Do you have codeword GHAST? If you do, there's no reason for you to explore here further- turn to **554**. Otherwise read on.

As you tread down the western path, you suddenly hear the frantic sound of footsteps echoing off the stone walls. Out of the shadows, a man stumbles towards you, his movements erratic and desperate. His face and hands are coated with a thick, glistening black slime, the substance oozing from his skin in grotesque rivulets.

Before you can react, the man collapses at your feet with a heavy thud, his body sprawled out lifelessly. You step back, horrified, as you watch his face begin to melt away, the features dissolving into a formless mass of black goo. The sight is nightmarish, and the air fills with a sickly, acrid stench. Despite the gruesome scene, something catches your eye—a black key dangling from the man's belt. It's a stark contrast to the decaying flesh around it, still intact and strangely clean.

Do you want to take the black key? If you want to do so, turn to **577**. He might have some valuable belongings on this body. If you want to search his body, turn to **206**. Otherwise you can ignore him and continue your journey, turn to **72** if you want to continue west. If you want to return east, turn to **229**.

459

You are at a junction- a passage to the south emanates with a faint, dark, blue glow, while both directions east and west are continuation of the main tunnel. Do you wish to head towards south where that faint light is (turn to **200**), head east (turn to **588**) or head west (turn to **503**)?

460

Not entirely convinced, the paladin ask you about your business here and why you want to trespass his privacy by opening the door. You try your best to convince him that you are here for the quest of the *Æther* and that you are merely curious in exploring this part of the dungeon to see what goes on over the other side of the door. You see the paladin soften his glance and relax his broken sword, as he struggle to sit back down on the floor. Turn to **283**.

461

You see *Grobb* ecstatically hurry to the shoreline, pleased with his newfound freedom. Just before he jumps into the river, he waves at you and shouts, "Thank you once again for the help!" After that a splash, and he is gone. He seems to be a pretty good swimmer. Record codeword **COBB**. There's nothing more for you to do here, and you shall also leave this place. Turn to **243**.

462

The southerly passage eventually lead into an alcove, and you are immediately captivated by a stunning painting of a white serpent hung on the wall. This painting exudes an air of ancient regal. You're reminded that *Sir Elandor* had mentioned before, about a skiff hidden in this room, and the details on how to find it. Take the **associated number of ZENGIS**, and **subtract it from the number of this section** to get a **new number**. Then **turn to that section** corresponding with this number. If you're not sure how to do this, you have no choice but to leave this place (turn to **407**).

463

Deciding to explore the room further, you meticulously scan every corner, your eyes adjusting to the dim light. Amidst the scattered debris, you notice a small pouch tucked away in a shadowy nook. Picking it up, you open it to reveal ten gold pieces, their dull gleam a stark contrast to the room's gloomy atmosphere. **Add 10 Gold pieces**. The unexpected discovery brings a brief moment of satisfaction. Noting nothing else of value in the room, you shall leave it and continue your journey. Turn to **508**.

464

Just as you are about to go through the lair to figure a passage of exit, you are surprised to see the once-inactive portal starts pulsing with purple light snaking around its edges, crackling with arcane power. The centre of the portal swirls with a deep, mesmerizing violet, almost like liquid amethyst. You figure this sudden activation must have been triggered by the death of *Ornias* or perhaps the mere presence of the *Huntsman*. Either way, the portal now stands as your escape from the *Huntsman's Lair*. Without a second thought, you step towards the teleporter. Turn to **404**.

The Huntsman- A Formidable Opponent

465

You decline *Ornias'* offer. The goblin shrugs, a sly grin playing on his lips. "Nevermind," he says nonchalantly, "you can come back to me later if you change your mind." His eyes gleam with a knowing look as he turns back to his wares, leaving you with a lingering sense of unease. There's nothing much else for you to do here and you decide to take leave. Turn to **195**.

466

As you attempt to sweet-talk *Ornias*, your words dripping with honeyed persuasion, his expression remains unchanged. He tilts his head slightly, an eyebrow raising in scepticism. When you finish, he leans in, his eyes narrowing. "Cut this nonsense, you glib-tongued disciple of the Harlot," he snaps, his voice devoid of any amusement. "I've dealt with enough smooth talkers to last a lifetime. And quite honestly speaking, a NECROMANCER can never be too charming. If you want something, you'd better be prepared to pay for it, not try to cheat me with your fancy words." Do you wish to review the items he was offering again (turn to **383**), or decide to move on (turn to **250**)?

467

The *Huntsman*, a slim yet imposing figure, calmly pulls the bloodied spear from *Ornias'* lifeless body with a sickening squelch. He stares intently at you, his eyes glow a menacing amber, piercing through the shadows that cling to his pitch-black skin. His lithe, athletic frame radiates a predatory grace, muscles rippling beneath his dark, sinewy flesh. As he steps closer, the air grows heavier, the tension thick and suffocating. His fangs glint in the dim light, and a twisted smile curls at the corners of his lips, revealing the true savagery that lies beneath his calm exterior. This is a very dangerous opponent- take heed. The *Huntsman* moves 2 squares in a turn. You will begin the turn.

Huntsman	
Life	20
Offence (Melee)	35
Defence	10

Huntsman's Probability Table

Outcomes	Exact Hit	Exact Hit	Exact Hit	Critical Hit	Critical Hit	Critical Hit
Dice Number	1	5	2	5	3	6

If you win the battle, **gain 50 Exp points** and turn to **223**.

468

You return to the north-eastern corner of the lair, which veers sharply to the right towards south, changing your course southward. Turn to **308**.

469

The stench of rat-droppings become stronger the further south you venture. The oppressive silence is gradually broken by an unsettling sound — chattering, faint at first but growing louder as you advance. The noise echoes off the tunnel walls, a cacophony of high-pitched squeaks and guttural clicks that set your teeth on edge. Turn to **333**.

470

Record codeword **VORNH** and turn to **122**.

471

Kolgrim's expression shifts as you confidently answer his question. His smirk fades, replaced by a look of grudging respect. For a moment, he's silent, studying you with narrowed eyes, as if weighing your worth. Finally, he nods, a slow, deliberate movement. "Well, well. Looks like you're not just some fool wandering in here." His voice lacks the mockery it held before, now tinged with a hint of approval. "Alright, follow me." *Kolgrim* turns on his heel, and you trail behind him as he leads you into the quarters, the air thick with the scent of smoke and sweat. As you pass by the brigands lounging in the dimly lit quarters, they barely give you a second glance, their attention still fixed on their own affairs.

"*Kanwulf's* room is all the way to the end on the eastern end," *Kolgrim* says as you approach a large wooden door at the end of the corridor. "Frow now on, behave yourself." Turn to **530**.

472

You are at the western side of the tombs, with paths leading north and south. Do you want to go north (turn to **563**), or south (turn to **580**)?

473

You arrive at an area where an embankment to the east forms a shoreline, along the north-south channel you are currently in. Do you wish to head east towards the shoreline (**533**), head north (turn to **298**) or head south (turn to **596**)?

474

You are in a corridor, with black stone hewn walls. There's a turn at the west end of the corridor, veering towards north. Do you want to follow the turn and head up north from here (turn to **403**), or head east (turn to **247**)?

475

Do you have either codeword HISH or PROSE? If you do, you had already visited here before, and shall turn to **122**. Otherwise read on.

You step into an alcove, and is immediately greeted by a warm golden light that seems to emanate from the very walls. The floor is inlaid with intricate mosaics of thunder and lightning. Within this space, a statue stands sentinel in the centre, and you quickly realize you have entered the shrine of *Hish*, the Wise One, the wizened Grand Benefic. The statue of *Hish* is crafted from radiant gold, depicting the god in majestic robes that seem to ripple with life. His eyes, set with precious gems, exude an aura of wisdom and power, watching over all who enter, and he might literally be watching you. While this deity is just and kind, he tends to behave otherwise towards his enemies.

If you are a follower of *Hish*, turn to **398**. If you follow *Barat* turn to **341**. If you pledged allegiance to other deities, turn to **210**. If you do not have a deity, turn to **512**.

476

Before you lies the dead paladin, finally at rest. A finely crafted plate armour adorns the body of *Sir Elandor*. If you want to take this armour, **add Plate Mail of Solaris (Shd: +6, Gp: 50)** to your inventory. A pouch of gold also lies in a pocket. **Add 30 Gold pieces**. You are however not so keen on his broken long-sword.

Also, if you are depraved enough, you might not want a body to go to waste. You may choose to defile the corpse to get some bones for your necromantic spellcasting. If you want to do that, turn to **276**. Otherwise you leave the this poor soul to rest and turn to **93**.

477

Sensing *Grobb's* hunger after being confined in the cage for so long, you offer him a ration. He devours it heartily, his gratitude evident. "I cannot thank you enough!" he exclaims between bites. "You are very kind, and for that, I must share more vital information with you." He pauses to catch his breath, then continues, "*Mortis* the Great Lich has become god-like and cannot be slain by ordinary weapons, and likewise, he wields tremendous power that can easily slay any contender.

There are two items that are crucial in your fight against him. First, there is the *Spear of Signonul*, a god-killer weapon. It is located in the north-eastern part of the *Inner Chambers*, within the lair of the *Huntsman*, who is a formidable enemy. Second, there is the *Draco*, a dragon armour. Unfortunately, its location is lost, but rumours suggest that hints about it can be found within the pages in the *Library*." After you take note of above, turn to **461**.

478

A tongue hangs out from the mouth on the gate, now still and silent. The once vigilant '*Librarian*' guarding the gate is dead, possibly tied to the death of the *Homunculus*, which may be a living extension of its self. With a shove on the gate, it swings open effortlessly. Turn to **201**.

479

Are you on a skiff? If you are, turn to **370**. Otherwise, turn to **277**.

480

Before the *Demonomancer* could unleash his fireball, you quickly calm him down with a soft voice, your words laced with hypnotic manipulation. His eyes, once filled with malicious intent, begin to glaze over, and his stance relaxes, the fiery glow in his hand dimming.

A dazed expression spreads across his face as he blinks slowly, seeming confused. "I'm... I'm sorry," he mumbles, his voice softened. "I didn't mean to frighten you. That was... unkind of me."

He looks around, as if trying to make sense of what just happened, then reaches into his robes. "As a gesture of goodwill," he continues, his tone now strangely apologetic, "please accept this." From the folds of his crimson cloak, he produces a small, glass bottle filled with a pale liquid. "I... I took this from some brigands I encountered, led by *Kanwulf*. It's an antidote. Should you find yourself poisoned, this will help. I... hope it can be of use to you."

He hands the bottle to you, his fingers trembling slightly as they release it into your grasp. Then, still in a trance-like state, he steps back, awaiting your next move. If you want this item, **add Antidote** to your inventory. You **gain 20 Exp points**. Record the codeword **DEMONOS**. You decide to leave the *Demonomancer* now, before he comes back to his senses. Turn to **403**.

481

As you move into this area of the river, you sense that the speed of the river is increasing, and seems to flow westward. The meander curves the river, and you can choose to either head south (turn to **150**), towards stiller waters, or westward, where the water is flowing towards (turn to **590**).

482

The labyrinthine tunnel stretches for a significant distance west before you come across an L-junction with a path to your left. There seems to be a faint greenish light emanating from that direction. Do you continue west (turn to **22**), or do you turn left towards the diversion where the light is (turn to **317**)?

483

"You're back!" *Grobb* exclaims, his voice echoing off the cavern walls. He rattles the bars of his cage more vigorously. "I'm so glad to see you. Can you help me out of this cage now?" His voice trembles with urgency, and you can see the strain and fear etched into his features.

If you have the Black Key, **remove the Black Key** from the inventory and turn to **163**. Otherwise, you can attempt to pick open the lock (turn to **366**), leave him again (turn to **243**) or even try to kill him (turn to **551**).

484

The Rabbit's Matrix: In a world where countless religions promised salvation and eternal truth, the faithful clung to their beliefs with unwavering devotion. Each religion proclaimed to know the path to enlightenment, the way to paradise, or the secret to ultimate transcendence. To their followers, these were more than just teachings; they were the very essence of existence, a beacon of hope in a world filled with uncertainty.

Yet, unknown to the believers, these religions were like the parable of the elephant and the blind men. Each faith grasped only a fragment of the truth, offering a piece of the grand tapestry that wove the universe together. The gods, revered and worshiped by millions, were far from the benevolent guardians they appeared to be.

For those few souls who had crossed the threshold of life into the afterlife and returned, a darker, more sinister reality was revealed. These travellers, touched by death yet not fully claimed, saw the truth behind the veil: the gods were not the omnipotent beings of love and justice that their scriptures depicted. They were petty contenders, locked in an eternal battle, competing to gather as many souls as they could.

In the vast expanse of the afterlife, these gods clashed in a never-ending war, each seeking to harvest the energy of the souls that flocked to them. The prayers, sacrifices, and unwavering faith of the living were the currency of their power, the fuel that fed their divine fire. The more souls a god claimed, the stronger they became. But the truth was even darker. The souls of the faithful were not rewarded with eternal bliss; they were consumed, their essence devoured to feed the insatiable hunger of these gods. The promises of salvation were lies, mere tools to lure the living into surrendering their souls willingly.

And so, the war of the gods raged on, unseen by mortal eyes, a cosmic battle fought not for justice or salvation but for the simple, brutal hunger of power.

485

The ground beneath your feet begins to slope gently downward, hinting at a shore lying to the west. The black-stone tunnel has also curved into a gradual turn. Do you head towards the shoreline at the west (turn to **169**), head north (turn to **4**) or head east (turn to **407**)?

486

Between you is a decorated wall to the south with a large symbol of *Utrarius*, and a wall at the north that recedes into an alcove, which houses an open sarcophagus made of the finest mahogany wood. This sarcophagus must have belonged to one of the deceased *Regii*. However, you realize the sarcophagus is empty! The body of the *Regii* seems to have been removed. There's nothing you can do here, except to move on towards east (turn to **411**) or west (turn to **116**).

487

You pause, considering *Kanwulf's* offer, and finally nod. "Alright," you say, "I'll stay." A slow smile spreads across *Kanwulf's* face. "Excellent," he says, clapping his hands together. "You won't regret it." He motions for you to follow him, leading you to a seat beside the roaring fireplace. The warmth is welcoming, and the smell of roasting pork fills the air. Soon, *Kolgrim*, *Lorelei*, and *Brutus* join you, each taking a seat around the fire. *Kolgrim* settles in with a grin, while *Lorelei*, with her fox-like features, sits quietly, a sly smile playing on her lips. *Brutus*, plants himself heavily on a stool, his eyes already fixed on the food. As the meal begins, the roasted pork is served, its succulent aroma making your mouth water. The first bite is tender, juicy, and seasoned to perfection—easily the best meal you've had in days. You find yourself savouring each mouthful as the others dig in with gusto. **Add +5 to LIFE** score.

The conversation is sparse, mostly focused on tales of past exploits and *Kanwulf's* grand plans. *Brutus* occasionally throws in a hearty laugh, and even *Lorelei* joins in with a few wry comments, her eyes gleaming in the firelight. *Kolgrim* eats in silence, as if in anticipation of something. For a moment, you forget where you are, caught up in the warmth of the fire, the camaraderie and the delicious food. It's almost easy to believe you're among friends.

"How can we forget the good stuff?" exclaims *Kanwulf*. *Lorelei* nodded and retrieve several flagons, putting one of it infront of you. "Now, this is the famed *Flureic* from *Tharach*, brewed from the finest elderberries. Drink it up" said *Kanwulf*, his eyes fixed on you.

Do you want to drink the *Flureic*? If you do, turn to **211**. If you refuse to drink it, turn to **549**.

488

You rotate the statue right again, and before you could react, a stream of scorching red flame shoots out from the mouth of the dog-head towards you! **Deduct 2 LIFE** points. If you are still alive, you notice the sound of ancient mechanisms grinding to life fills the chamber, and a section of the wall beside the statue shifts. Slowly, a secret door creaks open, revealing a hidden passageway beyond. **Gain 20 Exp** points. Cool draft wafts from the darkness, beckoning you to enter the secret room. Turn to **575**.

489

As you descend the final step, the passage opens up into a vast chamber, its sheer size almost overwhelming in the encroaching darkness. The air is thick with the weight of centuries, and the silence is so profound that even your own breathing seems an intrusion. As your eyes begin to adjust, faint outlines of the chamber start to emerge. The chamber stretches out before you, its walls lined with towering sarcophagi, each adorned with intricate carvings of regal figures—kings, queens, and warriors of old, their stern visages etched in stone, watching over the tomb in eternal vigilance.

Massive pillars rise from the floor, disappearing into the shadowy heights above, and the floor beneath you is a mosaic of worn tiles, their patterns long faded but still hinting at the grandeur that once was. You are in the *Tombs of the Regii*, where these ancient kids are interred. The stillness is unsettling, as if the tomb itself is holding its breath, waiting for something—or someone—to disturb its ancient slumber.

Suddenly, your torch flickers once, then sputters out, plunging you into total darkness. Do you still have a torch? If you do, **deduct 1x Torch** from your inventory and turn to **319**. If not, turn to **233**.

Thokk the Merchant showcasing his wares

490

The door swings open into a dimly lit and well decorated chamber, and you are surprised to see a man sitting by a large table, his presence utterly incongruous in this forsaken place. He is stocky, with a rugged appearance, his face shadowed by a scruffy beard. His eyes gleam with a shrewd intelligence, and he wears a tattered tunic that once might have been fine. A makeshift stall is set up beside him, laden with various items, from weapons to potions.

"Well, well, look who we have here," he says, his voice a gravelly baritone, filled with a mix of amusement and cunning. "A NECROMANCER, no less. My name's *Thokk*. And you must be here for the *Æther*, just like all the others." You narrow your eyes, still wary of this unexpected encounter. "*Thokk*? What are you doing here, in the depths of the *Necropolis*?" Thokk chuckles, the sound echoing eerily in the chamber. "Ah, you see, I've made it my business to be where the action is. The *Necropolis* attracts all sorts—treasure hunters, fools, and the occasional ambitious NECROMANCER like you. They all need supplies, and that's where I come in."

He gestures to his makeshift stall with a flourish. "I've got wares to trade, the finest you'll find in these forsaken depths. Weapons to cut through the monsters, potions to heal your wounds, and tools that might just give you the edge you need to survive. All for a price, of course."

You step closer, inspecting the items on display. *Thokk* watches you with keen interest, his eyes never missing a detail. "Why would you risk your life down here, just to trade with adventurers?" you ask, still skeptical. *Thokk* leans back, a wry smile playing on his lips. "Risk, you say? I've seen more danger in a tavern brawl. Besides, every adventurer who passes through here leaves something behind, willingly or not. I've learned to make the most of it. And who knows, maybe one of you will actually find the *Æther* and make it out alive. If that happens, I'll be rich beyond my wildest dreams."

He spreads his hands, as if presenting his entire philosophy in one gesture. "So, what do you say, NECROMANCER? Interested in a trade? I've got everything you might need to face the horrors of the *Necropolis*."

If you wish to trade, turn to **359**. Otherwise, you can leave the room (turn to **327**).

491

You are at the north-eastern corner of the tombs, with paths leading south and west. If you want to go south, turn to **572**. If you prefer to go west instead, turn to **539**.

492

"To access the *Repository*," it whispers, its voice trembling with the weight of its last moments, "there are two identical keys. *Mortis*, the desecrator, has found one. But the Great Wizard, in his wisdom, hid the other as a safeguard."

The spirit's translucent form begins to flicker, but it continues, "This key... it lies in the sarcophagus of *Yorlak*, who bears the emblem of *Utrarius* the Water Bearer. A secret compartment... within the tomb... there it rests, the spare key." The spirit's form wavers, becoming more ethereal by the second. "Find the key... and you may yet have a chance... against *Mortis*. But hurry... my time... is at an end..." With a final, ghostly sigh, the spirit dissipates into the darkness, leaving you alone in the tombs. **Add 50 Exp points.**

When you come upon the tomb of *Yorlak*, **add 16** to the **number of the section** and the **summed number will be the new section** to access the secret compartment. Turn to **339**.

493

"Fool!" *Lorelei's* voice rings out, dripping with contempt. Her fox-like face twists into a sneer as she catches your wrist in a vice-like grip. "Did you really think you could steal from me, from us, and walk away unscathed? You forget, graveworm, that you're dealing with people who does it for a living, hardened brigands like us. And we don't take kindly to tricks."

She releases your wrist with a shove, sending you stumbling back. Her voice rises, echoing through the quarters. "We've got a thief who needs to be taught a lesson!" The heavy footsteps of the brigands fill the air, accompanied by the clatter of weapons being drawn. The curtain is flung aside, and you see *Kolgrim*, *Kanwulf*, and the rest of the crew, their faces twisted with rage and excitement at the prospect of a fight. "You should have known better," she hisses, as the brigands surround you, ready to strike. Turn to **544**.

494

You are between walls, with paths leading north and south. Do you want to go north (turn to **538**), or south (turn to **439**)?

495

The tunnel opens up into a small alcove, illuminated by a shimmering, bluish-iridescent portal, its surface rippling like liquid glass. The portal emits a soft, pulsating glow that illuminates the surrounding rocks with an ethereal light, casting long, dancing shadows. Do you wish to step through this portal (turn to **583**), or do you decide against it (turn to **394**)?

496

The very moment you return south, you see a massive net falling onto you, sprung from a figure in the proximity. The coarse ropes tangle around you, pulling tight and knocking you to the ground. Panic floods your senses as you struggle against the net, but your movements only seem to make it tighter.

Your eyes widen in horror as you spot this figure, advancing slowly towards you, his slim built, black skin and an unholy looking spear in his hand looking menacing as it casts a silhouette against the dim lights. You have no doubt—this must be the legendary *Huntsman*. Without a word, the figure hurls the spear at you with deadly precision, aiming at your heart. The spear closes in, and you only feel an instantaneous piercing pain before your consciousness fades. You are immediately killed by a weapon what many referred to as a 'Godkiller'- *The Spear of Signonul*. Your quest ends here.

497

You are at row three of the tombs, on the western side, and in a junction where you can travel in all directions. The sarcophagi are situated in the walls along east and west. Do you want to go north (turn to **578**), south (turn to **386**), east (turn to **384**), or west (turn to **267**)?

498

You hesitate for a moment, then shake your head. "I can't afford it," you admit, trying to keep your voice steady.

Brutal Brutus' eyes narrow with disdain. "Can't afford it?" he sneers, his massive hand suddenly shoving you with surprising force. You stumble backward, the ground slipping from under your feet as you lose your balance. Your back hits the floor hard, and you barely manage to stop yourself from crashing into the roaring fireplace. Laughter erupts around the room, harsh and mocking. The other brigands are thoroughly amused by your misfortune. Even from the eastern room, you can hear *Kanwulf's* deep, booming laugh echoing through the quarters, as if he knew exactly what transpired.

Brutal Brutus looms over you, his sneer turning into a cruel grin. "Out of your league, squealer. Stay out of my way." The laughter continues to ring in your ears as you pick yourself up. Turn to **530**.

499

You navigate through the narrow passage beyond the opening. The path ahead is uneven, with jagged rocks jutting from the ground, forcing you to step carefully to avoid a misstep. In the distance, a flicker of movement catches your eye. As you draw closer, you recognize the familiar figure of *Ornias*, the goblin hustler. His sharp features are illuminated by the faint light seeping through the cracks in the rocks, and he grins widely as he sees you approach.

"Well, well, look who made it," *Ornias* cackles, his voice dripping with mischief. "I was wondering when you'd show up. So, here as promised, I shall bring you into the *Huntsman Lair*." His beady eyes glint with a sly confidence as he gestures toward the colossal stone gate looming ahead. "You see that big old stone gate? Looks mighty insurmountable, eh? But old *Ornias* knows a thing or two about secret mechanisms, he does." He winks, tapping the side of his nose with a long, crooked finger.

Without waiting for your response, *Ornias* hobbles over to a section of the rock wall beside the gate. His hands move quickly, feeling along the surface until he finds a barely perceptible indentation. With a grunt of satisfaction, he presses his hand against it, and you hear the faint sound of grinding stone. Slowly, the massive gate begins to lift, revealing a dark passageway beyond. "There you go," *Ornias* says, stepping back with a smug grin. Turn to **59**.

500

You arrive at a junction, with an east-ward path forming out of the north-south corridor. Do you want to head east (turn to **599**), go north (turn to **247**) or south (turn to **14**)?

501

Do you also have a Rope + Grappling Hook? If you have, you manage to swing the grappling hook to a good spot above and successfully climb the rope out of the hole, before retrieving it back into your inventory. If not, you fall several times in your attempt scale the side of the jutted rocks towards the hole, which costs you **3 LIFE** points, although you eventually succeeded. Turn to **3**.

502

You slide open the secret compartment within the sarcophagus and found a crimson key. If you want to keep this item, add **Crimson Key** to the inventory. When you are done, turn to **486**.

503

You are in the middle of a dungeon passage. You can either go east (turn to **459**) or west (turn to **442**).

504

Record codeword **ALEX** if you haven't done so. Reading this book is flouting the rules set by the *Library*.

The heavy book, embossed with cryptic runes titled "*Elemental Magick*" is authored by *Zathar*, the *Great Wizard* and Preceptor of *Krator*, and in his service to the *Regii*, has meticulously detailed the use and mastery of elemental magic.

As you turn the pages, you delve into the origins of this system, tracing it back to the Five *Elemental Deities*. Each chapter reveals the intricate symbolism and significance of the elements—Water, the source of life and adaptability; Earth, the foundation of strength and stability; Fire, the force of transformation and destruction; Air, the breath of freedom and intellect; and Spirit, the binding force that unites them all. It also discusses the alchemy through the use of *Five Artifacts*, and the *Riddle of Transmutation* to activate the *Philosopher's Stone* in a pentagram, although there's no description of the exact steps to solve the riddle. Most importantly, you learn the different elemental symbols.

▽̶ is Earth. △̶ is Air. △ is Fire. ▽ is Water. ⊕ is Spirit.

When you are done reading, turn to **320**.

505

You are at row two of the tombs. A stairwell is situated on one part of the eastern walls. You can head north, south, east or west. Do you want to take the stairs to the east (turn to **263**), go north (turn to **595**), go south (turn to **447**) or go west (turn to **328**)?

506

While *Sir Elandor* takes care of *Kolgrim* and *Brutus*, the remaining crew consisting of *Kanwulf* and *Lorelei* are not easy to deal with either. You will begin the turn.

Lorelei (A)	
Life	15
Offence (Melee)	10
Offence (Range)	20
Defence	8
Radius	2

Kanwulf (B)	
Life	20
Offence (Melee)	15
Defence	8

Lorelei (A)'s Probability Table

Outcomes	Missed Hit	Exact Hit	Exact Hit	Exact Hit	Reduced Hit	Critical Hit
Dice Number	3	5	6	4	2	1

Kanwulf (B)'s Probability Table

Outcomes	Missed Hit	Reduced Hit	Exact Hit	Exact Hit	Critical Hit	Critical Hit
Dice Number	1	2	4	6	3	5

If you win the battle, **gain 100 Exp points** and turn to **214**.

507

Do you have the codeword PROSE? If you do, turn to **194**. Otherwise, turn to **162**.

508

You continue north, down the majestic corridor, the marble underfoot cool and smooth, the air heavy with an ancient, solemn silence. As you walk, you notice a room to your left, its doorway partially ajar, as if beckoning you to enter. However, your eyes are drawn further ahead, where a colossal gate looms in the distance, its massive structure both intimidating and intriguing. Do you wish to open the door to check out what lies beyond (turn to **309**), or walk further down towards the massive gate (turn to **62**)?

509

You dash back towards the south. As soon as you reach the east-west corridor, you see a massive net falling onto you, sprung from a figure that is standing just right before you on the right, to the west. The coarse ropes tangle around you, pulling tight and knocking you to the ground. Panic floods your senses as you struggle against the net, but your movements only seem to make it tighter.

Your eyes widen in horror as you spot this figure, advancing slowly towards you, his slim built, black skin and an unholy looking spear in his hand looking menacing as it casts a silhouette against the dim lights. You have no doubt — this must be the legendary *Huntsman*. Without a word, the figure hurls the spear at you with deadly precision, aiming at your heart. The spear closes in, and you only feel an instantaneous piercing pain before your consciousness fades. You are immediately killed by a weapon what many referred to as a 'Godkiller'- *The Spear of Signonul.* Your quest ends here.

510

With your understanding of traps and secret lock mechanisms, you discover that this statue can be rotated, in a succession of two times to open up a secret door. However, each wrong move may also trigger the mouth to unleash a trap. Upon more detailed examination, you think the only option is to rotate the statue right, then right again, where the last step will still inevitably trigger a trap but also open up the secret door. Making a careful note of your observation, you can decide on your next steps. Turn to **415**.

511

You appear in a room, and this time you realize that there are no teleporters in sight. It is surrounded by four walls, and beneath you are piles of skeletons at your feet. Soon, it dawn upon you that you are going to be trapped here for the rest of eternity. Your quest ends here.

512

Suddenly, through the statue of *Hish*, you hear a voice resonating in your mind. "I am *Hish*, the Wise One and the Grand Benefic, Eldest of the Elementals and Heir Apparent to *Solaris*. I see that you've been unjustly punished by your previous master, the Great Harlot *Ked*, and I offer you refuge, by chance of conversion and embracing my rule, righting your follies with wisdom. Accept my benevolence, and you shall be blessed as one of my followers."

Since you currently do not have a patron deity, perhaps it is best that you convert to *Hish*. Turn to **94**.

513

The corridor is long and leads east and west. Along the way, you chance upon a small wooden box, positioned neatly to the side of the wall, as if someone intentionally left it there for you. Upon examination, you realize the contents are reagents for spellcasting. **Add +2 Nightshades** and **+1 Grimwood Bark** to Reagents if you haven't done so. Do you wish to head east (turn to **227**) or head west (turn to **207**)?

514

As you stand before the statue of *Taph*, the greenish aura pulsates more intensely, and the air around you grows heavy with a palpable sense of menace. You notice the mischievous grin on the jade figure's face widens, and a voice seems to pierce into your head.

"Ah, what an unexpected pleasure to welcome the most unlikely guests to my humble abode," *Taph's* voice chimes, each word laced with a mocking undertone. I do hope you find my shrine to your liking." "Allow me to extend my most gracious hospitality," *Taph* continues, his tone dripping with false politeness. "As honoured guests, you shall experience the full extent of my… generosity." You feel a strange sensation coursing through your body, as if stricken by certain curse. Gradually, you feel an increased vulnerability and affliction by ill luck. Your default Protection is reduced! **Deduct 1 from PROTECTION**. "I have just bestowed upon you a gift of humility! Humility really goes a long way, and this knowledge will save your skin!" exclaimed *Taph*.

Do you have lockpicks? If you do, turn to **30**. Otherwise, you hurriedly leave the shrine before more misfortune befalls on you. Turn to **22**.

515

As you swing the weapon at the rapidly approaching apparition, in anticipation of a combat, you realize that this spirit is impervious to it as your weapon passes through its body. The ghost moves with a terrifying speed, its howl turn into hysterical haunting cackle, and it passes directly through your body. An icy chill invades your very core, making you feel an overwhelming sense of weakness. Your strength drains away, leaving your limbs heavy and your breath shallow. **Deduct 2 POWER** points. The room spins around you, and you struggle to remain upright, your senses reeling from the ghostly encounter. When you look up again, the ghost is gone. Turn to **331**.

516

As you rush down the corridor south, you see a path opening up towards east before you, accompanied by rapid footsteps. The *Huntsman* seems to have changed course in his pursuit and before you can react, you see a giant net unfurled towards you; the coarse ropes tangle around you, pulling tight and knocking you to the ground. Panic floods your senses as you struggle against the net, but your movements only seem to make it tighter.

Your eyes widen in horror as you spot this figure, advancing slowly towards you, his slim built, black skin and an unholy looking spear in his hand looking menacing as it casts a silhouette against the dim lights. You have no doubt— this must be the legendary *Huntsman*. Without a word, the figure hurls the spear at you with deadly precision, aiming at your heart. The spear closes in, and you only feel an instantaneous piercing pain before your consciousness fades. You are immediately killed by a weapon what many referred to as a 'Godkiller'- *The Spear of Signonul*. Your quest ends here.

517

You glance upward and your breath catches in your throat. Above, three imps hover with twisted, malformed faces and bulbous, insect-like eyes that glint with malevolence. Their skin is a mottled, sickly green, and their mouths stretch into grotesque grins, revealing rows of jagged, yellow fangs.

The imps' wings, thin and veined like those of a bat, beat furiously, creating a chilling cacophony that echoes through the cave. They swoop down toward you, their movements quick and erratic, like nightmarish wasps guarding their nest, and they obviously are not pleased that you are approaching too close to the mysterious glow. With no choice, you ready yourself for combat. The *Imps* move 2 squares in a turn, one of them has the ability to cast fireball and they will begin their turns before you. Grey square denotes blocked area.

Imp (A)
Life	8
Offence (Melee)	10
Defence	5

Imp (B)
Life	8
Offence (Melee)	10
Defence	5

Fire Imp (C)
Life	8
Offence (Melee)	10
Offence (Range)	15
Defence	5
Radius	2

Imp (A)'s Probability Table

Outcomes	Missed Hit	Missed Hit	Exact Hit	Exact Hit	Reduced Hit	Critical Hit
Dice Number	6	5	1	2	3	4

Imp (B)'s Probability Table

Outcomes	Missed Hit	Missed Hit	Exact Hit	Exact Hit	Reduced Hit	Critical Hit
Dice Number	3	2	4	1	5	6

Fire Imp (C)'s Probability Table

Outcomes	Missed Hit	Exact Hit	Exact Hit	Exact Hit	Reduced Hit	Critical Hit
Dice Number	3	5	6	4	2	1

If you win the battle, **gain 20 Exp points** and turn to **171**.

518

The walls along the northern passage gradually transform as the rough black stone begins to give way to smooth, polished marble, each side adorned with ornate carvings and murals that depict scenes of ancient warfare and conquest. As you continue, your eyes are drawn upward to a plaque, or epitaphion, overhanging the top of the passage. The inscription, etched in intricate *Xenochian* script, reads "*Askir Shekor.*"

With each step, the passage widens until you find yourself standing before a massive stonegate. A giant pentagram is featured on the surface. Do you step forward to examine the pentagram and the stonegate (turn to **141**), or do you want to return to the main tunnel (**313**)?

519

You tell the *Demonomancer* that you have the stones and are willing to hand them over. His eyes, which were cold and calculating just moments before, suddenly widen in surprise and excitement. "Do you really?" he breathes, his voice trembling with a mix of greed and anticipation. "Hurry up then—give them to me!" He steps closer, his hand outstretched, fingers twitching with eagerness. His entire focus is now locked onto you, the desperation in his eyes making it clear that he is not someone to be trifled with.

Do you have any of those stone artifacts with symbols etched on them? If you want to give any of it to the *Demonomancer*, **remove that item** from your inventory and turn to **422**. If you refuse, turn to **591**.

520

As you move into this area of the river, you sense that the speed of the river is increasing, and seems to flow northward. The meander curves the river, and you can choose to either head west (turn to **298**), towards stiller waters, or up north, where the water is flowing towards (turn to **590**).

521

You are at a corner of the *Library*. You can either head towards west (turn to **320**) or head towards south (turn to **437**).

522

The river soon meanders into a curve before you. Do you head north (turn to **596**) or east (turn to **74**)?

Nyx- The Damned Merman of the Depths

523

You approach *Kolgrim* with a confident stride, your words measured and deliberate. "*Kolgrim*, I come not as an enemy, but as a friend. I wish to offer my assistance to *Kanwulf* and his crew."

Kolgrim raises an eyebrow, with scepticism written all over his face. He crosses his arms, a smirk tugging at the corner of his lips. "Offer help, eh?" he repeats, his voice laced with amusement. "And what makes you think *Kanwulf* needs your help? We don't take in just anyone." You stand your ground, meeting his gaze without flinching. "I've seen things, fought things, that most wouldn't dare face. I've skills that could be of use to *Kanwulf*. If you let me through, I can prove it." At this very instant, *Kolgrim* laughs before composing himself again. "You do not need to offer what we don't need. I just need to test you to see your worth. I shall be asking you questions concerning the numerations within the things in the *Necropolis*."

Do you know the associated number with the symbol ▽ on a stone artifact? If you know that, add its number to the number in this section, and turn to the new section according to the summed number.

Do you know the associated number with a Funerary Bell? If you know that, add its number to the number in this section, and turn to the new section according to the summed number.

Do you know the associated number with Rites of Evocation or codeword RITES? If you know that, add its number to the number in this section, and turn to the new section according to the summed number.

If you don't know any of these, turn to **598**.

524

The skiff starts rocking violently on the water, and you sense that something underneath the boat is trying to capsize it. As you shine the torch over the water, you see the form of a humanoid thing, swimming in the waters. All of a sudden, it emerges and tries to latch itself onto the skiff! You are shocked by the ghastly sight of a shrivelled and ugly form of a hag with a fish torso. It's a *Nyx*, the damned merman of the depths! **Roll a dice**. If you get **1, 2, 3** and **4**, turn to **423**. If you get **5** and **6**, turn to **340**.

525

You are between walls, with paths leading north and south. Do you want to go north (turn to **439**), or south (turn to **116**)?

526

You are at row three of the tombs, with walls to the east. You can head north, west and south. Do you want to go north (turn to **572**), go south (turn to **595**) or go west (turn to **455**)?

527

After walking a short distance, you notice an iron door to your right. It appears to be unlocked. Do you enter the room (turn to **292**), or do you continue your journey east (turn to **440**)?

528

The "*Necromantic Spells Compendium*" is written by *Vermes* the Elder Necromancer, and it is a grimoire filled with ancient yellowed pages of dark incantations and forbidden spells. You are familiar with most of the spells discussed herein, but there's a particular spell which you were previously unfamiliar with. You may want to take note of this spell.

Spell	Function	Reagents Used	Mana Cost	Add to Section
Skire Umas	The Modest Mouse moves the Cheeses.	1x *Bones* 1x *Ghost Caps* 1x *Nightshade*	8	66

When you are done reading, turn to **183**.

529

You are at the south-eastern corner of the tombs, with paths leading north and west. If you want to go north, turn to **418**. If you prefer to go west instead, turn to **230**.

530

You find yourself standing in the dimly lit quarters, the air thick with the smell of roasting meat, which makes your stomach growl. The soft crackle of the fireplace fills the space in the middle, its warmth a stark contrast to the chill that seems to linger within the *Necropolis*. To the north, you notice an alcove partially concealed by a heavy curtain. Within, a woman is seated on a chair. To the south, a burly man sits slumped against the wall, his arms crossed over his chest, and in a state of relaxation. To the east, a sturdy wooden door stands closed. According to *Kolgrim*, *Kanwulf* should be inside this room. Do you want to first talk to the woman (turn to **253**), talk to the burly man (turn to **52**), enter *Kanwulf's* room (turn to **332**) or leave this place (turn to **299**)?

531

A large symbol of *Ophiuchus* hangs atop the majestic looking alcove (symbolic of he who conquered the serpent), which houses an open sarcophagus made of the finest gold. This sarcophagus must have belonged to *Kralj*, the first *Regii*. However, you realize the sarcophagus is empty! The body of the *Regii* seems to have been removed. There's nothing more you can do here, except to return to the corridors in the *Tombs*. Turn to **380**.

532

As you move upward to the northern path, you notice that the skeletons, whole or fractured, with bits and pieces of themselves, gathering at the end of a wall with an open faucet, drawn together to a mysterious liquid with silver sheen streaming out of the tap- the prized *Æther* in its liquid form! You witness the bones and the skeletons begin to fuse together, clattering and scraping as they meld, their forms become increasing tangled. Flesh begins to grow over the fused bones, bubbling and stretching in unnatural ways. What was once many distinct bodies is now an abomination—a writhing, monstrous creature composed of multiple *Regii*. It looks menacing and may become hostile.

Instinctively, you have to get out of here before this *Abomination* come after you. Your only way is out of here, back to the junction, then the path towards east. Turn to **556**.

533

From the shore, you step onto a long stretch of sedimentary plateau formed on top of the embankment. This east-west land route ends on either sides. Along the way, you chance upon a small wooden box, which contains some ingredients that are important for spellcasting. **Add +1 Charnel Ash** and **+1 Grimwood Bark** to Reagents if you haven't done so. If you've already added them before, you will not be able to add them again. Either way will lead you back to the river. Do you want to head east (turn to **150**) or west (turn to **473**)?

534

You agree to *Ornias'* condition, handing over the 20 gold pieces. His eyes light up with a mix of greed and satisfaction. "Good," he says, pocketing the gold. "Just head north along the same route after you exit, go all the way to the end, and you'll find the lair. I'll be there, waiting for you." He gives you a cunning smile, turning back to his wares as you steel yourself for whatever may unfold.

Record the codeword **GYARG**. There's nothing else for you to do here and you decide to take leave. Turn to **135**.

535

You answered correctly. Turn to **471**.

536

You answered correctly. Turn to **471**.

537

You step through the exit and heave a sigh of relief, having survived the *Grand Hall*. **Gain 20 Exp** points. As you walk down a narrow passage heading east, you notice its walls are adorned with vivid, sinister murals depicting black serpents spewing fireballs. Your temporary relief became ephemeral as you suddenly hear several clicks behind the walls. You start to fear for the worst. Do you have the codeword VRIL? If you do, turn to **381**. If not turn to **290**.

538

You are at row three of the tombs, on the central side, and in a junction where you can travel in all directions. The sarcophagi are situated in the walls along east and west. Do you want to go north (turn to **441**), south (turn to **494**), east (turn to **258**), or west (turn to **384**)?

539

You are at the northern side of the tombs, with paths leading east and west. If you want to go east, turn to **491**. If you prefer to go west instead, turn to **565**.

540

You answered correctly. Turn to **471**.

541

You are at a junction. Do you wish to head south (turn to **403**), go west (turn to **588**) or go east (turn to **404**)?

542

You crouch before the door, and insert the lockpicks into the lock, manipulating the delicate mechanisms within. For a moment, it seems you're making progress, the subtle clicks signalling your success. Then, with a sharp snap, the pick breaks off inside the lock, rendering it useless. **Remove Lockpicks** from your inventory. You stare at the broken piece in frustration, realizing your attempt to open the door has failed. Now, your only option is to simply move on. Turn to **508**.

543

The spirit's fading eyes lock onto yours with a grave intensity. "To defeat *Mortis*, you must wield a powerful enchanted weapon, as no normal weapon can harm it. I do know of a certain *Spear of Signonul*, which is otherwise known as the 'Godkiller' and it is rumoured to be somewhere in the *Necropolis*," it whispers. "But the spear alone will not be enough. You will also need powerful armour, like *Draco*, forged in the hide of a powerful dragon. Both the spear and the armour can be found within the *Necropolis*, though their exact locations elude me." The spirit's form flickers, growing fainter with each word. "Seek these artifacts if you have not already… They are your only hope."

With that, the spirit's light dims entirely, and it fades away into nothingness, leaving you alone in the quiet tomb. Turn to **339**.

544

Do you have the codeword ZENGIS? If you do, turn to **385**. Otherwise, turn to **215**.

545

You panic as you are plunged into an utter pitch-black darkness, lost and alone in the underground river complex, and worse, in a dreadful circumstance, floating in the dangerous waters. Actually, you are not quite alone. The *Nyx* soon return to be in company with your misery. Your quest ends here.

546

Between you is a decorated wall to the south with a large symbol of *Astraea* and a wall at the north that recedes into an alcove, which houses an open sarcophagus made of the finest mahogany wood. This sarcophagus must have belonged to one of the deceased *Regii*. However, you realize the sarcophagus is empty! The body of the *Regii* seems to have been removed. There's nothing you can do here, except to move on towards east (turn to **439**) or west (turn to **294**).

547

Nothing happens at the shrine, so you decide to leave the shrine and go back to the main tunnel. Turn to **459**.

548

You dash southward, towards the east-west corridor, but unbeknownst to you, you run right into a trap. You see a massive net falling onto you, sprung from a figure that is situated to your right, from the west. The coarse ropes tangle around you, pulling tight and knocking you to the ground. Panic floods your senses as you struggle against the net, but your movements only seem to make it tighter.

Your eyes widen in horror as you spot this figure, advancing slowly towards you, his slim built, black skin and an unholy looking spear in his hand looking menacing as it casts a silhouette against the dim lights. You have no doubt—this must be the legendary *Huntsman*. Without a word, the figure hurls the spear at you with deadly precision, aiming at your heart. The spear closes in, and you only feel an instantaneous piercing pain before your consciousness fades. You are immediately killed by a weapon what many referred to as a 'Godkiller'- *The Spear of Signonul*. Your quest ends here.

549

You try to politely refuse the drink and you can see the frowns on the faces of the brigands. Suddenly *Kanwulf* laugh out heartily and say "Alright, spare this weakling!" The tension in the air is lifted, and everyone reverted back to the merriment. Soon, it gets late at night, and it is time to retire. Turn go **65**.

550

Your return to the guard-post is certainly even less welcoming this time; *Kolgrim's* expression darkens as soon as he sees you. His eyes narrow with suspicion, and he growls, "You again? You must be up to no good." Without warning, *Kolgrim* brings a sharp whistle to his lips and blows. The sound echoes through the corridor, and within moments, a rough-looking crew emerges from the shadows, with menacing grins and drawn weapons. Among them, a hulking figure steps forward, his presence commanding. He throws his head back and laughs heartily. "So, you've come back for more, eh?" he sneers. "I'm *Kanwulf*, and I don't take kindly to intruders. Now, we'll see how you like being quartered!" Turn to **417**.

551

"Wait, what are you trying to do? No! Aiyeee!!!" *Grobb shrieks* as you poke your weapon through the bars of the cage. After repeated attempts, you are pretty sure that he is dead, where an eerie silence and the stillness of the air permeates the cavern with deadly calm. There's nothing else you can do, as you can't access his corpse, and there's no treasures here. You're a disgusting miscreant **NECROMANCER!** Record the codeword **COBB** and turn to **243**.

552

After walking for a while, you arrive at a T-junction. You can choose to turn left towards west (turn to **8**) or turn right towards east (turn to **115**).

553

Between you is a decorated wall to the south with a large symbol of the *Vesica piscis*, and a wall at the north that recedes into an alcove, which houses an open sarcophagus made of the finest mahogany wood. This sarcophagus must have belonged to one of the deceased *Regii*. However, you realize the sarcophagus is empty! The body of the *Regii* seems to have been removed. There's nothing you can do here, except to move on towards east (turn to **418**) or west (turn to **411**).

554

You arrive at a junction, with a path to the west, along a north-south tunnel. Do you want to head north (turn to **197**), head south (turn to **100**), or go west (turn to **458**)?

555

At the end of the passageway with black serpent murals, it takes a sharp turn to the left, changing course to north. At this point, the flickering light of your last torch sputters and dies, plunging you into darkness. Do you still have any torches left? If you do, you hastily fumble for another torch, knowing that without it, you would be ensnared in utter blackness. **Deduct 1x Torch** from your inventory, and turn to **351**.

If you don't, you will be trapped in this utterly dark and forsaken corner in the labyrinth, quite indefinitely. Your quest ends here.

556

Before you stretches a vast passage leading eastward, where the rough stone walls begin to give way to more deliberate structure. As you peer down this path, you notice the space beyond is immense, with the faint outline of towering pillars and a raised dais barely visible in the gloom—this must be the throne-room where *Mortis* the Great Lich is situated.

To your left and right, narrower paths branch off from the main corridor. Do you want to head east towards the throne-room (turn to **573**), left towards the northern path (turn to **241**), or right towards the southern path (turn to **95**)?

557

You are at a corner of the *Library*. You can either head towards north (turn to **158**) or head towards east (turn to **396**).

558

You move silently towards the *Huntsman*, whose back is facing you. As you pass by a junction, you glance briefly to the side, while your focus remains on the figure ahead. As you ready to lunge forward for a sneak attack, you see the *Huntsman* spin around with a lightning speed, as if he had been expecting you all along, and before you can react, he hurls a massive net at you with practiced precision. The net unfurls in the air, and in an instant, you're ensnared, your limbs tangled and immobilized. Your attempt is foiled.

Without a word, the figure hurls the spear at you with deadly precision, aiming at your heart. The spear closes in, and you only feel an instantaneous piercing pain before your consciousness fades. You are immediately killed by a weapon what many referred to as a 'Godkiller'- *The Spear of Signonul.* Your quest ends here.

559

You are at the southern side of the tombs, with paths leading east and west. If you want to go east, turn to **226**. If you prefer to go west instead, turn to **453**.

560

Do you have codeword OBFUS? If you do, turn to **478** immediately. Otherwise, read on.

The corridor narrows slightly, leading you to a bizarre gate that looms ahead. At its centre of the gate is a massive, grotesque mouth is carved into the stone, its lips resting in a comical, sulky pout. Then, to your astonishment, the mouth begins to move. Its stone lips part with a grinding noise, and a deep, echoing voice reverberates through the corridor. "I am the *Librarian*," it bellows. "To enter the *Library*, you must present a Library Pass." The gate seems to breathe as it waits for your response, the mouth slightly ajar, ready to either grant you passage or deny you.

Do you have a Library Pass? If you do, and want to present to the mouth, turn to **391**. If not or you refuse to, there is no way you can enter the Library, and you have to turn back (turn to **14**).

561

Without the mean to access the *Repository*, you steel yourself, believing that with all the power you've acquired, you might stand a chance against this monstrosity. But as the *Abomination* steps closer, you realize with dawning horror that it is far more powerful than you could have imagined.

Before you can even react, the *Abomination* surges forward with terrifying speed. Its massive, fused limbs swing down with the force of a falling mountain. You barely have time to raise a hand in defence before the crushing blow lands, the sheer power behind it overwhelming your defences in an instant. Pain explodes through your body as you are squashed on the ground, and just before you are turned into a bloody pulp, you caught sight of the *Abomination's* many faces leer at you, a cacophony of voices laughing in cruel triumph. Your quest ends here.

562

You decline *Kanwulf's* invitation, shaking your head slightly. "I appreciate the offer," you say cautiously, "but I must continue on my way."

The room falls silent, the crackling of the fire the only sound as *Kanwulf's* smile fades. His eyebrow arches, and a flicker of anger sparks in his eyes. "You refuse?" he asks, his voice low and dangerous. "In my own quarters, you refuse? This is an affront, a blatant disrespect."

Without another word, you turn on your heel, heading back towards the door. As you reach for the handle, you hear the scrape of a chair against the floor behind you. *Kanwulf* is on his feet, his boots thudding against the ground as he gives chase. "You dare walk away from me?" he snarls. You keep walking across the quarters until you arrive at the entrance, but *Kolgrim* steps into your path, blocking the entrance. A grim expression on his face shows. "Going somewhere?" he asks, his voice dripping with menace.

You glance back over your shoulder, only to see the rest of *Kanwulf's* crew rushing toward you, their faces twisted into sneers and grins, eager for a fight. *Kanwulf* himself advances, his hand resting on the hilt of his sword, his eyes locked on you with deadly intent. You're surrounded, and likely outnumbered. Turn to **544**.

563

You are at row three of the tombs, with walls to the west. You can head north, east and south. Do you want to go north (turn to **597**), go south (turn to **472**) or go east (turn to **267**)?

564

Do you have THIEVERY skill? If you do, turn to **347**. Otherwise turn to **542**.

565

You are at the northern side of the tombs, with paths leading south, east and west. If you want to head south, turn to **365**. If you want to head east, turn to **539**. If you want to head west instead, turn to **335**.

566

"Listen NECROMANCER, I had the pleasure of dealing with many squealers in the past, and some of them predisposed to feeble pursuits like reading. One of the squealers had revealed that there's a secret access within the *Library* that will lead you into a 'control room with weird things inside', before I crushed his skull. If you ever come across a tapestry with a lion wearing a crown in the *Library*, it is likely a façade to a secret room behind it. Now, that's all I know," grunted *Brutus*.

Next time when you see that tapestry in the *Library*, **add 145** to that **section's number**, and turn to the **new section with the summed number** to enter the secret room. When you are done, turn to **530**.

567

The eye rapidly shuts the moment it sees you swing your weapon towards it. The weapon bounces off the hardy stone material of the eye and the gate, barely leaving any mark on it and the gate stands as strong and unyielding as ever before. You are left with no choice but to retreat into the *Library* to figure another way out of here. Turn to **201**.

568

You decided to try your luck, hoping to charm her into giving you one of the items for free. You flash a confident smile and weave a few flattering words, but as they leave your lips, you see her expression shift. Her fox-like eyes turn into an icy stare. "Don't bother," she says, her voice as cold as the wind before a storm. "I'm not so easily swayed. If you think you can charm your way into a freebie, you're sorely mistaken."

"Now, leave my alcove before I change my mind about letting you walk out of here." Realizing there's no further point in pushing your luck, you quietly step back and exit her alcove, her cold gaze following you until you're out of sight. Turn to **530**.

569

You step cautiously into a narrow passageway, the air growing warmer and more oppressive with each step. The tunnel is dark, but a faint red glow beckons you forward. As you move closer, the source of the light becomes clear: a small alcove, bathed in an eerie, crimson radiance.

The alcove is carved into the rock, the walls adorned with intricate, ancient carvings depicting scenes of brutal warfare and elemental fury. At the centre of the alcove stands a statue, imposing and foreboding. It's a depiction of *Barat*, the Bloodied One, the fearsome God of War. *Barat* is sculpted in an intimidating pose, his massive, muscular form towering over you. His eyes, inlaid with rubies, glint with an unsettling lifelike intensity. He is clad in ornate armour, each plate etched with battle scenes and runes of power. His right hand grips a colossal sword, its blade stained with crimson, as if eternally wet with the blood of his enemies.

You realize with a shiver that this is a shrine to *Barat*. The alcove seems to hum with latent power, a tangible reminder of the god's might and the devotion of his followers. The statue's ruby eyes seem to follow your every move, and the air grows thicker, almost stifling. You can feel the weight of *Barat's* presence, a silent challenge from the god of war himself.

Are you a follower of *Barat*? If you are turn to **435**. If you are instead, a follower of *Hish*, turn to **342**. If you are none of the above, turn to **295**.

Mortis- The Great Lich in Regained Human Form

570

As you rush down the northern path, you see a giant crimson gate loom before you at the end of the corridor. This must be the *Repository of Æther* and the ultimate prize that which you seek now lies beyond this gate. You notice a keyhole on the gate, and also a low rumbling from a distance- each footstep heavy, deliberate and ominous.

As you turn over your head, you notice a silhouette of mishappen grotesque form advancing towards you through the shadows. The *Abomination* is coming after you and it seems to know that you also covet the *Æther* like *Mortis* before you!

Do you have a Crimson Key? If you do, turn to **112**. Otherwise, turn to **561**.

571

You are in the middle of a north-south passage. Do you intend to head north (turn to **404**) or go south (turn to **247**)?

572

You are at the eastern side of the tombs, with paths leading north and south. Do you want to go north (turn to **491**), or south (turn to **526**)?

573

You walk past the vast chamber carved from the igneous rock, with towering pillars that reach up to the ceiling. In the centre, upon a grand throne, sits an imposing figure—a tall, fearsome man with regal bearing, his face as angular as a statue, crowned with a gleaming golden circlet. His eyes gleam with an unholy light, and his presence exudes an aura of immense power.

You realize that this man must be *Mortis*, the Great Lich who has somehow regained his human form by the use of the *Æther*. He laughs, a deep, resonant sound that echoes through the throne-room. "So, you have made it this far, NECROMANCER," he says. "You have proven your worth, navigating the trials of this forsaken place. I understand that you harbour grand ambition, which likely has my demise as part of your plan- but unfortunately that mean is far beyond your capability. You might want to consider a more viable option, an offering from my magnanimity. Because I can deeply empathize your position." *Mortis* rises from his throne, his eyes narrowing as he regards you with a knowing look. His voice takes on a more impassioned tone. "Tell me, NECROMANCER," he begins, pacing slowly before his throne, "have you not, too, felt the sting of injustice?

The cold, heartless judgment of those who shun us for our mastery of the dark arts? We are not the monsters they make us out to be. We are seekers of truth, wielders of power that they fear, not because it is evil, but because it is beyond their control."

He pauses, his gaze piercing through the gloom, his presence almost magnetic. "What I have done here," he continues, gesturing to the tombs, the chasms, and the legions of undead, "is not a crime, but a rightful act of vengeance against a world that turned its back on us. A world that reviled us for our knowledge, our power. They cast us aside, branded us as outcasts and heretics. But we are the ones who hold the true power."

Mortis clenches his fist, his voice swelling with righteous fury. "This is justice, NECROMANCER. The world will pay for its arrogance, for its ignorance. And you, like me, have the chance to rise above, to take your rightful place in the new order that we will create together. They called us villains, but we are the ones who will reshape this world." He extends his hand forward. "Join me…my Son… in this quest for world domination," he offers. "With your skills and my power, we can reshape this world. And as a reward, I shall share with you a portion of *Æther*—enough to grant you powers beyond your wildest dreams."

You contemplated your options, and decided to reject his proposal. You notice a furrow between the brows of *Mortis*, but a cold sneer is also forming on his face. "So be it graveworm- prepare for your doom!"

Do you have the codeword ANIMA? If you do, turn to **416**. If you do not have the codeword, turn to **265**.

574

"Thank you NECROMANCER," *Grobb* says, visibly relieved. "You have given me my freedom, and I will repay you with what I know. Firstly, I must warn you about *Kanwulf* and the brigands. He is the leader of this renegade soldiers turned criminals and they want to find the *Æther* for its purported power. These scumbags are despicable and never to be trusted- they are quick to backstab you, so always watch your back when dealing with them. *Kanwulf* was trying to set me up to deal with a group of crazed bloodthirsty imps in the eastern part of the *Inner Chambers*, which I strongly resisted, and that led me to this state. The scumbags are currently residing in the western part of the *Inner Chambers*, and I think they've succeeded in getting one artifact out of five, that are critical for accessing the *Tombs of the Regii*. I believe you are after the *Æther* like most of those who ventured here. The Great Lich *Mortis* and the *Æther* are hidden within the sanctuary known as the *Tombs of the Regii,* where the thirteen *Regii* are buried, and it is located at the southern part of the *Inner Chambers*.

This place is sealed by a giant pentagram at the gate, which can only be opened by those who possess all five artifacts and understand the secrets of solving its riddle."

Grobb's tone grows more serious. "*The Great Wizard*, whose grave lies somewhere northwest of this underground river complex, holds the secret to solving the pentagram's riddle for it was he who devised them, and I suspect that he also holds one of the artifact. To summon him, you will need the Funerary Bell and also the steps of the Rites of Evocation. The Funerary Bell can be found at the northern side of the *Inner Chambers*, a passage to the netherworld, amidst a ghostly procession which takes place perpetually, as new spirits are drawn into the *Necropolis*. You must take it from there, probably by mean of magic and not by force, from the undeads, who use such bells to shepherd the spirits. As for the Rites of Evocation, I can teach them to you." **Add 50 Exp points.** You listen intently as *Grobb* details to you the different steps of this ritual. Record the codeword **RITES** and the associated number **12**. At the location where you think lies the grave of the *Great Wizard*, **add the associated number of RITES**, with the **associated number of the Funerary Bell**. Deduct this **summed number** from the **section number** where the grave of the *Great Wizard* is, to arrive at a **new section**.

You sense that *Grobb* is grimacing, with hands over his stomach as if suffering from hunger pangs. Do you have any rations with you? If you do, and can spare one ration to *Grobb*, **deduct 1x Ration** from inventory and turn to **477**. Otherwise turn to **461**.

575

A small pedestal sits within the secret room. Atop this pedestal rests a ring, its surface glinting with a mysterious allure, as if it holds untold power within its delicate band. This ring is a Ring of Protection, and it is something which can permanently affect your PROTECTION score. It is not an ARMOUR so it cannot be placed there. As long as this item is in the inventory, it will fulfil its function. Surrounding the pedestal, scattered across the floor, are also a few gold pieces, their dull shine speaking of long-neglected wealth. Interspersed among the coins are clusters of translucent mushrooms. **Add +2 Ghost Caps** to Reagents, **10 Gold pieces**, and a **Ring of Protection (add +1 beyond current default PROTECTION score, Gp: 50)** if you want any of them. Feeling pleased with your find, you exit the secret room, and head back to explore the eastern tunnel. Turn to **115**.

576

Before you, three paths diverge into the gloom, a northern path, a gently sloping southern path, a path to the east, with its end obscured by thick darkness. If you want to head to the northern path, turn to **371**. If you want to head to the southern path, turn to **110**. If you would prefer to walk to the east, turn to **556**.

577

With trembling hands, you carefully reach down and grasp the black key from the man's belt. To your relief, it's clean—untouched by the vile slime that covers the rest of his body. If you want to keep this item, **add Black Key** to your inventory. As you straighten up, you notice the man's body beginning to dissolve further. His form, once human, now collapses into a grotesque puddle of black slime, the last remnants of his flesh melting away in sickening slurps.

You can continue to head west (turn go **72**) or return to the main tunnel (turn to **229**).

578

You are between walls, with paths leading north and south. Do you want to go north (turn to **368**), or south (turn to **497**)?

579

You bow before the statue of *Zakl* and feel an immense surge of energy coursing through your veins. By the blessings of your Patron Deity, you are healed and restored. Restore your **LIFE**, **MANA** and **POWER** to their maximum values.

Suddenly you hear a voice in your head, a low and graven one. "Seeker of fate and faithful servant," the voice intones, slow and deliberate. "Your quest is one that threads through the very fabric of time, and it is not without peril. But I see the path you tread, and I deem you worthy of a boon." The statue's eyes, once hollow and lifeless, now flicker with a faint light, growing brighter as *Zakl* continues. "I shall impart to you a skill, one that will be crucial to your journey. This skill is called Scrying."

"Scrying will allow you to pierce the veil of time and space," *Zakl* explains. "With it, you may gain knowledge of the directions of targets which you seek. You feel another surge of energy and this time, it feels like you've just downloaded a new knowledge into your head. **Add SCRYING** to your Skills.

When you are done, you leave the shrine. Turn to **459**.

580

You are at row two of the tombs, with walls to the west. You can head north, east and south. Do you want to go north (turn to **472**), go south (turn to **297**) or go east (turn to **414**)?

581

Kolgrim's eyes land on your armour, and his demeanour shifts abruptly. His stern expression melts into a wide grin, and he lets out a hearty laugh. "Ah, what do we have here? The esteemed paladin from the *Order of Solaris*! My apologies for the rough welcome. Come on in, come on in!"

He gestures for you to walk ahead of him. "I'll take you to *Kanwulf* myself. He'll be pleased to meet such a distinguished guest." You nod and proceed down the corridor, *Kolgrim* following close behind. As you walk, a sudden, searing pain erupts in your back, taking your breath away. You gasp in shock, stumbling forward as your hand instinctively reaches for the source of the agony. *Kolgrim* had driven his sword straight through your back. "Hey everyone, we've got another one here!" *Kolgrim* shouts, his excited voice echoing through the corridors. You collapse to the floor, your vision blurring from the pain. Through the haze, you see a tall figure striding toward you, flanked by a group of brigands with cruel smiles.

The figure stops just before you, looking down with a sneer. "I'm *Kanwulf*," he growls. "And you've just made a terrible mistake, paladin. Let's see if my gang can slice you up into a thousand pieces." The brigands around him chuckle darkly, their weapons ready, as they close in on you. Your quest ends here.

582

You appear in a room, painted entirely in crimson red. Within this room are three teleporters, placed in different directions. Do you take the one to the north (turn to **434**), to the east (turn to **104**), or to the west (turn to **208**)?

583

As you step through the portal, you feel a kaleidoscopic field swirling around you, sucking you into the vortex. The next moment, you realize that you are teleported to a small chamber. Ahead of you is a corridor lined with rather impressive-looking majestic columns. Turn to **87**.

584

As you try to discreetly slip an item into your pocket, *Ornias'* sharp eyes catch the movement. In an instant, he springs a trap, and a rusty cage appears out of nowhere and falls down from the ceiling, crashing onto the floor, trapping you in place. *Ornias'* face contorts with a mixture of anger and amusement. "Thought you could outsmart me, did you?" he sneers, stepping closer to the cage. "I've dealt with too many of your type before. But stupidity has its consequences, especially with zombie-brained NECROMANCER." He laughs darkly, his voice echoing through the chamber. "I'll pass you to my master, the *Huntsman*. He always needs new practice targets." His words hang heavy in the air as you realize the gravity of your mistake. Your quest ends here.

585

The eye on the gate appears lifeless, its once-vigilant gaze now hollow and vacant. The pupil has rolled back, leaving only a blank, eerie whiteness where there was once watchful intent. You think the '*Librarian'* is probably dead and it appears that the death of the *Homunculus* could be related to this. With a careful shove on the gate, it swings open without any resistance and you step out of the *Library*, back into the tunnel. Turn to **14**.

586

You arrive at a lower section of the *Library*. You can either head north (turn to **201**) or head towards west (turn to **457**).

587

You find the body of *Sir Elandor* on the floor, obviously deceased. Do you have, or had before the Plate Mail of Solaris? If you do, turn to **392**. Otherwise turn to **476**.

588

This passageway leads east-west, with a diversion to the north. A draft of cold air seems to waft in from the north. Do you wish to head east (turn to **541**), go west (turn to **459**), or head up north where the cold draft is coming from (turn to **121**)?

589

Soon you find yourself at a tense crossroads. To the north, you catch a glimpse of *Ornias* standing in the shadows of a dimly lit alcove, his sly grin barely visible in the gloom. But your attention is quickly drawn to the south. There, far down the corridor, you spot the unmistakable figure of the *Huntsman*. His black, slim form cuts through the darkness, sprinting toward you with alarming speed, his footsteps echoing ominously off the stone walls.

Caught between the cunning goblin and the relentless predator, you know you have only moments to decide your next move. Do you want to rush down south to confront the *Huntsman* (turn to **429**), dash north towards the direction of *Ornias* (turn to **448**), turn back east towards the north-eastern corner of the lair (turn to **468**) or run west, away from where all the actions are (turn to **318**)?

590

You are at a confluence, where water seems to be flowing rapidly towards north-west. You still have time to get back to the stiller waters towards south and east. Do you want to move towards north-west (turn to **479**), head south (turn to **520)** or east (turn to **481**)?

591

"Ah, I see," he sneers, his eyes narrowing with wicked delight. "You think you can defy me? Foolish. You truly believe you have a choice in this matter?"

He steps closer, the shadows of the chamber seeming to grow darker around him. "Actually, you have no option. I could search your lifeless body for the stones if I wanted. It would be easier that way, wouldn't it?" As he speaks, his hand begins to glow with a fiery orange light, the heat of the impending spell already radiating from his palm. "Prepare yourself," he hisses. "I will enjoy watching you burn."

Do you have CHARM? If you do turn to **480**.

Otherwise, turn to **452**.

592

Do you have the codeword GYARG? If you do, turn to **54**. If not, turn to **101**.

Ornias- The Goblin Merchant & 'Fixer'

593

As you head east, the passageway opens into a large chamber, unexpectedly well-decorated with tapestries and ornate furniture. The air is heavy with the scent of incense from exotic origins. In the centre of the room sits a goblin, his green skin contrasting sharply with the black fez hat perched atop his head. A plume of smoke curls lazily from the pipe he holds, adding to the room's exotic atmosphere.

The goblin's eyes glint with a mischievous spark as he spots you. His mouth stretches into a wide, cunning grin, revealing sharp, yellowed teeth. "Ah, welcome, traveller," he says, his voice oily and smooth, tinged with a sly undertone. "I am *Ornias*, a humble trader and 'fixer' at your service. It is not often that I have the pleasure of meeting a NECROMANCER in these parts. Might I interest you in these wares, and services that I can provide?"

Curiosity piqued, you ask *Ornias*, "How did you manage to get into the *Inner Chambers*, through all those traps? It wasn't exactly a leisurely stroll." *Ornias* chuckles, the sound low and raspy. "Ah, my dear NECROMANCER, not all paths are laden with peril, the same peril which you took! I took a different route, a river passage that flows through the underground caverns. It's a treacherous way, but one that bypasses many of the traps you encountered, and a much easier route! A cunning goblin must know his shortcuts, after all."

His grin widens as he continues, "And let me tell you, there's more than just traps and monsters down here. You'd be surprised that you are not alone here, and how crowded the *Inner Chambers* is, hardly a lonely god-forsaken place! Lots of adventurers like yourself, all trying to figure how to beat *Mortis* to his game and quest for the *Æther*. And they all came here like me through a more 'clever' way, accessing here by that same river passage!" With a sly smile, *Ornias* says, " That's precisely why I came here to ply my trades. Where there's danger, there's opportunity, and these chambers attract all manner of treasure seekers and thrill chasers. It's a bustling hub of commerce and peril, perfect for a hustler like me." To add insult to injury, *Ornias* starts mocking you with a condescending tone. "You might not be as sharp as the others who took the water passage," he sneers. "But that's no surprise; you NECROMANCER often relies too much on your gravewit. You're bound to need more help. Lucky for you, I've got just what you need—at a price, of course."

If you want to see what wares *Ornias* has to offer, turn to **383**.
If you want to attack *Ornias*, turn to **82**.
If you decide to leave, turn to **195**.

594

The northern corridor leads up to what appear to be a subterranean pool at a distance, with an unusual black shimmer. Do you want to move up ahead to explore the pool (turn to **285**) or do you want to return to the main tunnel (turn to **229**)?

595

You are at the eastern side of the tombs, with paths leading north and south. Do you want to go north (turn to **526**), or south (turn to **505**)?

596

This river passage stretches for a considerable distance, with sharp and irregular rock formations lining both sides of the tunnel. Do you wish to head north (turn to **473**) or south (turn to **522**)?

597

You are at the western side of the tombs, with paths leading north and south. Do you want to go north (turn to **334**), or south (turn to **563**)?

598

"You don't know, do you?" *Kolgrim* bursts into laughter, a deep, mocking sound. "You really thought you could just waltz in here without knowing a thing? You're not even worth the time it takes to swing a sword at you!" His laughter fades into a sneer as he waves a hand dismissively. "You're not fit to breathe the same air as *Kanwulf*, let alone stand before him. Now, get out of here before I decide to use you for target practice."

He turns away from you, his back a clear sign of his dismissal. "Scram," he calls over his shoulder, his tone dripping with disdain. "And don't let me see your sorry face around here again." Record codeword **GNAWER**. Left with no choice, you retreat back to the main tunnel, in disgrace. Turn to **49**.

599

The black-stone corridor curves before you. Do you wish to head north (turn to **207**) or west (turn to **500**)?

600

With newfound power from the *Æther* and the triumph of crushing the last hopes of *Krator* and the *Regii*, you walk mightily back to the throne room, your steps echoing with authority. The skeletal warriors that once served *Mortis* now stand in your path, their empty eye sockets following your every move. But you pay them no mind as you push through their ranks, feeling their bony forms parting before you like a wave before a mighty ship.

As you approach the throne, your gaze falls upon the shattered remains of *Mortis*, now nothing more than a broken mess on the cold stone floor. The once fearsome lich-turned-king is no more, his ambitions crushed along with his body. The skeletal warriors turn to you, their heads cocked in a quizzical manner, awaiting your command. You stand tall before them, your voice echoing through the cavernous hall as you declare, "The *Last of the Regii* has come! The prophecy of the *Reckoning* has been fulfilled! You, who have served the fallen kings, shall now obey the new master—myself, the **Master of Dark Arts**!"

Without hesitation, you ascend the steps to the throne, the seat of power that now rightfully belongs to you. As you sit upon it, the ancient stone cold beneath you, a sense of destiny washes over you. You look out over the vast legion of skeletons, their heads bowing low in submission. The entire army, countless in number, kneels before you, acknowledging your dominance.

A dark chuckle escapes your lips as you revel in your newfound power. You understand now that you have the might to command this undead army, to shape the world to your will. But before you even begin to plot your grand schemes of world domination, a thought creeps into your mind—a grudge long held, a soul you intend to torment.

Sladder.

The memory of his betrayal burns in your mind, and you grin wickedly as you contemplate your next move. Before the world bends to your will, you will settle this score. You will return to the desert, anticipating *Sladder's* return, and when he does, you will kidnap him, drag him back to the *Necropolis*, and make him suffer as only the *Master of Dark Arts* can.

The story ends here, but your dark reign is only beginning.

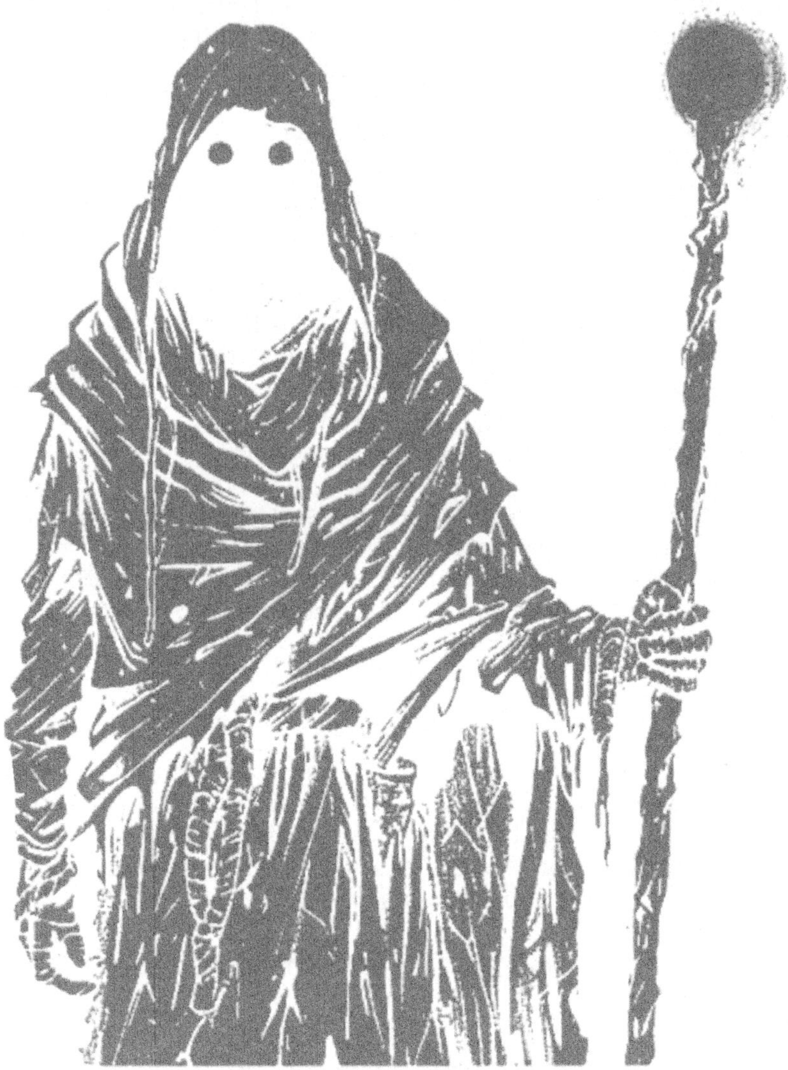

About the Author

Rex Talionis, a self-proclaimed anachronist, esotericist and occasional vagabond, revels in mythology, role-playing games and writing. Though a hermit struggling in many circumstances, he has a wealth of fantasy and world-building in his head, incessantly creating stories and games, largely for personal satisfaction.

This is his first gamebook and a quasi-autobiography.

Website: https://rextalionis.wordpress.com
Email: rextalionis666@gmail.com

Check out Black Circle Collective.

blackcircle.press

Like what you read? Consider a donation.

bitcoin

ethereum

Printed in Great Britain
by Amazon